CHASING FROST

ISABEL JOLIE

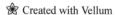 Created with Vellum

For the man who melts my frost

ONE

CHASE

The mammoth diamond on her ring finger disperses rays of light, spinning magenta and yellow flecks of color across the marble ballroom floor. She alternates between patting and fondling my forearm, while her ring-bearing hand lifts the champagne glass unnaturally high. My bow tie constricts around my throat, and my feet ache in these stiff dress shoes. If I get my way, these overpriced oxfords will never be broken in.

I search the crowd for my boss, and the arm patter's husband, Tom Bennett. My boss, the CEO of the accounting firm I work for, is the whole reason I'm here at this charity event. It's a good cause, and I remind myself of that every time Tom buys several tables at these fundraising dinners and fills them up with BB&E employees.

Senator McLoughlin is his buddy. I get it. They went to college together. Someone McLoughlin loved died from cancer. I get all of it. Support your friends. But does every charity event require participants to dress like dolled-up penguins?

Bennett's wife continues, pausing to adjust her dress before she has a wardrobe malfunction of the Janet Jackson variety. My buddy Cal looks over, and I raise my glass to him, sending silent pleas for him to rescue me.

This is cocktail hour. In an estimated ten minutes, the over-sized oak banquet room doors will open, and I'll get a chance to see how I'm faring in my boss's eyes. Today, I'm hoping he's thinking I'm doing a shit job and I get the table with the company peons. Bennett's wife is too touchy-feely for my taste. I doubt he cares what she does, based on how he acts when he's out with his buddies, and the fact he stands nowhere near her when I see them together, but there's no reason to test his hypocrisy.

Cal joins us, and Bennett's wife shines a commercial-worthy white smile his way. Multiple sparkling tennis bracelets slide down her arm as she reaches out for him. *Thank fuck for the diversion.* As Cal engages her in conversation, I tabulate the estimated value of the diamonds dripping on Mrs. Bennett. I know how much one of those tennis bracelets cost because my dad bought my mom one for their fortieth. She's got large diamonds on her ears, around her neck, fingers, and wrists. For Tom's sake, I hope some of that shit's fake, 'cause if it isn't, the dude's either going broke or he's into something illegal. But, then again, maybe our CEO fares better at bonus time than I realize.

If all that's real, the woman must give a damn good blow job. Plump and glistening in gloss.

Mrs. Bennett lightly squeezes my bicep. "What do you think, Chase?"

I have absolutely no idea what she's talking about. Cal saves me, and his shit-eating smirk tells me he knows he's doing me a solid.

"Maitlin, didn't you try the keto diet once? You weren't a fan, were you?"

"Years ago. I tried it. Very difficult to keep up. But what are you talking to us about diets for?" I flash her my charming, but purposefully not flirty, smile. "You're lovely. You keep eating healthy and exercising, as you obviously do, and you'll keep making all the ladies jealous." She smothers a giggle and tilts her head while batting her extremely long eyelashes, and the save is complete. But then she inches closer, and we have at least six more minutes before the doors open and the dinner portion of the evening begins, when the sentimental videos play and the tears and checkbooks follow.

"So, I've been asking all the men, doing my own sort of survey. Do you use those dating apps? It's been so long since I've been single, and I'm so curious about the dating world these days."

"Yeah, I use a few," I dutifully answer. Cal smirks.

"Oh, can I see your profile? I'm so curious. I read about these apps, but I've never interacted."

The answer to her question would be a hell-to-the-no, but I'm saved when Evan Mitchell, our CFO, walks up with a twenty-something femme fatale in a sleek, form-fitting gown. She is not his wife, and she just made this boring charity gala worth attending.

"Good evening." I nod to Evan. I reach my hand out to the hot commodity at his side. "I don't believe I've had the pleasure. Chase Maitlin."

Her slender fingers slip into mine, and hot damn. I'm not even sure where to look first. She's all-natural, with glossy, pale pink lips and a rosy blush to her cheeks. Her glossy, dark hair is pulled back, revealing an elongated neck and demure solitaire diamond earrings. Her arms are lightly sculpted. Not in a weightlifter kind of way, but a way that says this girl can do some push-ups and pull-ups and probably run a marathon too. As a fellow gym rat, color me intrigued.

"Sydney Frost." Her hand leaves mine, and her dark gaze sweeps over the others in our group. Frosty. I like it.

"Sydney will be joining our firm, filling Tad's role."

"Welcome." I grin. Excellent. She's gorgeous. Probably out of my league. But, as my main man Michael Jordan says, you lose one hundred percent of the shots you don't take. I'll need to play it right. Working together will be a great opportunity to get to know her. Get in the best position for the free-throw line. Of course, these days, working together can also be a highly sensitive situation and makes it easier to foul.

Cal extends his hand. He's got a gold ring on his finger, that omnipresent ball and chain, so he's no competition, no matter how much Frosty here seems to prefer him right now. Evan excuses himself, saying something about needing to find his wife and to please introduce Sydney to any other BB&E employees we run across.

Unfortunately, when Evan leaves our little group, Mrs. Bennett takes a step closer, almost separating us from Cal and my newfound shiny object.

"So, your phone? Can I see?" she says softly as if the other two can't hear her if she lowers her voice.

Frosty raises one dark, thick, perfectly shaped eyebrow.

"Mrs. Bennett is curious about the online dating scene," I explain. "She's taking a survey, trying to ascertain how today's singles meet."

"Oh, I'm sure someone like Sydney must have a boyfriend waiting in the wings." Mrs. Bennett's words are civil, but there's something about her stance that's reminiscent of a feral lioness.

"No." A barely-there smile graces those pale pink, shapely lips. "No boyfriend."

"Oh." Mrs. Bennett's response has a hard edge to it.

Cal breaks the tension. "Can I get either of you ladies something to drink from the bar? We should be sitting soon."

Both women smile graciously, declining his offer while sizing each other up.

"So, what about you, Sydney? Does a single woman like you resort to dating apps? Are you one of those girls desperately seeking a husband?"

Sydney's shoulders shift back, and her breasts rise. Cal turns his head, seeming to scan the crowd for someone as the two women glare at each other like opponents before the whistle blows.

"A husband? No, I can't say that's something I want."

"Probably for the best. So, no dating apps? No desire to meet a partner of any sort, for any *activity*?" Mrs. Bennett rests her fingers along my forearm and inches closer to me. My collar tightens when it hits me she's insinuating some kind of activity with me.

"Me? No. If I want sex, then I have sex. No app required."

I almost spit out my gin and tonic as Sydney twists and walks away, her tight ass swaying beneath her silk slip gown, sans panty lines.

It's official. I'm in lust.

TWO

SADIE

Sunday afternoon, I ring the buzzer on a nondescript Park Avenue office building. The basement row is filled with small offices for a variety of medical practices, such as physical therapy and chiropractor services. A small index card taped on the outside touts the therapeutic benefits of massage and the hours for unit 6A. Above the offices, condos reside.

The buzzer rings, and I look into the camera above the panel. A man's voice comes through the speaker.

"Yes?"

"Frost here."

The buzzer sounds, and I lift the stainless-steel handle and push on the door with one last glance down the wide city street. At the end of the hall, toward the back of the building, is the office the FBI occasionally uses for meeting up with undercover operatives. I won't return to the NYC field office until I'm off this case, to ensure my cover isn't blown.

Agent Hopkins opens the door before I reach it. He holds his hand out. "Agent Keating."

His voice is low, and no one is in the hall, probably even in any of these offices given it's a Sunday, but all the same, I'd prefer he not use my real name. But what do I know? This is my first undercover case.

I step past him into the small room. There's a square faux wood table, four black standard office chairs, and several cabinets along two walls. The office has no window, and I happen to know it has reinforced soundproof walls. It's a discreet, protected meeting place. A door to a bathroom is in the far corner, near the small hotel-like kitchenette, with a microwave, Keurig, and mini-fridge.

"How'd last night go?"

I pull out the nearest black chair and set my folder and notepad on the table.

"No issues. McLoughlin raised over three million. Impressive haul." His blank expression tells me this is not news to him. "Evan Mitchell introduced me to several key players. He had me seated at a table with many of the accountants." The balding middle-aged Chief Financial Officer had been nice enough. Tall with a noticeable slouch and a wide girth.

"Anyone of interest yet?"

"No one not already on our radar. None of the employees I met said anything of relevance to the case. I got the feeling Tom Bennett's wife might be having an affair with Chase Maitlin." The tall, skinny Chief Executive Officer had barely acknowledged my existence, so any conversation hadn't been possible.

"Really?" This seems to amuse Agent Hopkins as much as anything, based on the smirk on his face. Men.

"I don't have any evidence. But she acted like a woman defending her lover when I came around. She couldn't keep her hands off Maitlin, and her husband was in the room. I never noticed Bennett watching them, though, so either he doesn't care, or I might be off track. All of Bennett's attention centered on Senator McLoughlin." The Illinois senator starred as the biggest celebrity in the room. Bennett was hardly the only attendee clamoring for the charismatic Senator's attention. "I didn't get a good read on Maitlin. He sat at the table with all the executives, including Bennett and Mitchell. I found that interesting because when looking at the org chart, I wouldn't have expected he'd be seated with all the bigwigs." It wasn't difficult to see why Mrs. Bennett would seek Maitlin out. He was a good-looking guy. He didn't seem to be returning her interest, but doing so at an event with her husband present would be the height of stupidity. And, even though Maitlin didn't appear to be attracted to her, he did give her more attention than her spouse.

"Who all was at Maitlin's table?"

I push my summary to him. He's also got it uploaded on the intranet.

"Cooper Grayson, John Fischer, and their wives. All Chicago business executives. There was another guy I hadn't seen before who was there without a date. His name is Elijah Mason."

"Yeah, we're looking into him. He owns a medical supply business."

"Did you check to see if he's a Stanford alum? That seems to be a connection between all of them."

Operation Quagmire initially started as a public corruption investigation into Senator McLoughlin. The senator is a rising political star and a Chicago bigwig with ties far and wide. As the Chicago public corruption team uncovered more about his business dealings, the operation expanded to include investigating an additional business, a real estate development group. Coincidentally, that business is also owned by a Stanford alum and close friend of the senator.

"Elijah Mason's name didn't come up in the alumni directory. His business is a major contributor to the McLoughlin Charity, and the charity is one of their big clients. One more circular business. McLoughlin remembers his friends. You set in your new apartment?"

"Yes." I transferred to the New York field office one week ago. I'd been tempted to use my real apartment during this operation. This is a white-collar crime case, and it's unlikely anyone's going to be following me home to ensure I am who I say I am. But it turns out the FBI apartment is somewhat close to Maitlin's place, and he's our prime suspect. Being in close proximity could allow for some impromptu run-ins.

When I met Chase last night, he didn't strike me as a criminal. However, dating his boss's wife would be indicative of low integrity and poor judgment. And, as we all know, criminals don't have a look. They come in all shapes and sizes.

My job, in this case, is to determine who within BB&E Accounting is responsible for falsifying records. Operation Quagmire has uncovered that several of the senator's largest campaign donations come from companies his charity buys from, whether it's land, pharmaceutical drugs, or even patents. Senator McLoughlin has granted over $30 million in state projects to one of the real estate groups. And his charity, in turn, has bought renovated real estate at above market prices. They each feed the other. As Hopkins said, it's circular.

This started as a corruption case, with suspicion that the charity was being leveraged for funneling campaign funds and potentially illegitimate payments to the senator. The Chicago team discovered falsified financial records that impact several companies, not just the senator's charity. It's a convoluted case, and I'm still getting my head around it as the newest member on the team.

The DA wants to go after the guilty BB&E employees, the ones responsible for falsifying the financial records. The "how" piece will strengthen his case. But, in the DA's words, he doesn't "want another Enron." He's not going to charge thousands of employees with misconduct as they did in that case. He wants to know *exactly* who the individual culprits are.

The FBI has one contact within BB&E Accounting—Evan Mitchell, the soft-spoken balding man who took me around introducing me to everyone. A small team met with him to disclose the suspected fraud. He was apparently distraught when informed illegal activity might be going on within his company. He offered up filling a currently vacant role within the company with an undercover agent. The FBI team hadn't been angling for an undercover agent. They really were looking to get his take and to hopefully gain access to firm records.

But I was told Mitchell seemed so eager to find any bad apple within the company, the FBI special agent in charge agreed to the undercover idea. I expect Michell sees participating with the FBI in a covert operation as a way to avoid BB&E going up in flames from a public investigation on an Arthur Anderson scale.

"What did you think of Mitchell?"

"No red flags." The guy seemed like any middle-aged dad. He showed me photos of his kids.

"Good." Hopkins fiddles with his laptop. "Did you get the sense he's trustworthy?"

I did sense he was handling me with kid gloves last night as he led me around the gala, introducing me to BB&E employees. Not that that's unexpected. People generally find FBI investigations enthralling. I could be wrong, but I'm fairly certain he kept glancing at my gown, trying to determine if I was carrying a concealed weapon. And I was not. There was no need. This isn't that kind of case.

"I didn't trust him enough to tell him anything he hasn't already been told."

I am certified for undercover, but this is my first case. I wasn't with Evan Mitchell long enough to make any kind of personality assessment. My specialty is forensic accounting. A different guy on my team probably would've gotten this assignment, but his wife's due in the next month or two, plus I'm new to the team and to the city, so less chance of being recognized out and about. It's a good case for me to transition to the New York office. And it should be a short undercover stint.

Agent Hopkins lifts a black computer bag onto the table and unzips it.

"BB&E will give you a company computer with access to its network. You've already received your identity documents, correct?"

"Yes." He's fully aware I received my identification with my undercover name, Sydney Frost, last Friday when I was assigned this role. "I wish they'd let me be Sydney Bristow. Would've been so much cooler." Sydney Bristow from the TV show *Alias* is one of my all-time favorite undercover operatives.

"Am I the only one who thinks Sydney Frost sounds like a made-up name?" Agent Hopkins asks the question in a teasing tone, his body language indicating he's ready to wrap up this Sunday afternoon meeting.

I don't offer a response to his question. So many names in the world. They only sound off to us because we're trained to pay attention to details. Not many people out there would hear someone's name and think *undercover agent*.

"Ready for tomorrow? Anything you need? The warrants cleared, and we've planted listening devices. Surveillance has begun."

I can't think of anything. To start, I won't be wearing a wire. One less thing to worry about. Goosebumps spread on my arms, and I hope Hopkins doesn't notice. My first undercover role. It's a pretty straightforward plan. I'm filling the role of the CIA, or certified internal auditor, for the firm. I fully expect that as I home in on these accounts that I know have cooked books, I'll be able to pick up on some discomfort level from the guilty parties. And, with network access, I'll be able to see who is accessing the files for these firms the most.

When I was a kid, my sister and I would play secret agents. We'd bullet point our plans as if they were a shopping list.

Find evidence

Break into bad guy den (which we'd built ourselves)

Call chief (who was a plant pot with a smiley face)

Solve case

Put bad guys away

I zip up my laptop bag and think of this case in the same childish fashion.

Fill in the role of a certified internal auditor (CIA) for the firm

Home in on accounts with cooked books

Look out for guilty parties

Use network access to observe who is most often accessing the files for these two firms

Identify said guilty parties - A.K.A. Catch the bad guys

If I do my job well, I'll make the case stronger. We're dealing with a sitting US senator and several wealthy CEOs, so the prosecutor's case needs to be airtight. These men will hire a stellar defense team.

Agent Hopkins lightly taps his pen on the table as I prepare to leave.

"Is it true you were Top Gun?"

"Yes, sir." My claim to FBI fame. It's a Quantico honor. I hoist my bag over my shoulder. Respect flashes across his features. Then he's back to business.

"Anything suspicious, let me know. If at any point you don't feel comfortable, you get out. You understand?"

I refrain from rolling my eyes, but internally, they're doing three-sixties.

"Got it." I give him a reassuring smile. It's white-collar crime at an accounting firm. And I caught our prime suspect checking me out multiple times during dinner last night. He didn't come across as overly confident, as he'd look away quickly when I returned his gaze. Our covert glances back and forth almost became a game. The classic black tuxedo complimented his broad shoulders. It wasn't exactly a hardship to throw a few flirty glances his way. And the fact that doing so seemed to piss off that socialite Mrs. Bennett made it borderline fun.

"You know, now that I think about it, look into Mrs. Bennett too."

"What're you thinking?" Hopkins asks, pen in the air.

"It's a hunch. I don't think her marriage is a happy one. Or at least, if it is, it's an open arrangement. The woman was dripping in diamonds. I know you'd normally check into her background anyway when looking into him, but I'm curious which one of them is the money source."

"You got it. We're already working on accessing financial records for all the executives."

There's something about Mrs. Bennett. The other wives weren't particularly noteworthy.

We're almost positive Tom Bennett, another Stanford alum and close friend of McLoughlin's, is orchestrating the falsifying of the financial records. But the chances that the CEO is doing it all on his own are slim. He's got to have at least one employee in on it. We strongly suspect that person is Maitlin, as he's the client relationship manager on all the accounts we are investigating.

"Does Mitchell know you've bugged the office?"

"Yes. He offered it up. Well, he doesn't know where we placed devices. He said he wanted to work with the FBI in every way possible. Why?"

"Tom Bennett and Evan Mitchell are close friends. I saw that last night. And they both went to Stanford. Did no one find that to be a risk?"

"Agent Blakely swears by Evan Mitchell. A personal friend. But we've put bugs in Mitchell's office too. Blakely has us doing full surveillance for insurance." Agent Blakely is the SPIC, or special agent in charge, on Operation Quagmire. He works out of the Chicago office.

This really should be a simple case. If Maitlin's guilty, I'll figure it out quickly. And, if we're wrong, I'll flip him and recruit him to help us catch the bad guys.

My goal is to have this case closed out in less than two weeks. I transferred to this field office in the hopes of building a more fulfilling life outside of work. Undercover is hardly a step toward meeting my personal goals.

When I push open the door to the FBI apartment on King Street, my new short-term home, it feels like I'm stepping onto a movie set. As one would expect, the team did a good job setting it up. It could be any single person's New York one-bedroom apartment. The wear and tear on the end of the sofa arms suggest the furniture is rental. One sofa, one side chair, one coffee table, two sofa end tables, two matching lamps, a queen bed in the bedroom, one dresser, and one side table. I can envision the rental form and the checked boxes beside the rooms of furniture.

They didn't fill it up with photos, as my cover role has no family and no boyfriend, and I shouldn't have a need to entertain anyone here. They did hang landscape poster art, so at least I'm not stuck staring at blank white walls.

I pull out my laptop to review my cover story one last time before I fall asleep tonight. As a new employee, most likely I'll be meeting a lot of people and could face a variety of random questions about my past. Where I came from, when I moved, how I found my apartment. I need to be consistent.

My phone rings. My personal phone sees little activity. I hesitate then read the screen. Aaron. I don't particularly want to talk to my ex. We haven't talked in weeks. But it might be important. I pull my legs up under me and answer before it goes to voicemail.

"Aaron, hi."

"I heard you're working UC now?"

"Yes. In New York."

"What the hell?"

"What do you mean?" I ask at the same time I notice my blinds are open and people from the building across the street can probably see me sitting on the sofa.

"I work undercover."

"Yes."

"You know relationships don't work when both partners are undercover. We'll never see each other."

I hold my phone out and look at the screen as if it's going to divine answers. Then I put it back to my ear.

"Aaron. We broke up."

"That was temporary. Until I finished this case."

"You've been on this case for over six months."

"And so what? You're walking away?"

"Aaron. I moved. I now live in New York."

"It doesn't matter where you live. I don't have that much time off between cases, anyway. Unless you meant it this time? We're done?"

I exhale, searching for strength. "Aaron, yes, I meant it."

"Sadie, are you asking me to stop working undercover?"

"No. No, I'm not. You love working undercover. But I didn't love us. And I especially didn't appreciate you telling everyone about us."

"That really pissed you off?"

I grit my teeth, refusing to get into this with him again. I worked hard to get where I am. The FBI is accepting of women. But that doesn't mean dating a colleague was a smart choice. Aaron didn't understand. Told me I was being *sensitive*.

"How long's your op?"

"Indeterminate." As if I'm going to tell him anything. "Who told you I'm UC now?"

Typical Aaron, he disregards my question. "When we're both off our cases, let's take a weekend. Talk. Don't take another case until then."

"There's nothing to talk about. We're done."

"I've been calling you every month. I've been calling you instead of my mom."

"Here is why that piece of information is disturbing. One, in all those conversations, I never had any clue you still thought we were dating. Not one. Think on that, Aaron. And call your mother."

I end the call. Angry at him...and myself. Him for opening his mouth and making me uncomfortable in the D.C. office. Me for putting up with him for as long as I did. The man is emotionally barren.

Wait. When was the last time I spoke to my mother? Or father? I check the time. Pot, kettle. It's too late to call them now. But it's not too late to call my little sis.

She answers on the first ring.

"Sadie? Are you okay?"

"Yes. Why wouldn't I be?"

"I don't know. You don't usually call me. And it's late here." I hear music in the background.

"Are you out?"

"Yeah, wait, I'll go outside."

"No, it's okay. I'll let you go hang with your friends." She's in college. She should be out enjoying herself. She's in Cambridge, so it's quite late her time, but she's a big girl.

"Well, tell me why you called?"

She knows me. If I call, I have a reason.

"Aaron called."

"Let me guess. He's back in D.C., and he wants you back. For the weekend."

"Well, not exactly. I moved to New York last week."

"What?" Her shriek pierces my eardrum.

"Go back to your friends."

"When were you going to tell me you moved to a different city?"

"Now. I called you. Remember? Now, call me tomorrow." Then I remember I'll be working and won't have my personal phone with me. "Scratch that. I'll call you."

"Don't forget."

"I won't. Promise."

THREE

CHASE

"Good morning, sunshine! Are you raring to go on this bright, beautiful Monday morning?"

"Yes, I am. Did you have a good weekend?"

Rhonda, my assistant extraordinaire, follows me into my office with a steaming cup of hot coffee just for me. I've already had one coffee on my way to work, but I love having a warm mug on my desk.

"Rhonda, you are too good to me. Best assistant on the planet." Her smile boosts my mood. She's so easy to make happy. I like having happy people around me. Life is too damn short to be pissy.

My laptop blinks to life as there's a tap on the doorframe, and Evan Mitchell and hot Frost crowd the doorway. Rhonda nods to them both as she backs out. "Let me know if you need anything."

"Sure thing. Thanks, Rhonda. You put the sun in my day."
She beams in response.

Evan steps forward, looking like himself in his drab suit and
tie, but Ms. Frost has some sort of wartime expression going
on. Once again, she's in black, only today she's in slim-
fitting, ass defining slacks and a black suit jacket over a
demure black blouse that could be so much more if she
unbuttoned one more button. I peer over the table, curiosity
getting the better of me. Yep, black high heels.

"Chase, do you remember Sydney? I introduced you both
Saturday night."

"Of course."

Ms. Frost stands behind my office guest chair, one hand
resting on the back of it, as the other holds a notebook. It
could be my imagination, but I'm fairly certain her fingers are
pressing hard into the back of the chair. I do a quick mental
rundown of what I've said that might have already pissed her
off but come up emptyhanded.

"As I mentioned, she's stepping into Tad's old role. HR has
cleaned up his office, but his files are a mess. It seems he
wiped his laptop before leaving, too, so Sydney here is
starting fresh. Do you mind helping her out? I know she's not
in your group, but you know this place like the back of your
hand, and I can't think of a better person to introduce her
around."

Evan's not lying. If they held a firm-wide popularity contest,
I'd win hands down. And there are over two thousand
employees in our New York offices. I'm an extrovert in a
cubicle minefield of uptight introverts. It works for me.

Case in point—everyone here wears suits. Men always wear ties. Me? T-shirt under a jacket, usually khakis, but sometimes I push it and go jeans. And you know what? My refusal to fall to an outdated wardrobe protocol hasn't hurt me *at all*. If anything, I stand out. I'm everybody's buddy. No one thinks I'm trying to climb the corporate ladder, because no one dressed like me is ambitious, right? Wrong. I've risen through the ranks faster than any of these other CPAs. My clients *love* me, probably because I'm a hell of a lot more fun on the golf course. But, at the end of the day, all the bosses care about is how happy the client is. And I'm in the business of making people happy.

"I'd love to help her get the lay of the land." I flash her my flirty smile, the one I usually break out if I'm introducing myself to a stranger in a bar. Solid dark eyes, so dark they're almost black, regard me with a studied coolness. A frost so chill it's spooky. This woman's perma-frown is a sign she needs a little of my brand of sunshine. I'll happily warm her right up. Of course, I'll do so in a completely professional and appropriate way.

"She's starting at ground zero. We can't find any of the work Tad did for the first two quarters of the year. Can you show her around our intranet, how to access our accounts, that kind of thing? I've told her if she runs into any issues or has any questions, she can come to you. I know you don't handle all our accounts, but if she has a question you can't answer, you'll know how to get the answer."

"Sure thing."

Evan exhales and runs his fingers along the top of his head, and the small patch of hair he has up there shifts. Rhonda and I use that patch as a meter for his mood. If it's lying down flat, everything's groovy. If the front has shifted a tad up, then something's brewing and you gotta keep it to business. If it's perpendicular, then we stay the fuck away. That's not an entirely fair assessment, as it could just mean he scored some office sex, or at least, that's what I like to imagine. To be safe, when the patch's upright, I follow Rhonda to the copy room.

Frost openly inspects me, and I get the distinct feeling she's trying to decide if she's going to reject Evan's offer for me to help her.

But then she says, "IT has me set up on my laptop. I should have access to everything now. Do you think it might be best if you come with me to my office? If you can show me around the intranet, then I can navigate and come up with a game plan and come to you if I have any questions. Does that work?"

The corners of her pale pink lips lift into an awkward smile. It's the most warmth she's shown me since I met her. I'm not worried. She'll grow to like me. All it takes is a little time around me, and eventually, I grow on people.

As we pass Rhonda's desk, I rap my fist against it and say, "Patch Level Two. Level Two." I shoot her with my finger, and she smothers a laugh. Sydney's walking in front of me, leading the way, all business, like any new employee learning the ropes.

We round the corner into her sterile office. There are no personal items at all, which is what you'd expect from a new employee. Other than the laptop and a large monitor to the side, and a cup holder with pens and pencils, there's nothing to indicate anyone occupies this office.

She points at my shirt. "Do you always dress like that?"

I glance down at my tee. It's a white t-shirt with a Batman mask and black font below it that reads *I'm not saying I'm Batman, I'm just saying no one has ever seen me and Batman in a room together*. I think the black works well with the black sports jacket I'm wearing today. But I get it. She's a conformist. She wants everyone to look the same and follow all the same rules. To her credit, my jacket covers part of the text, and therefore she can't fully appreciate the humor.

"Not a DC Comics fan?" I ask, holding out hope she's a huge Marvel fan.

"What is DC Comics?" she asks in a way that makes it clear she's not flirting with that answer. She genuinely has no idea.

I don't even answer because there's no real reason to. If she's reached adulthood and doesn't know the basics, then there's little that can be done. She's one hundred percent professional, not a joke to be found, as I sit down behind her computer and type away.

Hotness level be damned, she's coming across like an accounting stiff. It's not looking like we'll be hanging out after work drinking brewskies. This woman is not a PLU. I'll inform Rhonda. PLU is our inside code for *people like us*. You gotta be a PLU if we're including you in the after-work invite. That lust I felt Saturday night is shrinking the same way my favorite limb shrinks when thrown in Lake Michigan.

I show her around on the network, leave some notes for her, and jot down my office extension should she have any more questions.

I'm barely back in my office when my phone rings. No name shows up, but I hazard a guess that's because HR hasn't fully set her up yet.

"Hello."

"I clicked to access the accounting reports, and it's saying I don't have access."

Yeah, it seemed improbable she'd have full access on day one. Our IT department is competent, but far below outstanding.

"Tell you what, let me call my main man, Tommy, and send him your way to get you fully set up."

"How long do you think that will take? Do you have any paper files I can look through?"

I actually do have a gazillion files, which she probably surmised when in my office, as one wall of my office is file cabinets. The entire area behind Rhonda is also file cabinets. I'm the only guy in the place who keeps printed records of everything. Rhonda's nickname for me is tree killer. But it's not a good idea to hand the files over to Frosty. They could be outdated, and she'd be spinning her wheels. And she'd only have access to my accounts. BB&E is a shit load bigger than the twenty-five accounts I oversee.

"I'll get Tommy to make you priority number one. He'll be at your office in five minutes."

A brief huff crosses the phone line, making it clear five minutes does not meet her expectations.

After I dispatch Tommy, I call my good friend Anna to make lunch plans. If I'm going to end up spending more time today with little miss serious-as-can-be, all-work Frost, I'm going to need a relaxed, happy lunch.

As I chat on the phone with Anna, my desk calendar catches my attention. I'm in the office every day this week. That's problematic. I shoot a text to Rhonda to see if she can schedule some tee time for later in the week.

After Anna and I agree to a lunch spot, I head to the twelfth-floor conference room for Monday morning status with my team. Rhonda passes me a fresh cup of joe as she steps in place beside me on the way to the elevator. The elevators slide to close until a notebook thrusts between them, activating the safety catch to open the doors. Sydney steps inside as she mumbles an apology, or maybe it's thanks.

"What floor are you going to?" I ask, polite as ever.

"Twelfth? For your status meeting?"

"My status meeting? Why would you—"

"Evan suggested I attend all of the team status meetings today, or at least as many as I can. Several all happen at the same time, but he gave me a list of the ones he thought I should prioritize. You know, to get the lay of the land?"

What do I care if she attends my status meeting? She's coming in here as an internal auditor. To some, that means she's looking for screw-ups. But I know better than that. If she finds a mistake, she's really saving my ass. I'd much rather a colleague find a mistake than it be splashed across the nightly news as an accounting scandal that's tanking a client's stock.

As a CIA, she may be used to people treating her like the IRS. Maybe that's why she's all business. That would suck to fall into a career where everyone thinks of you as the enemy.

I exhale loudly, call on my inner camp guy, the one who reaches out to every loner, just as the elevator door opens.

"Ms. Frost, it will be our honor to have you attend our Monday morning status meeting."

Rhonda heads on into the conference room, saying hellos on the way in, as Sydney stops right outside the door, blocking my entrance. She looks me directly in the eye, but there's a soft blush to her cheeks that undermines her confident stance.

"I'm sorry if I was a bit brash this morning. Sometimes I can be a little abrasive."

Frosty, abrasive, tomato, tomatah. I smile and hold out my arm, directing her into the conference room. My team awaits.

"No problem. You've been fine." Really, she's been beyond uptight, but I knew I'd wear her down eventually. Everybody's got a soft side, some you just gotta work a little harder to soften 'em up. And, these days, I suppose I could stand to take a page from Ms. Frost and be a tad more professional.

Status passes issue-free. Sydney's pen writes down almost every word spoken. Something tells me she was the student who filled up multiple notebooks for each subject.

It takes forever and a day for lunchtime to arrive. The end of the quarter is coming up, and my phone has been ringing off the hook. Several of my clients want extensions or are calling with questions.

One account, an account I haven't yet really figured out, wants to go out Thursday night. It should be a pretty straightforward business, but the guy doesn't seem to have any office employees. I only deal with Joe, the owner. The guy disposes of biohazard waste, so I guess he hasn't felt the need to hire anyone to help with the accounting. I have this vision of his employees wearing rubber gloves and face masks as they dump chemicals somewhere in the dark of night, possibly in a river. I try not to think about it. He's this gold-chain-wearing guy straight out of Scarface, lives in Chicago, and whenever he comes into town, he handles the plans. My week is looking up.

When I step up to Osteria Delbianca, the small Italian restaurant we favor, Anna greets me with her signature, "Hey you!" and I pick her up and whirl her around. Anna's one of my oldest friends from Chapel Hill, and now she's chained down my good friend and grad school roommate, Jackson. Not to brag, but I was their *yente*. Yep. When he moved to New York, I set him up with a place in her building and orchestrated a few meet and greets to rekindle the old college flame. I've mentioned to Jackson more than once that I should be his firstborn's namesake. Seems fair. Or…maybe godfather.

We're seated in our normal table by the back window, but I see a better table out on the coveted terrace—or, well, roped-off sidewalk. It's the end of summer, and I'm not sure how much more time we have for outdoor seating, so I ask. The hostess loves me, so of course, she smiles as she leads the way to the only available *al fresco* table.

As Anna holds the menu, I do my habitual scan of her fingers. No engagement ring yet. I know Jackson's bought the damn thing. I was with him when he did it. And I wish I hadn't been because the guy's been waiting forever, and it might shock some people to learn this about me, but I don't really like having to keep secrets. Especially big-ass secrets.

"So, are you ready for this Saturday?"

I'm torn between going healthy-ish with a Venetian salad or going all out and getting a chicken parm sub. "What are you getting?" I ask, because if she's ordering a salad, that means she's planning on eating half my order. We've been doing the lunch thing for years.

"I think I might be bad and order the lasagna."

The waitress comes up, and I order the chicken parm. My hour run this morning, plus some evening weight time, and I'll earn it.

When Leigh Ann, our waitress, leaves, Anna kicks my ankle.

"So, this weekend? You're in, right?"

"Oh, yeah. Why wouldn't I be?" We have this cheesy bachelor-slash-bachelorette party that our friends are throwing. I don't know the couple well. Not a surprise, since any close friend of mine would *not* agree to have his bachelor party combined with the ladies. If that isn't a recipe for lame, I don't know what is. I hope Jackson doesn't get any crazy ideas from this shindig, because when it's his turn, I'll be the one planning his party, and it's going to rock the motherfucking casbah.

"Sam said you didn't RSVP. I told him I'd check in and make sure you're coming."

"What was I supposed to RSVP to?"

"The email that went out?" Anna sounds exasperated, which is hardly needed. It's our friends. Of course I'm going to show.

I snag a piece of bread from the basket, dip it in olive oil, sprinkle some salt and pepper, look up, and she's staring at me.

"What? Yes, I'm going. Jeez. I didn't realize Sam was being all girlie about it. I'll text the guy."

"It's not that big of a deal. I'll let him know. It's just Olivia is throwing this together last minute. She found out they were coming into town like a week ago, so she's stressed."

"Okay. Fine. I got it. Aren't we just meeting at Sam and Olivia's apartment?" I really do not see how anyone is stressed about this.

"We're meeting there, and then they have a whole night planned. It'll be fun."

Yeah, whatevs.

"Are you bringing a date?"

"Do I ever?" I snag another piece of bread as a loud bus rides by and a plume of exhaust floats out across the sidewalk. Oh, yeah, that's the reason I don't always sit outside.

"What about the wedding? You did RSVP for the wedding, right?"

"I wasn't raised in a barn. Of course I mailed back the RSVP card." I think. Pretty sure I did. Maybe. "I booked the hotel you said you and Jackson are staying at. In Iowa. I've never been there. You?"

Anna breaks down and reaches for a piece of bread. It was only a matter of time.

"No. But it looks lovely. Maggie is such a sweetheart. I'm really happy for her." She pauses. "You know, you should consider bringing a date to the wedding."

"Are you out of your mind? Out of town? No fucking way. Nothing says *I'm serious* like *come with me to an out of town wedding.*"

"Well, bring a friend. I know you have tons of them."

"You tired of me being third wheel?"

"No. Not at all. But it's gonna be a long weekend of couples. I want to make sure you have fun."

"Are Delilah and Mason bringing pipsqueak?" All our friends have coupled off recently at the speed of light. Mason has a daughter from a previous relationship, and a lot of times when we all get together, she and I end up hanging. I'm the fun uncle. Every kid's gotta have one.

"No. She's staying with Mason's mom. Delilah's pretty psyched about an adult weekend away."

Yeah, I know what that's code for. So, it's gonna be me with three lovey-dovey couples. Seventh wheel in the middle of Bum Fuck. Fabulous.

FOUR

Chase Maitlin's desk sits empty. Most everyone has stepped out for lunch, possibly down to the cafeteria, or they're behind closed doors in meetings. The top of Rhonda's head can be seen over the cubicle wall, and I can faintly hear the hum of her phone conversation. Unseen, I step inside his office.

Tall file cabinets line the back wall. A collection of signed baseballs, basketballs, and one soccer ball sits on top. To the side of his desk is a bulletin board packed with mementos. I step around his desk, curious.

Given the Mets schedule on the bulletin board, I'd assume he's a Mets fan, but I look back and see Yankees crap mixed in with the sports memorabilia on the top of his file cabinets. Upon closer inspection, Mets junk is mixed in too. There's no clear allegiance. There are a few New York Giants ticket stubs sticking out from the edge of a bulletin board, and on further examination, I discover those tickets aren't used.

They're for an upcoming game. I count the tickets, and there are six of them.

Everything on his bulletin board appears personal, and other than a photo of a dog, everything is sports-related. He has a desk calendar, and I'm about to pull out my phone and snap a photo of it when Rhonda calls out to me.

"Are you looking for Chase? He's at lunch."

I point at his bulletin board. "He's got quite the collection of interesting stuff."

With a fond smile, Rhonda surveys all the stuff crowding Chase's office. "Yeah, glancing around, you'd think he's a big sports guy. And, don't get me wrong, he likes his sports. But, for Chase, it's about the people he's with. He doesn't really care what team he's watching. He's not one of those guys who's in a bad mood after his team loses. He doesn't really care. He just likes being around people."

This is a woman who clearly likes her boss. She's probably in her mid-forties, and her wedding band and kid photos indicate their relationship is completely platonic, even if outside the bounds of a strictly professional one.

"I can call you when he's back from lunch?" she offers, hovering by the door.

I glance at my watch to check the time.

"His lunch meeting is probably running a little late. I can have him come by your office later this afternoon? I think he has an opening after three p.m.?"

I'd love to be able to continue looking through his office, and I glance wistfully at the day calendar left out openly on his desk. But Rhonda shows no sign of leaving me in here, so I thank her and leave.

When I make it back to my office, I pull out my phone and type into my notes app.

Chase Maitlin - long lunches, everyone's buddy. Takes clients to sporting events. Only employee in a t-shirt, no tie. How?

It's clear to me, if Maitlin is our guy, he's not stressed. Probably because someone up top is covering for him. He's the client relationship manager. I could tell from the status meeting that he has accountants on his team who do all the real work.

This morning's status meeting ran smoothly. One thing I'll give Maitlin, he has happy employees who know the drill. They ran through updates without any tension or drama. There was only one guy on his team who didn't joke around much. I even caught him rolling his eyes at one of Maitlin's jokes.

I flip through my file from the status meetings this morning. Garrick Carlson. He's the accountant who handles the pro bono work for the McLoughlin Charity, plus he handles four other business accounts, all based in Chicago. And two of those four accounts are the reason I'm undercover at BB&E Accounting.

I add one more note to my app.

Garrick Carlson - not too friendly. Didn't joke around with others.

There's a knock on my doorframe, and I swipe up to close out of the app.

"I heard you missed me." At five foot eight or nine, Chase is about my height in heels, but he somehow fills the doorframe with his smile and persona. He spreads his arms out wide, and as he does so, his t-shirt tightens across his chest, revealing muscular lines. As an FBI agent, I've spent a fair amount of time around gym rats, and looking him over, I realize he must be one.

"Long lunch meeting?"

"Nah. Met up with a friend. She's in advertising, though, and tends to eat lunch on the later side. Most of the folks at BB&E are heading out the door for lunch at noon sharp." He pulls out a chair and sits. "You know, it's your first day. We should have taken you out to lunch. I always do that for my team."

"I'm not on your team. It's not a problem."

"Yeah, you're not on my team, but I'm the one who's supposed to be welcoming you. Tomorrow?"

More time to get to know him? "Sure."

"I'll text Rhonda and ask her to schedule with my team. We'll go around the corner. You can get to know everybody." His fingers fly across his phone.

Perfect. "I'd love that."

"So, I know you're replacing Tad. But I'm not entirely sure what his objectives were. Are you simply double-checking to ensure our work is correct? Or are you evaluating resource needs as well?"

All traces of the friendly jokester are gone.

"Resource needs? You mean, personnel?"

He nods, lips in a straight line.

"Ahm, yes, technically, that is a part of the job description posted on the human resources board." His right eyebrow lifts, and I add, "The job I applied for. But, no, Evan hasn't highlighted that as a pressing priority right now."

He crosses an ankle over his knee and leans into the corner of the office chair. In a flash, jovial Chase returns. Interesting.

"Good to know. It's usually in the fourth quarter when BB&E identifies poor performers and layoffs happen."

"You have annual layoffs?"

His shoulders lift slightly as he considers my question. "BB&E isn't a strict Six Sigma firm, but they do adopt the approach to some degree. Are you familiar with it?"

"A bit."

"Well, the theory is you can trim about ten percent of your weakest performers each year, and bring in new blood, to build the most effective and efficient team."

"And yet you're still employed here." The snark slips out of my mouth before I can stop it. He grins.

"Yes, I am. It may surprise you, but I'm good at my job."

"That's what I've been told." The question is, Maitlin, are you gonna land yourself in prison for being too good at your job?

He taps the armrest. "So, what did you need to see me for?"

"Oh, I can't seem to access the pro bono accounts."

"You're starting with our pro bono accounts?" His tone says he doesn't approve of my tactical choice. Just like a man to be judgmental.

"I'm not starting there. I'm simply trying to ensure I can access everything. Today has been all about navigating an intranet from the eighties. Whoever handles your IT should be fired."

He comes around the side of my desk to view my computer. "I can't say I entirely disagree with you, but from what I can tell, it's multiple people, not just one. And IT's not a core competency or priority for the firm."

He zooms around, clicking options at lightning speed, and then frowns. The same error message I've received a dozen times flashes on my screen. Access Denied. I don't try to hide my amusement, because he was so confident I simply didn't know what I was doing.

He reaches across and taps a few numbers on the keypad for my phone.

"Tommy, you need to give Ms. Frost full access."

"I did."

The frustrated expression on Chase's face is priceless, but you'd never know it from his warm, friendly tone.

"Tommy, my man, I'm sitting here at her computer. She doesn't have full access."

"I'll be down in thirty." The line clicks.

Chase and I stare at each other for a moment, and then he dramatically holds his arms out wide and looks to the ceiling as if praying to the gods. I can't stifle a giggle at his exasperated facial expression.

He grins then asks, "Did you find the cafeteria?"

"You mean the break room at the end of the hall?" There's a full-size refrigerator in the small room, a coin-operated Coca-Cola drink dispenser, and a microwave and coffee maker on the counter.

"Nah. Come with me. Evan did a crap job showing you around and making you feel at home, huh?"

I follow Maitlin to the elevator bank, thinking about Evan Mitchell. He's been nice enough, and he seems to genuinely want to root out any corruption in his company. But I don't think he really knows how to deal with an FBI agent. It's not a big deal. A lot of people freeze up around agents, and I did get the distinct impression Evan's not the one who normally handles onboarding. But he's handling me himself because we all agreed the fewer the number of people who know there's an undercover investigation going on, the better. The head of HR, an older woman in her late fifties, is the only other person who knows I'm FBI. None of the employees in her department know the truth. They all think I'm a personal connection of Evan's who happens to be a perfect fit for their open position.

We're quiet on the ride down, as several other people are also in the elevator. When we reach Level C, the doors open into a large cafeteria. It's mostly empty, given it's midafternoon, but there's a deli, a pasta bar, an enormous salad bar, a griddle for hot sandwiches and fries, and one area with a sign that reads *International*. I point at the sign, and Chase explains.

"Supposed to be international cuisine. Changes daily. There's a menu for the month over there. You can also find a link to it on the portal home page. Some of the food here isn't that bad. The salad bar is always pretty fresh. It's packed down here during lunch. Anyone from the building has access, not just BB&E employees." He strides over to a coffee bar, which proudly serves Starbucks coffee. It's great and all, but there's a real Starbucks on the corner of our block. Chase opens a refrigerator and pulls out a large bottle of water then asks me if I want anything.

I bypass the soda fountain and select a bottle of water, too. Chase lifts it out of my hands. "I gotcha."

He continues talking as we head to the lone active cash register.

"So, do you live nearby?"

"Not far. Chelsea area. You?"

"Same. What street?"

"King Street."

"Hmmm. You know, we actually don't live far from each other." He sets the water down and pulls out his wallet from his back pocket. "Hello there, Ms. Wallace. How're you doing today?" The cashier smiles at him, and they act like friends for a minute as she swipes his credit card. When we're past her station, he asks, "So, what gym do you go to?"

Yep, nailed it. He's a gym guy. "I don't have one yet."

"Yet? That's right. Evan mentioned you recently moved here."

"Yes. From Los Angeles."

"Oh, you're one of those."

"What is that supposed to mean?"

"Nothing. I'm just giving you a hard time. Hhmmm, so, you're not only new to the company, you're new to my city. You should've said. I'll help you get your feet on the ground."

"Well, you could start by recommending a gym."

"I like Chelsea Pier. There's a gym in this building, too, but they don't have classes or anything. HR gave you the packet on employee benefits and all, right? The menu for this place should have been in that, now that I think about it."

I actually did not receive a packet from HR, but I make a mental note to ask for one. I don't like being caught off guard. I should at least be aware of what new employees receive so no one gets suspicious.

The doors to the elevator close, and Chase says, "You know, I've got this thing coming up this weekend. Some friends getting together. You should come with."

I pause and study his posture.

"I mean, not as a date," he's quick to clarify, "but to meet some of my friends. I have some good friends who you'd like. Besides, if you don't know anyone here, what else ya going to do?"

"I'd like to go. Thank you."

I am sincere in my answer. If I'm going to crack this case in two weeks, I need to figure out how guilty Maitlin is, and spending time with him, and getting to know his friends, is a great way to pick up that kind of information.

We each return to our offices. IT hasn't yet arrived. I close my door and dig down into my briefcase for my personal cell. It's almost too late to call my sister, as she'll likely be out again or busy with friends. The five-hour time difference can be challenging.

"Sadie, you called." Surprise resonates in her tone, which is entirely deserved.

"I said I would."

"Yeah, well... So, do you like New York?"

"I do. It's been less than a week."

"And let me guess. You've spent essentially no time outside the FBI office building."

Quinn spent one summer with me in D.C., and I don't think she'll ever let me live that summer down. It was an especially busy summer, and I still had a lot to prove as a new agent, so I put in a lot of hours at the office, leaving her all alone.

"On that count, you would be wrong," I tell her.

"Wait, are you working undercover?"

"Yes."

"Damn. You're like Dad."

"Don't say that."

"I meant in a good way. But you'll be careful, right?"

There's a knock on the door.

"I gotta go. Sorry."

"You're being careful, right?"

"It's a nothing assignment. Seriously. Boring."

The door cracks open.

"Yes. I'll see you at four p.m. tomorrow. Eleventh-floor conference room, right?"

"Just like Dad," is the last thing I hear before I hang up.

I smile at the man standing in my doorway. I assume he's IT, as he's not wearing a jacket or tie, and he's also wearing black running shoes.

"I hear you need help."

"Yes, I seem to have limited access."

"Well, I'm your knight in shining armor."

Out of nowhere, Chase comes up behind him. "Don't go stealing my lines. Just fix her computer, Romeo."

I laugh as the man steps behind my desk.

Chase pulls out one of my guest chairs for me as the IT guy taps away on my keyboard.

"Here, sit. I'll make all your problems go away."

The guy rolls his eyes. "I'm the one fixing her computer."

"Yeah, but I'm her knight."

It's all in jest. Chase's brand of casual is fun, not at all what I'm used to, and he kind of cracks me up. But he's also clueless. He's not so much my knight as my target.

FIVE

CHASE

My office phone rings right as I'm about to power off my laptop. Evan's name lights up the thin, narrow screen. Fan-fucking-fabulous.

"Hey, boss man."

"Maitlin. How did today go?"

"Fine," I drawl. Today wasn't anything special. Another Monday for the books.

"Did you get Ms. Frost settled in okay?"

"I believe she has full access now, and I showed her how to get around on the portal."

"Did she give you any indication of what she's starting on first?"

"No." There's an awkward pause, and the seconds blink by on my digital clock. "Do you want me to find out?" *She's not in my group. Doesn't report to me.*

"Yeah, maybe try to keep an eye out on what she's tackling. Tad left us in a lurch, and she's got a lot of catch-up to do. I want to trust her, let her figure this out on her own, but I also want to keep an eye on things, you know, in case she needs some guidance. I don't want to come across like I'm a micro-manager. She told me she doesn't like that, but if you could keep an eye out, I'd appreciate it. If she comes to you about any concerns, please keep me apprised."

"Sure thing. Not a problem, boss." I'm in charge of maybe ten percent of our accounts, but if this half-cocked oversight plan of your new employee lets you sleep better at night, fine.

"Oh, by the way, Cooper's coming back in town. He has some business meetings and wants to go out Thursday night. Can you join us?"

The chicken scratch on my desktop calendar bears the word *Joe*, reminding me I've already committed to one client.

"I'm supposed to go out with Biohazard Waste Disposal Thursday night. He let me know earlier today that he's coming into town. Do you want me to cancel?" There's no doubt Cooper's Chicago Real Estate Development Group is the bigger client.

"Nah, keep your plans. You getting out of here soon?"

"Yep. You?" *Come on, wrap it up.*

"Yeah. Gracie wants me to pick up Maura from soccer practice, so I've gotta run to make the 5:32 train."

"Ah, the life of the commuter."

"Yeah, stay single."

"Oh, I plan on it."

He laughs into the phone, and I hear other sounds that indicate he's closing up shop. I stand and throw my laptop into my backpack, ready to make my escape.

"And remember, keep me apprised of Ms. Frost. I need to know that she's starting out on the right foot."

"You got it, boss."

When I head down the hall, I pass her office. It strikes me that it's odd HR put our new internal auditor right by my office. Maybe someone else had already taken over Tad's old spot. Fluorescent lights fill her office as I zoom past her open door for the elevators.

Her sing-song voice floats out into the hall calling, "Chase." I pause, my attention on my compadres gathering by the elevators. *Fuck. IT probably screwed something else up. Damnit. I'm gonna have to wait to get into my weight rotation.*

I exhale my frustration, plaster on a smile, and spin on my heel. "Yes, sweetie pie?"

Her face contorts, like, wrinkles literally form on her brow, and a deep one shows between her eyebrows.

"Do you treat all of your colleagues with that level of disrespect?"

Oh, fuck, she's one of those.

"Not all of them, no. I thought you and I were becoming friends. My mistake. What can I do to help you?"

A perfectly polished, short nail taps on the desk, and I can hear her huff. She's cute and all, but she's interrupting my gym time. I'm the one who should be huffing.

"I'm sorry. This office is more casual than I'm used to. You're being nice. I know you didn't actually mean to disrespect me or treat me as a lesser colleague." *Lesser, what?*

"No, you've got it all wrong. I'm casual with everyone. Not just women. It's not about disrespect. I just wanna enjoy my day. That's all."

She stares at the middle of my t-shirt. There's a giant red stain on it from where marinara sauce leaked out of my chicken parm sub earlier today. *Yeah. It's stained. Get over it.*

"Thank you for your help today. Are you headed to the gym?" She points to my gym bag.

"On my way right now." I smile, mostly to hide how frustrated I am that I'm not in transit to said gym at this very moment.

"Maybe I'll see you there."

And this is my chance to get out the door. I shoot her with my finger gun and shout out down the hall, "Have a good night."

SIX

SADIE

Chase heads down the hall toward the elevator bank, and a chorus of "night, man" and "see you later" floats down the hall.

I power down my laptop and pack up. This is my first undercover assignment, and I'm not exactly nailing it. Why on Earth is his *laissez-faire* attitude getting to me? This isn't where I actually work. He is not another agent not taking me seriously.

UC is not my thing. Yes, I've gone through the training, but when I transferred to the New York office, it wasn't supposed to be my role. But things change quickly, and this should be a short assignment. One of Dad's motivational postcards comes to mind. *Great things never come from comfort zones.* I can do this.

Nothing in the reports so far shows anything suspicious. I've got to dig deeper, but what I really need to learn is who specifically knows some of these businesses are essentially laundering money. We have enough to indict a senator. I need to close this loop. Identify who is involved, and I'm out.

My pep talk streams all the way to Chelsea Piers Fitness, the gym that made our suspect's eyes light up when he waxed poetic about it. I checked it out online, and the monthly fee is so high it should be fabulous. There are a few classes I'm looking forward to taking. And there's a pool for laps.

The place is mammoth, so I'm a little concerned about the ease of observing him here. He said tonight he's doing weights. After changing in the spa-like changing room, I follow the signs to locate the weight room. We have a gym at the FBI field office, but I can see myself keeping my membership here after this case is over. Besides, if Maitlin's guilty, he'll be doing ten to twenty, so it's not like I'll be bumping into the guy I helped prosecute.

When I enter the weight room, he's talking to a beefcake by the chest press machines. Neither guy is lifting weights. They're just standing there talking. I pull out a mat to observe from a distance as I stretch. It doesn't take long to fully grasp how Maitlin spends hours at the gym.

He does reps on a machine, a guy comes over and talks, they both stand and talk for longer than he did reps, then he moves to the next machine. This could be where his real business takes place. I don't recognize any of these men, but I do use my phone and covertly snap a few photos so the team can research them later.

I can only catch snippets of his conversations. It all seems rather benign. Sports, stocks. Sometimes he tosses in a question about how the kids are doing. He always seems to know the kids' names. Standard light conversation.

He moves over to the cable machine. To watch him, it might look like this is nothing more than a social circuit, but those muscles say otherwise. His biceps bulge as he curls his biceps up and the block of iron plates lifts. No, those muscles say he's the definition of a gym rat. He's not beefy, like someone taking steroids, but I'd bet he's consuming protein shakes regularly, and he's spending most of his free time right here in this weight room.

As an FBI agent, I spend my fair share of time in the weight room, too. It's a required part of the job, maintaining a basic level of fitness. I've seen plenty of men lifting weights. So, I can objectively say, Maitlin has a good program. He's fit. He's wearing a shirt, but the tight fit of his t-shirt hints at well-defined pecs and nicely shaped biceps, and I'd bet he's sporting an attractive six pack. Not a bad male specimen. Too bad he's most likely destined for prison bars. Chase peers around the shoulder of the guy he's talking to, and I instinctively turn sideways.

"Sydney, is that you?"

"Yeah." The observation game's over. "I love your gym."

"Right? So, you joined?"

"Well, I'm on the free trial. But, yes, I think I will."

He taps his buddy on his chest. "Roger, this is my new colleague at BB&E, Sydney Frost. Sydney, this is Roger Baldwin. He's a gym regular, too. He lives in Lower Manhattan. You'll find people from all over come to this gym. It's great."

"Hi, Roger. What do you do?" I ask as his large hand engulfs mine.

"Ah, I work for Fidelity. Nice to meet ya." He effectively dismisses me, turning back to Maitlin. "If you get a chance, stop by the box at the game this weekend."

Roger Baldwin moves on to the next machine in his circuit, and Chase grins. He looks me up and down. "Lookin' good, Frost."

I'm wearing leggings and a tank. We're in a gym. There's nothing about my outfit that isn't appropriate or warrants an open evaluation. I glare back at him, the exact way I'd shoot daggers at any guy in the academy giving me shit.

He catches on quickly, and his eyes return to my face lightning fast. Then he grabs a water bottle and chugs.

The guys at the FBI gym do show respect. He and I are still colleagues. I stand at attention, chest puffed out. The clank of iron on iron breaks my ire, and I remember my assignment. *Get to know him.*

He wipes his mouth with his palm, and his gaze falls to my shoes. "If you need spotting, let me know. I know most of the guys in here, too. Some of 'em are single. So, if you're interested in anyone, lemme know. I might be able to do ya a favor," he tells me with a harmless, boyish smile, and I soften. Maybe the whole him checking me out thing was all in my head. Maybe Aaron was right, and I am too sensitive.

"Thanks. But no, thanks. I'm not interested in finding a guy. But I might take you up on spotting. I'm mainly doing hand weights today, though. You come here every day?" I have a routine I follow, and I've been able to complete it and put in extra reps in the time I've been observing Maitlin.

"To the gym? Yeah, but not weights every day. I love the Python's Tuesday evening spin class. I usually do laps Thursday. Weekends, I bounce around. But yeah, I'm here almost every day doing something. You can't get better than this place."

"I agree. It's a good gym." You'd think he owns the place the way pride shimmers off him.

"Good? It's fan-fucking-tastic." He grins.

I'm in tennis shoes, not heels, and he's only about four inches taller than I am, but it's the first time he's had a clear height advantage. It's also the first time I notice the amber flecks in his irises, and a few light gray strands mixing in with his dark hair. He's gonna be one of those men who flaunts the salt and pepper look. Not that he wants to look distinguished, but want to or not, he will.

"Yeah. It's way better than what I had in L.A. Thanks for recommending it."

"No problem. I love making people feel at home in my home-town. Which, speaking of, you're still coming with me Saturday night, right? To meet the gang?"

"Yes." I'd love to ask him about Mrs. Bennett, but I can't figure out how to word that question and not come off like a nosy bitch, or worse, an insecure female.

"Great. You'll love my friends. Anna'll pull you right under her wing. You'll be settled here in no time." The real me loves the idea of having girlfriends to hang out with on the weekend. But here I am, once again, devoting every minute of my weekend to work.

I go to leave, and Chase stops me. "No water?" he asks.

Before I can explain I usually drink from the water fountain, he walks away, toward the far wall and a gym bag. He lifts a

Smart water bottle out of his bag and delivers it to me. "Drink it on the way home. It's important to stay hydrated."

It's easy to see why everyone loves this guy. When he's not playing the tool card, he comes across as genuine and outgoing. Like he's everybody's friend. Of course, I suppose there are quite a few mafia guys over the years who've had the same schtick.

Later that night, I pull out my phone and type in a few notes.

Maitlin - Chelsea Piers Gym. Seems to know all. Gym routine hours long. Locate Tad. Why leave suddenly? Clean his computer?

SEVEN

C<small>HASE</small>

I buzz outside Sydney's building, then shoot her a quick text to let her know I'm here. She didn't want me to pick her up. She couldn't have been any clearer; this is not a date. But like I'm gonna have her show up at my buddy's place not knowing anyone. I'm not an insensitive prick. I'm friends with chicks, I have a sister, and I know it's uncomfortable to show up to a place where you don't know anyone all alone.

As I stand there waiting on the bottom concrete step, a text from EJ comes through.

Elijah Mason/MSC: You're in for tonight. Text your location, and the car will pick you up around midnight.

Fuck. I told the guy I had plans tonight. But he's one of those clients who acts like he's the boss of me. And the thing is, I know where he wants to go. Thursday night we were in a strip club. The place they want to go tonight makes that place look PG.

I stare at the phone, contemplating my response. When I first started hanging out with Tom Bennett and his college buds, I thought it was all good. Only good things could come from schmoozing with the bigwigs, right? One by one, each of his buddies requested me as their client service manager for their businesses.

They're good guys. Fun on the golf course, maybe not so faithful to their wives. I really don't want to know, don't want to judge. They're acquaintances. Business associates. But this pressure to join them all the time is starting to feel...not good. Doesn't make sense either. These guys are wealthy as fuck. Even if they want me there to write it off as business, well, they can write it off as business without me there. Although, really, the place they wanna hit tonight shouldn't be on anyone's tax records.

The door pushes open, and I step back. *D.A.M.N. Sydney Frost can snazzy it up.*

I fall back two steps down, taking her in. She's in smoking high heels and a tiny black dress that shows off some mighty fine legs she's been hiding in pants all week. Her hair's blown out, sleek, showing off an angle that's not quite so evident at the office where she pulls it back into a low bun for the sexy secretary vibe.

Fuck. I've been respecting my colleague, keeping it friendly and harassment-free, but damn. I should've been putting on my A-game. She might be all business and know next to nothing about comics, but she is fine with a capital F. I'd backed off taking that long shot, but now I might re-strategize.

"You didn't need to come and pick me up. I told you." She sounds annoyed. Frosty.

"I'm aware I didn't *need* to. I wanted to."

I bow to her, ever so slightly, holding my arm out to guide her to her chariot. Well, the Uber I paid to make one stop before the final destination. She rolls her eyes as I open the back door of the tiny Chevy for her. *Rolls her eyes*. I've been piecing Sydney together like a puzzle. My running theory is she's so into the professional work scene that when she's with someone who doesn't follow status quo, it throws her. If I played the part of a perfect corporate executive, I wouldn't be getting under her skin.

When I round the car and slide into the seat next to her, she looks me up and down. And not in a let's-get-it-on kind of way.

"What?"

"Do you always wear t-shirts?" Her nose scrunches a bit when she asks the question.

"Well, if you're asking what I sleep in, the answer is no. I prefer commando."

She stares out the window, and I lean my head back on the headrest and close my eyes. I didn't have to invite her out. She's not my client. She's not even on my fucking team. I'm just being *nice* to someone who has no friends.

The Uber stops at a traffic light, and we sit in silence. I should just tell her to forget about it. Leave her skinny, tall, frosty, yet simultaneously hot ass on the curb near a bar where she can find the kind of man she wants, because I am not her kind of guy. I'm not the kind of guy she'd choose to hang out with at the office, much less go out on a date with.

Once again, I try to be the nice guy, and then everybody feels free to walk right over me. *I have plans tonight. Can't go out.* Pretty solid and clear. EJ might as well've said, *You little peon. I own your ass, and you're coming out if I say you're coming out.*

"I'm sorry. I don't know what it is about you that brings out the bitch in me." Her meek, quiet tone lulls me out of my stew. She sounds almost…contrite.

I stop staring straight ahead at the vinyl headrest and give her a hard look. Then I do what I do best and let the simmering anger cool and go for a joke.

"You know, I'm pretty sure the original lyrics weren't going for that." She pauses, and the corners of her glossy pale pink lips turn up a tad. "You know, it's supposed to be 'brings out the man in me.'"

"I got the reference," she assures me. "But, seriously. You're being nice. Doing me a favor by introducing me to your friends. And I'm…"

"Being a bitch." Her eyebrows almost hit her hairline, so I backtrack. "Abrasive. You're being abrasive."

"I'm sorry." She sounds genuine.

"So, what am I doing that's bringing this out? Is it just my presence? You really hate t-shirts? You have a thing against short guys?"

A smirk plays across her lips, and she looks away for a moment. "You know, I think it's that you remind me of one of those guys who doesn't take anything seriously. I had to work damn hard, and some people don't have to work hard, and it gets under my skin. You know?"

I think back to business school and group projects. There was always one slacker. That's about as close to understanding what she's talking about as I can get.

"You know, I might joke a lot, but I do work damn hard. Don't let the jokester routine fool you. As one of the shorter guys, growing up, it felt like I had to push it twice as hard as anyone else. And being in the sub-six-foot category definitely didn't play well with the girls. Joking's been my go-to thing for a long time. Usually, it makes friends, though, not enemies." That's a touch of honesty I don't normally share, but it feels like she and I might have something in common. Maybe she had to work super hard for her grades, or maybe she ended up at a company with a lot of male testosterone. In financial services, it's not unheard of, that's for sure.

She reaches out and touches my knee. Her touch sends a tingling sensation along my thigh and into my nether regions, and goosebumps rise on my arms. It's a reaction I'm pretty positive she didn't intend to create.

"Hey." Her voice is sultry. Sexy. I can't even swallow. Those glossy lips shine, reflecting the streetlights we're whizzing past. She flicks her tongue over the full lower lip in slow-mo. "You're not that short. You're taller than me. When I'm not wearing heels."

She pulls her hand back with a friendly smile, and damn if I don't need to get out of my own head because for the briefest of seconds I thought she was going somewhere she so clearly was not going. Fuck. Maybe it's a good thing EJ's taking me out tonight. It appears I need a release. With *anyone* I can find.

The car pulls up outside of Sam and Olivia's building. They live in the T1, a new build, high-end apartment with stunning views of the Hudson and Manhattan. The skyscraper towers over the Hudson river, its metal and glass far more modern and imposing than any of the nearby brick apartment buildings and low warehouses. I hop out, thanking our driver, and walk around to open Sydney's door. She's already stepping out of the car by the time I round the trunk.

Sydney matches my stride as we head into the iconic glass building. She hesitates.

"Wow. That's a gorgeous building."

"Yeah, it is. Sam's one of the founders of Esprit Corp. He's loaded." I glance at her, deciphering how she's taking that info. Just in case, I add, "His *girlfriend*, Olivia, is one of our close friends. Anna, Olivia, and Delilah are the women I was telling you about. The ones I want you to meet."

"But tonight's a gathering for your friends Maggie and Jason, right?" She sounds tentative, like she's attempting to remember the names. I didn't really offer many details when I invited her.

"Yes. Jason is Sam's good friend. They're like brothers. Go way back. The girls have known Maggie for a while, and they're close, but Maggie and Jason moved to Chicago. They came back so Jason could clear out his apartment. He sold it. Think he signed the papers earlier today."

The doorman waves us through, clearly expecting us. I come here quite a bit to hang with the guys. Sam seems to prefer to have everyone over to his place as opposed to going out, and I have to say, I don't mind at all. At least, it works for me for early hours, but if I wanna get lucky, I have to cut out and meet up with other singles later on. I like this group and all,

59

but they are one coupled up crew. It's only a matter of time before big rocks are placed on all their ladies' fingers.

It's kind of funny. When we first moved to New York, I was the only one in a serious relationship, and I felt jealous of my single friends. Now, the tables have turned. I'm the only one not in a relationship, and at times, I do find myself jealous of these guys. They never stroke an urge to bar hop, searching crowds, aiming for a connection. They have all they need now, wherever they choose to go.

The elevator opens into Sam's foyer. I guide her down the hall, where Anna greets us.

"Anna, this is my new colleague, Sydney. She's the one I told you about, who's new to the city." Within seconds, Anna's guiding her over to the others.

Sydney's in good hands, so I head straight on back to the terrace, where I know all my buds are hanging. I do stop by the kitchen and pull out a few beers in case anyone else needs one. As I round the corner of the kitchen island, I take a moment to appreciate all the ladies in the house. They are decked out.

I glance down at what I'm wearing. I've got a sports jacket on, and jeans, but they're dark jeans. Like super dark, almost slacks-like. Yeah, I've also got a t-shirt on, but who gives a shit?

When I join the guys outside, they're dressed like me. No t-shirts, but you know, sports jackets. No one's in a tie. Jason's not even here yet. Jackson, my college buddy, is over talking on his cell on the far end of the mammoth terrace.

Sam greets me, and we both sit. Sam's brother, Ollie, nods and takes a beer from me. I set the extra on the table.

After we've got all the niceties out of the way, I mutter to Sam, "Hey, am I dressed okay for what you've got planned?"

Of course, Ollie overhears. "You know, I was gonna tell you, man, your ass looks kind of big in those jeans."

I flip him the bird, and he just laughs. *Thank you, Sydney, for turning me into a girl.*

EIGHT

Anna, Chase's good friend, loops her arm around mine and ushers me into the kitchen, where other women are gathered around an island. From where I am, we can see through the glass wall onto the terrace. All the men are sitting on two facing sofas in front of a gas fireplace. I'm new to New York City, but I've lived in enough cities to know this apartment must be insanely expensive.

My immediate thought when surrounded by such excess is *how did they get this money?* Anna passes a gin gimlet to me as I put on a convincing smile and sharpen my senses. Time to start digging.

"So, help me understand how everyone here knows each other."

Anna pauses then points around the room as she speaks. "Delilah and I work together, and Olivia and I used to live together. Chase and I knew each other at Carolina. My boyfriend, Jackson, and Chase lived together in grad school. And then, Maggie's fiancé, Jason, is childhood friends with Sam. Sam is the guy out there with cowboy boots on. This is his place."

I point to Olivia, a woman who towers over me, and ask, "And Sam is your boyfriend?"

She finishes nibbling an olive before answering, "Yes. We live together. Jackson and Anna live together, Delilah and Mason live together, and well, obviously Maggie and Jason do."

"Interesting. There's no way I'm keeping all that straight." I point out to the terrace, where I do want to understand the connections. "So, do all of the men work together? Or are they just friends?"

Delilah, the blonde, laughs, and her hands flail out in front of her as she speaks. "Oh, no. Mason's a veterinarian. He didn't know any of these guys until we met. But he was Anna's veterinarian." She raises an eyebrow and in a firm tone directs, "And that's a story we will not be sharing."

"What about Sam's business? Esprit. Are they a BB&E client?" All the women look at me. Shit.

Olivia taps a nail on her glass, considering as she answers, "I don't know who Esprit uses for an accounting firm. But, really, Sam isn't the one who would be dealing with that. He'd see top-line reports. Sam's more involved now in investing in other start-ups, almost more like a spin-off of Esprit. But, you know, if Chase ever wanted to pitch BB&E to Esprit, I'm sure Sam would help him out." Her nose wrinkles. "Does Chase do new business for BB&E? Or do you?"

"No, he doesn't. And I'm not trying to look for new business opportunities. Chase is more of an account manager, like client services. I do internal auditing."

Olivia gazes out the window at the men. "Hmm. I can definitely see Chase in client services."

Anna sidles up next to me, tapping my elbow. "What about you and Chase? Are you guys…?" She lets the question trail.

"Colleagues." I make a point of looking her directly in the eye, so she knows I'm not being coy. "I recently moved here, and he brought me along so I could meet people. He said he wants me to like his city, and he had great things to say about all of you."

Delilah pipes up. "That's our Chase. He's like a one-man welcome wagon." With enthusiasm, she points to Anna. "That's how he got Anna and Jackson together. Trying to make Jackson feel at home when he moved here."

Anna gives a half-laugh. "I'm not so sure I'd say he got us together." Then she redirects the conversation back to me. "You know, Chase can come off as a bit of a jerk, but under all those jokes, he's a good guy. He's been a good friend through the years."

Delilah adds, "Yeah, we love our Chase. If you decide to give him a chance, be good to him."

"First, he's a colleague." I hold out my index finger as if I'm directing a class. "Nothing is going on. Second, he doesn't strike me as someone who's exactly looking for a relationship."

Olivia responds with a slight smile. "I tend to agree with you that he's a player. But we've been hanging out with him for years, and you're the first woman he's brought around us since his ex-girlfriend. All that said," she pauses to make eye contact with both Anna and Delilah, "leave her alone, guys. I understand what it's like to not want to date a work colleague. Drop it."

"It's okay." Ex-girlfriend. Maybe she couldn't handle corrupt dealings. Harder to be in a relationship when you're skirting the law. But what about Mrs. Bennett…? "So, the player bit. Do you know, has he dated anyone through work before?" I twist my heel back and forth, hoping to come across like a tentative, curious girl, someone who may be debating dating a guy.

Olivia and Delilah look to Anna to answer. She shakes her head slowly. "No. But I wouldn't know. It's been years since he told me about anyone." Her squint and tilt of the head tell me she's questioning if I'm asking for me, so I offer additional background.

"I met Chase at a function last weekend, and there was a woman there he seemed close to. I just wondered."

Maggie sets her glass on the counter and asks, "Were you at the McLoughlin Charity Gala last weekend?"

"Yes. Were you there?"

"I knew I'd seen you before." She snaps her fingers. "I was trying to place you. Yes, I was there. I work for The Health Foundation, but I used to work for McLoughlin. The group I work for now does some work with McLoughlin, and since it's my old company and a lot of my connections, they sent me out. We're planning a similar fundraising event this holiday season."

I step around the island to stand closer to Maggie. "When did you work for McLoughlin?"

"Up until, let's see…" She counts on her fingers for a moment. "I guess a little over nine or ten months ago. It's crazy how time flies. McLoughlin was my first job out of college. It's hard to find jobs in the non-profit sector, and cancer research is important to me, so I stayed there for a long time."

"So, is that how you met Chase? Because BB&E handles the McLoughlin Charity account, right?"

She shakes her head, which is the wrong answer. Because they absolutely do.

"I don't really know. I didn't handle that. I don't have any idea about that." She tilts her head and stares out the window as if she's thinking about something. My gut tells me she just realized something.

"What is it?" I aim for light and hope I'm coming across as if I'm making casual conversation.

She blinks rapidly as if dismissing an idea. "Nothing. It's nothing at all. So, which woman did you think Chase was close to?"

This right here is what makes being undercover so tough. If I were interrogating her, I could get right to the point and find out exactly the connection she just made between BB&E and McLoughlin. Instead, I've got to take it slow, meander through the conversation, and not raise any suspicions.

"She was beautiful. Decked out in diamonds. Purple gown."

"You mean Mrs. Bennett?" Maggie's mouth gapes open, and her face contorts into a look of mild disgust. "No way. First, I don't believe Chase would go out with a married woman."

Olivia angles her head. "Really? I could see it. It's the perfect non-relationship. No threat of commitment."

Maggie shakes her head, firm. "Not the CEO's wife. No one is that stupid."

"She's the CEO's wife? Yeah. No. Chase wouldn't. And the thing about his player status? He's more talk than anything. Trust me. I could tell you stories." Anna looks me in the eye, ignoring the others. For some reason, she wants me to believe her.

Olivia squeezes Anna's shoulder while smiling at me. "Anna sees the good in everyone. And Chase is like a brother to her. So, weigh anything she says with that background info."

Anna wrinkles her nose at Olivia then sets about refilling everyone's glasses. The conversation changes to Maggie's remaining wedding preparation.

My team thought it was great I was going out tonight. They briefly discussed if I needed backup, but for white-collar crime, it's not needed. It's not like I'm infiltrating a gang. This is hardly a dangerous assignment, but it is moving more slowly than I anticipated.

I've gained full access to the BB&E intranet and haven't discovered anything suspicious. I've shared tons with our team, who are currently doing additional analysis. There's a whole set of people listening in on audio in the building. We know someone at BB&E is falsifying records, but who? The most likely person is still Chase.

My gaze flits from face to face, circling the kitchen island, and out onto the patio. If he's indicted, his friends will be shell-shocked.

When Sam enters the kitchen to announce it's time for us to leave, the only one he looks to is Olivia. The saying *I only have eyes for you* comes to mind. All the couples have the goo-goo eyes thing going on. It's sweet. These seem like nice people. But, unfortunately, sometimes nice people make bad decisions.

All the couples pair up as we head out, leaving Chase and me together. When we exit the building, there's an extra-long limousine awaiting us. I notice a man in a black t-shirt and dark jeans hovering nearby. He's watching all of us, but standing back, out of the way. What catches my attention is the bulk on his hip. He's carrying.

No one else notices the guy. Why would they? They've all been drinking and are out to have a good time with friends. Sam's the last one to pile in, and he gives a quick nod to the man before ducking into the car. I watch as the man gets into the passenger seat of a black Tesla that's sitting behind our limousine. *Does Sam have security?*

We pull up in front of the Moxy hotel for dinner reservations at the Fleur Room, a rooftop club lounge. We're all admiring the panoramic skyline when Chase circles his arm around my waist. "Are you doin' okay?"

His proximity is unnerving, but Chase touches everyone. I exhale to relax into my role. "Yeah. Your friends are really nice." Be truthful when you can. Undercover 101.

"I knew you'd like them. You don't have to stay the whole night. From what I've been able to gather, Sam and Olivia have reservations for us at several places tonight, and they're planning on playing it by ear. Seeing what everyone wants to do. Knowing this crew, I wouldn't be surprised if this is the last place they make it out to. Rallying them to multiple locations is next to impossible. I mean, they might make it to three a.m., but they'll probably own their one table the whole night."

"No, I'm having fun. Are you afraid I can't keep up if it's a late night?"

"Nah, I just don't want you to feel obligated to hang. I have to cut out around midnight."

The others are making their way to a private table, specially reserved for us, but I lean into Chase to hold him back for a moment.

"What do you mean? Where are you going?"

"I've got clients I've got to meet." He looks pissed.

"Are you serious? On a Saturday night?" My tone becomes more shrill with each question, genuine surprise leaking through. Then it hits me, this is when the real business occurs. And I need to be there.

He shrugs. "Tell me about it. EJ's in town."

"Who is EJ again?"

"CEO of Medical Supply out of Chicago. He's in town for the week."

"Didn't you say you went out with him Thursday night?"

"Yeah, I did. Apparently, he likes the way I hold his hand."

Sam stands and waves us over. Chase places pressure on my lower back to guide me to the table. Two empty seats have been left vacant for us.

When we sit, I notice the man with a concealed weapon is standing back behind the hostess desk, near the elevator entrance. I lean closer to Chase and whisper, "Does Sam have security?"

He nods and adds, "Mainly to keep media clear. He used to have it everywhere. I don't think so much anymore."

Interesting. Our team will need to look into Sam. It doesn't seem someone whose job is to keep the media away needs a concealed weapon. There could be something more going on there.

Two waiters have arrived with plates of hors d'oeuvres and are setting them down in the middle of the table. A waitress makes her way around the table for drink orders, even though Sam has already ordered wine and champagne.

I stay close to Chase's side. Our legs touch beneath the table. He wraps his arm around the back of my chair, and it's tempting to lean into him, but I don't. Chase is at ease during the dinner conversation and pays careful attention to me, bringing me in and asking questions to keep me engaged. At one point, he offers me a bacon-wrapped scallop then feeds it to me. Back at Sam and Olivia's, he was keeping an eye on me. I know this because I've been tracking him, and every now and then, I've had to glance away quickly. There's an interest level that I can leverage.

Chase plays the role of the perfect host, making me feel like I'm a part of his crew, even though we just met. If this was real, if I really was simply a colleague, I'd be making friends in my new city. Girlfriends I could call on. Yet, I remind myself, this is work. These people won't have anything to do with me when this case concludes.

I'm careful with the alcohol, but after one glass, my shoulder muscles loosen up and the conversation flows more easily. As dinner progresses, Chase and I rub against each other. Not on purpose, but our knees knock. His arm grazes my back when he rests it on the back of my chair, relaxing. My body reacts each and every time. It shouldn't, but it does. The flutter, the burning warmth, the mild electrical current zapping me each time we bump. The sound of his laughter, a deep chuckle, warms me from the inside out. When he laughs, I laugh. It's infectious.

My physical reaction is disconcerting, but it's not like I'm in danger of falling for a guy about to do ten to twenty. Flirting will increase the chances he'll bring me along later on tonight, so I do it. Leveraging this attraction is part of the job. If I play it right and let Chase think he's gonna get lucky, maybe I can overhear some of what they talk about. A meeting late at night is definitely suspect. This is not standard client service. I should be there. *Whatever it takes.*

Chase's cell vibrates, and he excuses himself. He steps outside of hearing distance from the table. I excuse myself to go to the ladies' room and walk up behind him. He sees me, smiles, and nods. I slow down as I pass, hoping to overhear his conversation.

When I exit the restroom, he's still on the phone. I stand by the door observing him, unnoticed. He might be the gym's all-star social attendee, but he's lifting some weights during all those hours too. As I skim lower, I confirm that yes, he's sporting a firm torso and he fills out his jeans nicely. He says he runs or bikes every single morning before work. His trim waist proves he's speaking the truth.

"I'll be out in a few." He winks at me as he ends the call.

He drops his phone into his pocket. "I've got to go for that client thing I mentioned. But you stay out with everyone tonight and have fun. You're getting along with everybody, right?"

"Yes." I step up to him and do something the real me would never do. I press my body up against his and place my fingers on his chest. My cheeks heat at the absurdity of what I'm doing and my last-ditch effort to be included, almost like a real-life sparrow. "I want to go with you."

"Trust me. You don't want to go where I'm going." He glances down at my hand, and I pull it away, knowing this must seem like it's coming out of nowhere, but he captures my retreating hand and places a light kiss over my knuckles.

"Sydney, trust me, I'd love nothing more than to bring you along tonight. If you're up for it, maybe we can go to dinner another night?"

His hand loops behind my back, and his brown eyes fall to mine.

"I'd like to go to dinner sometime."

His eyes narrow. "As a friend or a date? Since we work together, I'll let you lead." His dark eyes focus on me, full of interest, and inside I flip, which is ridiculous.

I suck on my bottom lip to buy time. I could play this two ways. I could go back to acting like we're just colleagues, which is the role I'm supposed to play, or I could express interest and hope I learn something by going deeper under cover. Or, well, at least playing a more involved role.

"I'd love to go on a date with you." His gaze narrows on my lips. I inch closer, close enough I can breathe in his musk scent. My heartrate quickens.

"You let me know when you're available, and I'll plan a first date you'll never forget." With a glance at his wrist, he places pressure on my lower back to guide me back to our table.

I grab his hand, preparing to beg him to take me, but I stop myself. If I do more, it'll be suspicious, too out of character for Sydney Frost.

When we make our way back to the table, I can't help but notice all the smiles cast our way from the ladies.

Chase announces his departure. "Everybody, I've got to head out. Sydney's going to stay and hang out for a bit longer."

Jackson's the first to speak. "Where are you off to?"

"Pain in the ass client. Take care of Sydney, okay? Car's outside waiting, so I've got to run."

He gives me a quick nod, takes two steps, then backtracks and places a soft kiss on my cheek. "Looking forward to our date," he says so only I can hear. I watch him hustle out of the restaurant, pausing to say something quickly to Sam's security guard.

I stand before the table as all of his friends gawk at the stranded girl.

Anna breaks the awkwardness. "Sit down. Where's your drink? Are you drinking red or white?"

"I'm not. Thank you, guys. It was so wonderful to meet you, but I think I'm going to head out, too."

Maggie jumps up, arms out, as if she's going to embrace me or something, and I hold out my palm. "Seriously, I'm wiped, guys. It was so great to meet all of you."

Maggie smiles and proceeds to wrap her arms around me. As I'm hugging her goodbye, I congratulate her on her upcoming wedding, and she says, "Oh, you should come with Chase! It's going to be in my parents' back yard. It's not a big wedding, and I've been worried about Chase not having fun. Please come."

"Well, he hasn't asked me to come." You can tell she's one of those girls who's nice to everyone. She reminds me of my sister. She's super soft, whereas I've always been the harder one. Harder to get to know, slower to let you in.

"Oh, he will. He hasn't been able to stop looking at you all night. I'll work on him."

"That's okay. It's very sweet of you—"

"No. It'll be sweet of you if you come. I really hope you do. It's gonna be a relaxed weekend. It'll be fun, I promise. And everyone's coming out on Sam's private plane, so you don't have to worry about airline tickets."

"I've been telling Chase he should bring you," Anna adds. These guys are too much. Did they not see him leave me behind tonight?

I rush my goodbyes, and with a backward glance at the table, I doubt they'll be making it to any of the other locations Sam and Olivia planned. Delilah mentioned the disco balls up at Paul's Cocktail Lounge, but all the couples look too content to envision them heading out. Several customers stand waiting for the elevators. A small sign on a door farther down indicates an exit stairwell, and I push the door open and sprint.

When I exit the Moxy lobby, a dark sedan awaits us on the curb. The driver's wearing a suit, and I spy Chase slip into the back seat.

I step out onto the street and hail a yellow taxicab.

"Can you follow that car?"

The cab driver glances in front of him, to the black sedan, then back at me, and laughs. "Are you joking?" he asks in a thick, heavy accent I would place as New Delhi.

"No. I'm not. Please. Now." I stare straight ahead, determined not to let the black sedan out of sight. "I'll pay you twenty extra."

He presses on the accelerator, and we lurch forward, moving a couple of cars behind Chase. Traffic is heavy, but so as long as we don't get stuck behind a stoplight, we shouldn't lose him.

Inside, anticipation stirs. I'm giddy. My first chase. It's not high speed, and it's nothing like I imagined as a kid, but I'm in pursuit.

"So, he's cheating on you?" The taxi driver asks. He's facing forward, but he's watching me through the rearview mirror.

That's not a bad cover story, so I go with it. "I think so. I don't want to lose him. Can you stay close?"

I settle back into the seat, keeping an eye on both the black vehicle ahead and the street signs passing by. We're headed in the direction of the midtown tunnel.

"Keep following?"

"Yes. Please."

Shit. This isn't smart. I didn't put on a wire because it didn't seem necessary tonight. This was more of a get-to-know-the-friends night. I hadn't anticipated anyone would open up with any details I needed on wiretap. Now, I'm leaving the city. But it's fine. I'll just see who he's meeting. Snap some photos. He'll never know I'm there. There's no risk. No reason to call Hopkins.

The drive over continues about fifteen minutes after we exit the midtown tunnel.

"Slow down," I tell the cab driver once we're on more vacant city streets. Even a yellow cab following closely will get noticed eventually. My cab driver has a smile on his face, fully entertained.

The neighborhoods have disintegrated quickly the longer we've driven. Graffiti lines walls, and the streets are darker. The cars parked along the street are banged up and a mix of older models.

"Where are we?"

"Warehouse district. Jersey City. That way is Hoboken." The cabby points out the passenger window.

The sedan stops in front of a nondescript brick building. There are no visible business signs all along the rundown, poorly lit street.

"Turn right on that next block."

He does so, turning at the corner before Chase's exit point. "You sure you want to get out here?"

"Yes. I know the area. It's fine." I lie.

The moment we're out of sight of Chase, he stops the cab, and I toss him the money. I should get a receipt for reimbursement, but I don't take the time to do so.

"Good luck, lady," the cabbie calls before driving off.

I rush along the side of the building, returning to the street where I saw Chase exit the cab. I peer around the corner, hidden by the building. Cigarette butts and broken glass litter the sidewalk. A couple of sedans are parked farther down the street. There's a broken streetlamp on the corner, which explains the darkness. Farther down the block, a streetlamp is partially busted, and the light has gone spastic, flicking on and off.

Chase looks calm. He raps his knuckles against a heavy metal door. The door at one point in time may have been painted red, but it's heavily faded, and some of the paint has completely chipped away, exposing smooth stainless steel.

The door opens, and a tall, muscular man blocks the entrance. He takes one look at Chase, and a big smile spreads across his face. From my hidden perch, his teeth glow white. The guy is enormous in a bodybuilder kind of way.

Chase disappears inside, and the door closes again. The black sedan drives away.

I cross the street. My heels *click clack* across the pavement. A stumbling couple turn the corner and approach the door Chase passed through. The woman is giggling and leaning on the man for balance. The man appears fairly intoxicated himself. He pounds on the door, and the woman squeals. "I can't believe I let you talk me into coming here."

"You love it." When the door opens, he's sucking her face.

I stand on the corner of the street, fully aware that I probably look like a prostitute. But, standing on the corner, I can observe without gathering suspicion.

"What the fuck? Let us in, man."

"Members only. I can't letchu in."

"Come on. It's Caitlyn's birthday."

"How much have you had to drink? Fuck. Did you take a cab?"

The next thing I know, he's leading the woman and man over to the far corner. All three are shouting at each other. That's when I notice the door is slightly ajar. The bouncer left a wedge in place to keep the door open.

Headlights appear farther down the street, and the bouncer waves his arms. When the cab pulls to a stop, the woman falls backward, and both men huddle over her while peals of laughter fill the street.

I jump at the opportunity while the bouncer's back is to the door and he's working in tandem with the drunk guy to try to pick the woman up from the sidewalk and get her into a cab.

The last thing I hear as I slip past the door is the cab driver shouting, "Aw, man, I don't want no vomit."

A dark, velvety curtain hangs from the ceiling, feet from the door entrance. A pulsing beat with a deep bass plays and the lights are dim.

The bouncer will be back any minute. I need to move. Exhilaration courses through me, my senses on high alert. I slip past the velvet curtain and find myself in a bar.

I survey the area. Maybe ten small round tables line the perimeter. The front of the bar is wrapped in leather, and about fifteen bar stools are in front. A man and woman sit in one of the small tables with cocktails. Three men are seated at one end of the bar. A lone man sits about midway along the bar talking to the bartender. Club music pulses louder on this side of the curtain, uninhibited. Velvet curtains hang, covering all walls. There are no windows. It's difficult to discern where the door is as the heavy drapes hide all exits. No emergency signs light the way. This room is not to code.

I stand to the side, partially hidden by the velvet curtain. I don't see Chase. I watch as the lone man stands and pulls back the black velvet curtain on the far side of the room and disappears.

I straighten and nod to the bartender. He focuses on the drinks he's mixing, disregarding me. I stride toward the same panel I saw the man go through. Behind the curtain is another door. The music plays louder.

The man I followed is engaged in conversation with another man. They appear to be watching video on a phone together, with both heads bowed and focused on the screen. The man is standing behind something that looks like a hostess stand, and there are small cubbies behind him that are filled with phones and slim evening bags.

I inhale and go for it, stepping past the men, aiming for a confident air, and slip past another velvet curtain.

A blue light over a center stage lights the room. On stage, a woman is down on her knees, blowing a guy.

So, it's that kind of club. I've read about these places, but I've never been to one. I'm staring, transfixed. I force my gaze away from the performance and survey the room. Farther off is another dark stage, with a cross and swing. All along the perimeter of the room are dark alcoves. Rhythmic, low music pulses as a backdrop. The walls and floor are black.

One entire wall is a series of alcoves with leather semi-circle booths. A man sits in the back of one booth, his head tilted back, eyes half-closed and a look of ecstasy plastered on his face. His hand presses on the back of someone's hair, forcing the head down. The table is pushed back, giving them enough room. The space is dark, but the two are clearly visible.

A woman parades by dressed in heels and a black leather thong. The piercings on her nipples shimmer in the blue light. She smiles at me as she passes. In another booth, the woman crawls onto her companion's lap. She's wearing a looser skirt that drapes his thighs. His hands grip her hips, and he guides her up and down.

The carnal scene is an assault on the senses. It's dreamlike. A bizarre fantasy. I sink back against the black velvet curtain, thankful I'm wearing a black dress, but fully aware I'm not invisible. My demure, chaste black cocktail dress, as compared to the attire of the other women in here, hardly fits into this scene.

What the hell is Chase doing?

NINE

CHASE

"Do you wanna go in the back?" Brittney presses her barely clothed body up against mine, and her hand grazes my crotch.

I lift her hand, polite and all, but I'd rather she not fondle my junk. I'm not anywhere near drunk enough for this shit.

EJ sits back in the center of the booth, watching the show going on stage, while Blue Bell cradles up beside him. I step back. I have a hunch what her hand's doing underneath that table, and I'd rather not see it. Sure, voyeurism can be great, but this right here isn't my scene.

It's one thing to show up with a bunch of guys, sling some drinks back, watch some shows, get a few lap dances in. I've noticed the married guys are somewhat likely to take a chick into one of the back rooms. Me, I don't need to buy it.

Several of the domainers I do business with are Eastern European, and they fucking love this shit. EJ, the client who has been all over me to come tonight, is one hundred percent

American, but he's a bit guido. Can't say I was shocked to learn he knew about this place or liked coming here. For all I know, this place is how Tom and Evan won his business. Can't underestimate the value of networking.

Still, it's awkward as fuck. Me standing here holding Brittney's wrist, a sex act going on behind me, and EJ sprawled out like a kingpin getting fondled in front of me.

"EJ. Man. What the fuck am I doing here?"

"Come sit."

"Nah. Man. Come on, now. I was at my buddy's engagement party, and you made me come out here to sit?"

"Aw, don't be like that." He shifts in the booth and grasps Blue Bell's wrist, shoving her arm as if it's a napkin he needs to dispose of. Then he slips out of the booth and hands his cell over to her.

He zips his pants up and drapes an arm around me and, to Blue Bell, says, "Take a photo."

"What the fuck, man?" I shove his arm off me, careful to avoid touching his hand. "How'd you even get a phone in here?" They collect phones before anyone comes into this side. No one here wants photos commemorating this shit. It'd be powerful blackmail over half the suits that come to this place.

A stupid-ass, sloppy, drunk grin spread across his face. Fuck. *What a fucking waste. I had things going with Sydney, and this fuck...*

A bright camera light flashes, cutting through the blue wave strobe lights.

"What the fuck?" EJ and I say in unison.

"Dumb bitch. You can't use a flash in here." EJ reaches across the table and snags the phone.

He messes around with it then hands it back to her.

"Once more. For posterity." Then he reaches out and pulls Brittney over, positioning her beside me. The black leather straps across her chest leave her breasts and nipple piercings fully exposed, and the black leather thong doesn't cover much either.

Blue Bell smiles as she holds the phone up, angling it every now and then. EJ's so hammered he can barely stand straight. Brittney's hand roams over my chest, and once again I stop her from going lower, this time with a pointed shake of my head that clearly says *no*.

"Who else is here?" I ask without attempting to soften my annoyed tone.

"Bennett and Mitchell are in the back. They'll be out soon. Sit."

He gestures to the booth as a bouncer approaches.

"I need that phone. You know you can't have it in here."

"Fuck you're gonna take my phone," EJ slurs, getting all up in the bouncer's face. The muscle-bound guy shoves his chest out, my cue to back away.

One thing about Club Casablanca, they are on it protecting members' privacy. No need to worry about those photos, 'cause they'll never see the light of day.

The sex act on stage hits a climax, pun intended, and both men ejaculate all over a woman as she holds her tongue out like it's marshmallow creme. Annoyance and anger simmer, and the whole scene on stage has the effect of someone raising the heat level on an almost boiling pot.

Fuck EJ. Fuck these guys. This is all bullshit.

My shoes pound the concrete floor as I head to the exit. A bouncer has some chick cornered up against one wall, and her fist clutching the velvet drape strikes me as desperate. It's a small detail that barely registers. One step farther, and I see her face.

What the fuck?

TEN

Sydney

A firm hand grips my shoulder. "Ma'am. This is members only."

He roughly pushes me toward the exit, and I stumble.

"Sydney?" Chase's voice calls after me.

Busted. I close my eyes and breathe in and out deeply.

"Surprise," I offer up in a weak voice.

"You followed me here?"

"I wanted to see if you were meeting someone. You know, the girls said you were a player, and I didn't know if they were telling the truth."

"So, you followed me? Out to Jersey?"

"Crazy, huh?" I say, shrugging, hoping like hell he's buying this.

"Yeah, I'd say. You're making my ex look sane."

A new act has stepped up on the stage, and the two men and woman are taking turns kissing and fondling each other. The guy takes the other guy's dick out and the woman falls to her knees. I have to turn my back on the stage in order to focus on the situation.

Chase smirks. "I told you. This isn't your kind of place."

The bouncer steps right up to Chase and towers over him. "Is she with you?"

"Yeah," Chase answers, squinting, most likely full of questions.

"You got to check in your guests. Did she sign the agreement? And you can't have your bag." He gestures to my clutch.

Chase wraps his arm around me and guides me back behind the last set of velvet curtains. The bouncer hands me a clipboard and pen. I skim through a contract. It's a non-disclosure agreement. This place isn't at all legal, yet they are distributing NDAs? I sign and hand over my clutch, which happens to hold my FBI issued cell phone and credit cards. But there's nothing in it that can blow my cover. No, I seem to be doing a remarkable job of endangering my cover all on my own.

After I've signed what I assume is an unenforceable NDA, Chase guides me into the bar area.

"Would you like a drink?"

I shouldn't. I've already had several, but my pulse is racing along at laser light speed. "Yes, please."

We both sit at the bar, and he orders our drinks.

"What is this place?" I ask the moment the bartender walks away.

"Uh-uh. I get to ask the questions. How did you follow me?"

"I saw you get into the sedan, and I was getting into a cab, and I just wanted to see where you were going, and then I got more and more curious—"

"More and more curious, huh? And what would you have done if you had come in here and seen me with a woman?"

Chase leans forward, and I brace, unsure what he's going to do, but all he does is slide my hair behind my ear. I search for any sign he's threatening me, or considering hurting me, but his body language doesn't show any signs of aggression. If anything, the tilt of his head indicates a level of confusion.

"If I'd seen you with a woman, I would've been disappointed. I mean, I was just curious. I figured if I was entertaining crossing the line with a colleague, I should try to make sure it was worth it."

I lick my lower lip, remembering that earlier tonight, running my teeth across my lower lip had lured his focus and made me think he might kiss me. I hold my breath, waiting to see if he's buying it, while simultaneously mentally retracing my steps out the exit door, and weighing if the bar stool will work as a defensive weapon.

"You know, I didn't think you were interested in me."

"It's that we work together. I want to be taken seriously. And I'm a new employee."

"But yet you followed me?"

Desperate times, desperate measures. I move off my stool and stand between his legs. He cups my jaw, controlling. I match his position. My thumb strokes the grizzled late-night scruff along his jaw. We inch closer, eyes locked. The tip of my nose brushes his. I am close enough the warmth of his breath tingles. His hand caresses the curve of my ass and gently presses me closer. I capture his lips with mine.

The adrenaline coursing through me intensifies the kiss. I close my eyes and savor his intoxicating bourbon flavor. His fingers cup the back of my head, angling it to his liking, while his other hand massages the curve of my ass and rubs my core against his. Our tongues collide and spar, and it's as if a million synapses fire at once.

None of this is part of my assignment. My breathing quickens, as if I'm running. Danger heightens all my senses, but I had no idea the impact it could have on something as simple as a kiss.

He breaks the kiss but keeps me close. "Well, hello."

I give a breathless *Hi* back, playing the part better than I ever thought I could.

"Why don't we get out of here?" Dizziness clouds my mind, and I hold on to him, waiting for the room to stop spinning and for my breathing to calm.

"What is this place?" I ask the question softly, out of breath.

One of his hands remains on my ass, while the other caresses my hip. He smirks and brushes my disobedient strands behind my ear once more before answering. "It's what is referred to as a gentleman's club. If we were going anywhere else, I would've brought you, I promise. I didn't come here to meet another woman."

"You like it here?"

"It can be very erotic." Chase's lips brush my ear. "But we can go. The client who wanted me to come out is currently being entertained."

"What does that mean?" I trail kisses along Chase's jaw, to stay with my cover and defray suspicion. His cologne is attractive, a subtle deep woods scent. Stubble grazes my lips, and I lean into him.

"He's busy."

"With a lap dance? Do you get those when you come here?" I aim for sultry as I ask the question, hoping I come across as sexy, or tempting, and not like a weak, jealous girl.

He places a kiss on the sensitive skin below my ear, and goosebumps instantly rise all along my arms.

"Are you the jealous type, Frost?"

"No," I blurt.

He smiles. I don't get the sense he believes me.

"My ex, he wasn't faithful. I think it played with my head." He leans back, away from me, reaching for the drink the bartender set down. "Not that we are anything or going anywhere. I just wanted to be sure. You probably think I'm bat shit crazy and don't want anything to do with me." *Holy shit, I do sound crazy. Weak and stupid and crazy.*

I give what I hope is a somewhat girly smile, bow my head, and back away, searching for the section of the curtain that will take me back to my clutch so I can escape. My cheeks are flaming I'm so embarrassed by the make-believe crap that spewed out of my mouth. I scan the black velvet, searching for an exit point, and spot Mitchell and Bennett. Both men look like a man caught with his pants down.

Mitchell approaches, but he doesn't speak to me. He looks directly at Chase. "Are you two together?"

Chase shakes his head but doesn't offer more. I glance back, and Bennett is gone.

"Did you go in? The back?" Mitchell asks, this time directing his question to me.

"Not yet," I answer before Chase can answer for me. Shit, could this get any worse?

Mitchell runs his hand across the top of his head, and the remnants of hair stick straight up. His eyes are bloodshot and glazed, and I notice his zipper is down and his shirt tail sticks out of the gap.

Mitchell stumbles forward toward the exit. "My car service is here."

I watch him lift the velvet curtain and disappear, and sit back on my stool in a daze.

"Evan Mitchell comes here? You guys watch—"

"It's a voyeurs' club. A private club for the sexually adventurous. Some people find the sexual experience more intense with others watching." He sips his drink then adds, "Or while watching others."

"You bring your dates here? Or do you prefer the private entertainment?"

He rocks his head back and forth then repositions himself on his stool. "Some girls get into it. You saw couples in there, right?"

"Yes."

"Did it turn you on?"

"More like shocked the hell out of me." Play it honestly when you can.

"Yeah, I can see that, especially if you didn't know what you were walking in on."

"So, you do bring dates here?"

"No. I use this place for connections."

I find that hard to believe. He can tell.

"Seriously. It's been better for business than you can imagine."

"Business?" I scoff. This is not the kind of place I see as useful for business meetings or networking.

"Believe it or not, some very connected folks are members. It's all about connections in this town."

"Was this some sort of BB&E meeting tonight?"

He rubs his jaw. "No. It's just a night out. I didn't know who all would be here. Speaking of, Mitchell didn't look thrilled to see you. But I wouldn't worry about it. He was pretty lit. As long as you act normal on Monday, I don't think there'll be any issues."

"So, it's kind of a boys' club at BB&E? Women aren't allowed in the places where the men like to hang?" There's obvious disdain in my tone, but it works with my cover. Any woman working in a corporation would be upset to find out about this kind of boys' club networking. It's bound to give men in the firm an advantage for getting ahead.

"What? No."

I set my drink down and stare, waiting.

"Maybe. Maybe it is a bit of a boys' club. But I didn't join here for BB&E. I came here for a side hustle first. Mitchell and Bennett coming here...I had no idea."

"Do a lot of the men from work come here?"

"Some."

"Why did you have to come here tonight?"

"Sometimes clients need to remind you they own you." He tosses back the remainder of his bourbon.

"And which client owns you?"

"They all do, Sydney. They all do. Now, you ready to get out of here?"

ELEVEN

Chase

"Sleep tight, beautiful." That's the smooth move I pulled last night outside Sydney's door. Maybe I could have pushed to be invited in, but I think she was reeling from the whole sex club thing and BB&E executives being there. And, to be fair, she shocked the hell out of me by following me. That's a blaring red flag if I ever saw one. I made sure she got home safely, but I think we both needed some cooling off time.

That kiss, though. I can't shake it. The way she moved that tight little body right up against me. How she zeroed in for the kiss. I forgot where we were. Hell, I forgot everything. Lost in her.

Our chemistry is smoking. But she's still an enigma. Definitely one to take with caution. On the outside, Sydney's sexy as fuck, but she's also rocks a steep wall. The all-work-no-play vibe has never been my thing, but maybe she's one of those who you have to put in the time, dig a little to figure out what's underneath. After all, someone centered solely on work wouldn't follow me to Jersey to see what I'm doing. She can't be all work.

The sun is shining, and Post Malone blares through my earbuds. A few sailboats are off in the distance, circling the Statue of Liberty, and the subtle blow of a ferry horn skims the beat of my music. The wind blows in gusts, creating minuscule whitecaps on the river. Overhead, the sky is blue, marred only by a few clouds and the random passenger jet flying in the distance.

It's a gorgeous day, and my fellow Manhattanites are out in droves. Running along the Hudson River Greenway might be my favorite New York activity. The running paths go right along the river, so you can choose to watch the boats, check out apartments in the skyrises that line the edge of the city, or people watch. On a normal day, I like to watch joggers in tight Lycra with bouncing breasts. Today, though, my brain's on a nonstop sexy Sydney loop.

A motorboat follows a big tanker and jumps the wake. I watch the small boat chasing the big one. The tanker can't stop on a dime and bears a strong undertow. The move strikes me as unwise. Much like dating a woman who followed me before we'd ever gone out on a date could also be unwise. Maybe I'll give Anna a call later and get her take.

I run harder, pounding the pavement, pushing until my lungs burn. Before I know it, I'm dripping sweat and I've arrived at my gym.

"*Hola.*" Frankie's sitting behind the counter, but in an instant, he's grabbing a towel and tossing it to me.

"Maitlin. How you doin'?"

"Good. Gorgeous fucking day."

"I know it, man. I'm taking my lunch break outside. They're saying next week temps are gonna drop. Fall, man, it's coming." His eyebrows rise as he talks. He's got the shaved bald look going on, so his bushy eyebrows stand out.

"Seasons gonna keep changing. See ya, man." I shoot him with my finger and head down to the weight room. The crisp sound of iron on iron clangs down the hall. It's one of the best sounds.

I grab a mat to stretch before hitting my circuit and almost fall on my ass.

"Sydney?"

She's stretching her quads and twisting her torso, but I'd recognize that blunt, dark ponytail anywhere. She's got a light layer of perspiration along her chest, but she's not drenched like I am with telltale black sweat marks under her pits or stomach. Shit, I probably reek.

"Chase. I should've known I'd run into you here. Do you ever take a day off?"

"The gym? No. Use it or lose it."

She alternates legs. "But you're not supposed to lift every single day. That can't be good for you."

"Different muscle groups."

"Ah, you're one of those." The corners of those pale pink lips turn up. She's teasing me. Two can play.

"One of those? What? Men with a six-pack?"

She looks up to the ceiling while pulling her foot up to her firm buttocks for a deeper quad stretch. Sydney might like to tease about my gym time, but she's lean and strong. She works it, too.

At least she's acting normal. After last night, seeing my other club, it wouldn't've shocked me if she'd been in avoidance mode.

"Maitlin. What's up, man?" Tim Rothman calls across the gym, fist in the air. I wave back and scan the weight area to see who else I know. I've got a wide range of friends and business associates, and some walk on the skankier side of life. Hence the reason I joined that voyeur club in the first place. It's like a strip club on steroids. One of the best networking investments I've made, actually. But I'd like to try to get Sydney to go out with me, and if she thinks all I hang with are guys like Rothman, who go to clubs like that, well, any chance I have might combust.

And yep, now I'm waving to Johnny P, Matty, and a business partner from my uptown venture. It's Sunday. The gym's packed.

"You finished working out?" I ask, positioning myself so anyone here can see I'm busy.

"Yeah. I did the nine a.m. boot camp. Came in to round it out and stretch. What class did you do?"

"I went for a run. Came in to stretch. Can I talk you into an early lunch? Brunch? A walk?"

"You'd skip weights?"

"Nah. I'll come back this afternoon. It's Sunday. I got all day."

She stands and leans down and touches her toes. Her legs remain straight, zero bend in the knee. Baby's got flex. Then she rises, stretching her palms to the ceiling, exposing a slim middle and smooth, soft skin above the line of black Lycra leggings. I take it all in.

She shifts her head and catches me gawking. "Let's go for a walk. I'm not up for a greasy meal. I ate out too much last week."

"I hear ya. Last night's food alone was probably at least four or five thousand calories."

"Exactly."

"That's why we work out, right?"

"Yeah, that's why," she says with a daydreamy expression.

On our way out of the gym, Frankie calls, "Maitlin? You leaving already?" He's all drama, looking at his wrist like he's telling time.

"I'll be back. Breaking for lunch."

He nods, a shit-eating grin as he eyes the hot chick walking out the door with me. I slow my pace so I can step behind her and block his view of Sydney's ass. Yeah, I know what he's looking at.

We're barely past the Chelsea Piers building when Sydney's phone rings. She answers and listens while we make our way along a pedestrian packed sidewalk to the jogging path.

She doesn't say much on her end. Listens a lot and makes affirmative noises. Not many of the women I know act like that on a phone, so I can't help but wonder who she's talking to.

"Two p.m.?" She flicks her wrist, checks the time. "See you then."

I match her pace on the sidewalk and wait for an explanation.

"I need to run. I have to meet a friend later."

A friend, huh? "Gotcha."

We stop next to a bench on the sidewalk. She's not acting clingy. And I dig her. *Take the shot.*

"You know, I meant what I said about wanting to take you out on a date. This coming weekend, though, is the wedding. I know the girls and Maggie would love for you to come. Any interest in joining? You could get to know the crew better. You know, my normal friends." I lift my shoulders, unsure. She might shoot me down. I hate this part of asking chicks out.

"Normal? You mean not like the gym rats? Or not like the guys from the voyeur club?"

They're actually largely one and the same, but no reason to get into the nitty-gritty. "Yeah."

"I'll think about it. See you tomorrow at work."

"One night this week?" I doubt she'll actually go on a weekend away with me. I should probably drop pursuing her. We work together. She followed me. There are solid reasons to drop it. But here I am, chasing her anyway.

Her pink lips, glossy in the sun, lift into a small smile. She pushes a flyaway strand of dark hair behind her ear. "I'll think about it."

Her teasing smile has me mentally fist bumping the air, and she didn't even say yes.

TWELVE

S<small>ADIE</small>

Since I'm in the middle of an undercover op, I throw on an outfit I believe Sydney would wear on any given Sunday afternoon. Cargo shorts and a lightweight navy sweater with sandals. This outfit also happens to be what I'd wear in real life, too, but most importantly, if I happen to bump into Chase Maitlin or any other suspect, they won't think twice about my weekend outfit.

As I head up Park Avenue, I can't help but scout up and down and across the wide avenue for any sign I'm being followed or anyone is watching me. I thought being undercover would feel like the movies, that I'd be the up and coming Jamie Bond or something. Instead, it's more like I'm the one being hunted. Every moment makes me feel like a small child again. Everything I need to treat as 'normal' is unnerving, and I couldn't feel further from a kick ass world-class spy. I take a breath…and remember my training.

With one last glance up and down, I push the door open. Once again, there's no indication any of the offices on the hall are occupied. The door at the end of the hall opens, and Agent Hopkins smiles in greeting.

He's wearing khakis, dress shoes, and a button-down dress shirt with a jacket. On a Sunday afternoon, Hopkins is dressed like more of a businessman than Chase Maitlin on any given workday.

"How was the first week?"

"Interesting." I open my handbag and pull out my thin laptop.

There are manila files sitting on the table, and he already has his laptop open and set to review the new information the team came up with over the past week.

"Interesting on our end, too. SEC may be getting involved."

"Why?" The SEC gets involved when there's suspected stock fraud, but the companies we're investigating are private.

"Titan Pharmaceutical announced they are acquiring South Fork Research."

"That's not particularly suspicious. South Fork has been making progress on alternative cancer treatments. It was only a matter of time before they'd be purchased."

"True. But do you remember who the biggest shareholders of South Fork are?"

He's dribbling the information out like I'm a slow learner. I refrain from rolling my eyes as I answer, "The guys we're investigating. The Stanford crew. That doesn't explain the SEC interest."

"Well, those same guys also happen to be significant shareholders in Titan. For the most part, the men all acquired significant shares within the last six to twelve months."

I can see it's suspicious. But these are wealthy men, and they're heavily vested in the bio-med space. Regardless, it's good for me to be aware of, but I won't be the one investigating that angle.

I pick up my phone and make a few notes in my app as Hopkins continues. "South Fork Research is also the biggest beneficiary of funding from the McLoughlin Charity. And, coincidentally, BB&E does their accounting."

"I'll prioritize looking at South Fork's books on Monday. I'll need to anyway. BB&E will expect me to double-check everything given due diligence will be coming."

He nods as he peruses a yellow notepad. "Tom Bennett's wife didn't necessarily come from money. Middle class background. She doesn't work. We didn't find anything particularly interesting. We also located Tad Johnson. He died two months ago."

"How?"

"Drunk driving accident in upstate New York. He plowed his car into a tree. No suspicions of foul play. No autopsy completed, and he was cremated."

"That's…interesting."

"Yes. But the agents who drove up there to investigate further didn't find any leads to suggest anything other than Tad got behind the wheel of a car when he shouldn't have. We also gained access to Chase Maitlin's financial records." He slides a folder over to me, and I flip it open as he continues to talk.

"Maitlin has brokerage accounts with over $12 million in them."

"Wow. He didn't earn that from BB&E."

"No, he did not. He's a real estate investor and apparently also what's called a domainer."

I write the word down and wait, hoping Hopkins expands. If he doesn't, I'll have to ask, and I'd rather not admit I'm not familiar with the term.

"A domainer refers to someone who buys and sells domain names for websites."

"Ah. I've read about that." I snap my fingers. "Buying and selling website domains would be a great way to receive legitimate payments for illegitimate services."

Hopkins snaps his fingers right back at me. "Bingo."

"Who is buying domains from him? Are they at inflated prices?"

"Valuing domains is largely subjective. It's not like real estate where it's more obvious McLoughlin Charity was paying inflated prices on properties to Cooper Grayson's company. But the team is researching prior sales now."

Damn. Chase Maitlin's friends are going to be shocked when they find out everything he's into. I had thought he was a small player, but looking through this folder at his financial statements, he's not looking like he's such a low-level component anymore. I set the folder down.

"Last night, I went out with Maitlin. At first, with his friends. I didn't find any of them to be suspicious. They aren't related to BB&E or these Chicago firms. Actually, one of his friends,

Maggie Thompson, used to work for McLoughlin Charity. She and her fiancé recently moved to Chicago. You may want to look into both of them."

I jot down the names for him.

"I have some pics on my phone of them that I'll send you. Also, Sam Duke, one of the founders of Esprit Corp, is one of Chase's close friends." I write down his name as well. "I don't see a connection between his company and these guys, but—"

"He's a billionaire. Got it. Anyone else we need to look further into?"

"Jackson Hendricks works for Sam. He's a lawyer. His focus is on M&A. If I remember correctly, they're solely focused on tech, but given what's going on with South Fork, it might be worth researching exactly where they've been investing."

Shit. This case has far-reaching implications. It no longer feels like an in-and-out case.

"Oh, and after we went out with Chase's personal friends, he left to meet a client. I found it suspicious, so I followed him."

Hopkins snaps to attention.

"EJ Mason is the client who insisted Chase come out and meet him. They met at a private club. He called it a gentleman's club. I would call it an underground sex club."

"You weren't wearing a wire last night." He frowns. "Did they discuss anything incriminating?"

"I wasn't around them to hear. I did see both Evan Mitchell and Bennett. Mitchell had had a lot to drink. I didn't get a good look at Bennett." Fidelity is none of the FBI's concern, but given we're trusting Mitchell, at least in my mind, it speaks to his credibility, and I strongly suspect based on his open fly he'd been partaking in some way, but I don't say anything because I don't have proof. "Mitchell did not look happy when he saw me."

Hopkins gets on his laptop and clicks the keys.

"If you followed them—"

"Chase saw me first. I acted like I had been following him to see if he was meeting up with another woman." Hopkins stops typing. "He bought it. I think Mitchell assumed Chase brought me."

Agent Hopkins returns to typing.

"Are you letting Agent Blakely know?" I ask.

He peers over his laptop. "I'm setting up a meeting to update the team tomorrow morning. Blakely will be there. What's the name of this club?"

"I don't know." His eyes narrow. "There were no signs. It's private. Illegal. I had to hand over my phone to enter. Members only." Thinking back, I'm glad I wasn't wearing a wire. The music was so loud they wouldn't have gotten anything, anyway, and I sure as hell wouldn't have wanted to risk getting caught with a wire by those bouncers.

He clacks a few keys more slowly. "Where was it?"

"Jersey City. Backstreets. Warehouse district. Off Grand Street. I could locate it if you want."

"Probably not necessary. Did they discuss business at all?"

"No. Sex act on center stage. There was a back room, and I suspect the men were with prostitutes in the back. Chase mentioned EJ was busy being entertained with a private lap dance."

His fingers light up the keyboard.

"All of the men participated?"

"I don't know. I felt limited in terms of what I could ask, given I followed Chase there and he found me. But I'd guess Evan Mitchell participated in something. At the very least, he was drunk. I didn't get a good look at Bennett. As a matter of fact, he was standing far enough away I couldn't testify it was him."

"Interesting. And Maitlin didn't get suspicious?"

"I don't think so. He asked me out on a date."

"Okay. Listen, I expect the operation will remain intact. If Blakely has concerns about Mitchell after learning this, I'll reach out, and we'll pull you. For now, keep your wire on. Even when you're not in the office."

"The auditory quality won't be good in the gym. Or any nightclub."

"Yes, but if he says anything, we want it on tape." He's right. I should have worn the wire last night. "You're getting closer to Maitlin."

I look away so he doesn't see how much that hint of judgment angers me.

"It's not a bad thing. It's good. It's what we want. This could be a career case," he says.

That catches my attention. There's nothing in his demeanor that indicates he's joking or being a smart ass.

"Really?" That's not the way I interpreted this case when I transferred onto the team.

"Yes. The Illinois AG briefed the New York AG last week. SEC coming in? If this ends up expanding beyond the little Stanford clique, it's gonna be a big case."

"And Walters still wants to focus on BB&E?" Bill Walters is the prosecuting attorney. He's Mr. *'I don't want another Enron.'*

"Sadie, BB&E is the cornerstone. It's the how. This case is big. Get close to Maitlin, but if you get uncomfortable, let me know. Remember, my top priority is you. That's what it means to be your handler."

"Got it. Chase and his friends invited me to a wedding. It's for Jason and Maggie, his friends who recently moved to Chicago."

He glances over his notes. "Maggie is the one who worked for Senator McLoughlin's charity?"

I nod.

"You should go."

"It's in Iowa. I'd be riding on Sam Duke's private jet."

"Send me the details on where the wedding is. I'll look into getting backup in Iowa."

"I can't imagine backup will be needed." He looks at me like I have no idea what I'm talking about. "Seriously. It's a wedding in her parents' back yard. In Iowa. It's not going to turn into the Red Wedding *à la* Game of Thrones."

"Send me the deets. I'll let you know what the team decides."

"Okay. Oh, one more person to check out. I emailed you. Garrick Carlson. He's the guy who actually does the work on all the accounts we're suspicious of. And I got the impression he's not a huge fan of Maitlin."

"What do you mean?"

"Well, everyone else looks at Maitlin like he's a superstar. He'd win Most Popular hands down. Carlson treated him the way people normally treat colleagues."

"So, he might be the one guy who knows what he's up to. Maybe the guy we can convince to turn."

"Bingo." I shoot him back with my fingers.

When I leave my meeting, I deflate. There's little doubt Chase is involved, and I like him. If he wasn't a bad guy, he'd be easy to fall for. I mean, at first I thought he was one of those guys who half-assed everything and got by on his personality, but he has multiple businesses on the side. He might have a carefree persona, but he's driven. Unfortunately, I'm about to discover exactly how many lines he's crossed thanks to that drive.

———

Monday morning, I'm in my office, scanning the news while drinking my coffee. I might be UC, but there's comfort in routine and finding similarities between a person I'm pretending to be and the real me. That's one of the things they teach us.

This case isn't such a departure from my normal office dwelling self, but it's still tiring. So many times when chatting with Rhonda or when making small talk before meetings, it's been on the tip of my tongue to drop in comparisons between D.C. and NYC, and I have to swallow them because my cover story is I moved here from L.A. The other day, Rhonda was showing me pictures of her dogs, and I wanted to tell her all about my childhood dog Sam, but instead, I pushed it back and asked subtle questions about her dog. I was surprised to learn Maitlin has cared for her dog in the past when she's gone out of town on vacation with her husband and kids.

Rhonda knocks on my door and steps in, a conspiratorial crouch to her posture. "Word is there's a huge fight going on between Tom and Evan right now. Stay clear of the eighteenth."

"What do you mean?"

"Karen called from the executive floor to warn everyone." She smiles with clear pleasure over spreading gossip.

"Do they fight a lot?"

"Yes and no. But when they do, bad moods all around. Stay clear."

I pretend to check my calendar and in a conspiratorial tone say, "I think I'm in the all-clear. No executive-level meetings today."

Chase's booming voice echoes down the hall, along with a chorus of "hey, man" and "good weekend?" She wiggles her fingers goodbye and exits, presumably to greet her boss with his coffee and share the gossip.

I reach down and pick up my briefcase. I open it and, using my FBI issued phone, send a text to Hopkins to check the tapes from Evan's and Tom's offices from this morning. Our team auditing the wiretaps would eventually listen, but we have so many wiretaps going on in this operation, it could take them a while to get there. And I can't help but wonder if the Monday morning argument had to do with Saturday night. Or if Mitchell broke down and copped to agreeing to let the FBI into their offices. He swore to keep it private, but my gut tells me Mitchell doesn't deserve the trust the FBI has given him.

THIRTEEN

I lean forward, studying the numbers. Something is not right. Then I slip on my glasses, the glasses I'm supposed to be wearing periodically throughout the day to reduce eye strain when viewing the computer. I look back to my folder with the originals sent over by our client. The numbers remain the same. $14 million in expenses is missing.

I'm not sure exactly what he's done wrong, but the profit margin is substantially inflated.

I grab my desk phone, tap Garrick's extension, and ask him to come into my office.

I'm not a micromanager. I try to give my team the same respect I want from my bosses. Trust that they're doing a good job. But when it's announced one of your clients is being acquired and you know due diligence is about to be hot and heavy, then I figure I'm doing him a favor by looking over his work. Not to mention, Sydney's going to be all over this. While she hasn't told me where she's starting, it doesn't take a rocket scientist to figure out South Fork Research will be a priority. Egg on face.

Garrick comes into my office with a frown. He's never particularly happy, but this morning I can't help but notice his hands are balled into fists like he's looking for a fight. And he doesn't have a notebook or any way to take notes.

I point at the chair across from my desk. "Take a seat."

His chin juts out, and his posture is stiff. He's defensive, and I haven't said word one.

"I was going over quarterly reports and found some inconsistencies. I need you to review South Fork Research."

"I've already delivered everything they need for the acquisition."

"Without getting the okay from me?" *Seriously, dude?*

"You don't normally ask for approval for me to respond to a client request."

"Garrick, you have to see how this is different. They are being acquired by a public company." He's clutching those armrests so hard his fingers whiten. "Look, what's done is done. But I know there are errors. They've incurred some losses on patents they purchased in the past few years that are not reflected. Also, some significant purchases of medical equipment that should be amortized are not reflected."

"Losses in prior years."

"Yes...but they've still got the carryover liability. Where is it? And these revenues are three times higher than the prior year. Something which was not present on the original docs they sent over. Look, go through the numbers. It's not adding up. Here…here's the file from last year."

He reaches for the folder and holds it out like I've given him my sweaty gym clothes.

After flipping through the papers, he asks, "Where'd you get this?"

"I keep printed files of all originals. Look, I don't have time to go through it myself. I'm in back to back meetings. But they are being purchased. We need to get this shit straight. All it would take is someone comparing this year to last year's tax filing, and they'd suspect issues." His face contorts. "Garrick, man, I know you're the best at what you do, but everyone makes errors. I am telling you, we are missing some losses. And if I had to guess, something's not right in some Excel fields on those revenues. Find the errors, before our new internal auditor does when she double checks your work, or worse, before it's discovered in due diligence."

He scowls. He's on the scrawny side, but still, if I was out at a bar, I'd be backing up and giving him room. But we're in my office, and he's my employee, and the whole threatening look act isn't going to fly. I sit in my chair and throw him my best *I am the boss* pose.

"My last meeting's at five. Let's plan to regroup then, and you can let me know what you've found."

"Are you going through all my accounts?"

I wasn't actually planning on going through all his accounts, but I sure as hell am now. I can't tell if he's trying to intimidate me with his gruff question or if he's just pissed I found errors, but either way, his vibe doesn't garner trust.

"Yes. Need I remind you, we have a new CIA? She's going to be looking for errors on every account. That's her job." Having Sydney think less of me isn't something I want, so I'd rather we find the errors.

He stands, lips in a flat line, one hand holding the folder I gave him and the other balled into a fist once again. What's he gonna do? Pummel me? He's normally quiet and focused on work. This is a different Garrick. But, then again, I've never questioned his work before.

He leaves my office without a word. I swivel the chair toward my computer. The reflection on the large monitor serves as a mirror. I'm wearing my *With great beard, comes great responsibility* shirt. I could definitely have picked a worse tee for today's confrontation. The trouble with this one is I'm not currently sporting a beard, more like rough scruff, because I didn't feel like shaving. This morning in the closet, my pick made sense, but at this moment my two-day growth is markedly inadequate.

Shit. If there's any kind of sign like it's gonna be a bad day, it's when I find myself questioning my wardrobe choices. With perfect timing, Sydney herself taps on my doorframe. She's smiling and clutching several binders to her chest.

Both my laptop and monitor are open to South Fork Research documents. In a flash, I click on different windows. You'd think I was looking at porn, I switch out of those docs so fast.

She raises a perfectly sculpted eyebrow. Yeah, she probably thinks I was looking at porn.

"Did you have a good rest of your weekend?"

"I did. You?" I swivel my chair in her direction.

"Let me guess…you spent the rest of the afternoon at the gym?"

I check the time. Three minutes until it's time to head up for the first meeting of the day. She shifts her binders, and the black button-down blouse she's wearing shifts too, exposing the slope of one breast. She's dressed professionally, but there's something about the form-fitting blouse and the way it hints at what's beneath that lures me in. She makes a noise in her throat. Busted.

"Some at the gym. Went over for dinner at Anna and Jackson's."

"I like them."

"Yeah, they're good peeps."

I gather what I need for my marathon meeting day. Other than a regularly scheduled lunch with Evan, I'm in back to back meetings. Sydney shifts again. There's a pink hue to her complexion. It's not hot in here. The AC is cranking.

"So, I don't know if the offer still stands, but I've been thinking about that wedding…"

Holy shit balls. She's going to go away with me for a weekend.

"What?" She tilts her head with her question, and one leg bends in a way that pulls her black slacks and highlights the curve of her ass. Her pose is demure-like, yet flirty. She reaches out and touches my forearm. *Oh, yeah.* "Why are you grinning like that?"

"You want to go with me to the wedding. Of course I'm grinning. You just made my day."

"I mean, as friends."

"Yeah, okay."

"No, really, Chase. Friends. I'll pay for my own room. Send me the information, and I'll make my own reservations."

"No way. You come as my guest, I've got it." She huffs, and it's adorable. She may play the Frost Queen game, but she came in here all on her own. I know what's going on. And I have to say, I'm game.

I follow her out to the elevator where we meet up with Rhonda. The two ladies lead the way, which gives me a chance to fully appreciate Sydney's rear in her black slacks, sans panty line.

As we head to the elevator bank, Sydney asks, "Any word on what Tom and Evan were fighting about?"

Rhonda answers, "No. Not yet. But definitely steer clear of the eighteenth floor. According to Pam, Tom hasn't returned to the office yet."

She gives me her 'you poor boy' look because she knows I can't just steer clear. I've got not one, but two meetings up there today.

Fuck. With great beard comes great responsibility, indeed.

FOURTEEN

SADIE

It's almost eight p.m., and Chase's office light is still on. I've been hanging in my office, attempting to follow him out the door to randomly meet up at the gym again. He's been in meetings all day, but he piqued my curiosity this morning. It's completely possible he was just texting a friend or wasting time on a video game, but whatever he was doing, he most definitely didn't want me to see.

Everyone else has gone home. The office is empty, and the only sound is the faint buzz of the fluorescent hall lights. My neck muscles are sore, and the small button wire in my shirt is rubbing my skin raw. It's time to call it a day, but first I'll stop by and see if I can learn anything more about what has Chase Maitlin working late.

I pause in the doorway and watch him. A few pieces of hair stick out from the right side of his head as if he's been pulling on them, and he's wearing black frames I've never seen before. The black frames give him a studious persona. Yes, with those glasses, he's rocking a sexy book nerd look. His sportscoat hangs on the back of his office chair. There's a stack of file folders on his desk, a pencil in his mouth, one in his hand, one behind his ear, and his focus is on the large monitor on the corner of his desk.

I inch forward enough to see the screen. It's an Excel sheet. The folder on his desk is also open to report details in Excel format.

I softly tap on his desk. "Hey."

He sits back in his chair and removes the pencil from his mouth. There are dark indentations all along the yellow paint from his teeth. He frowns and glances between me and the monitor.

"Everyone's gone home. You going to be leaving soon?"

He glances at his wrist, then rubs the side of his face.

"Is something wrong?"

"Yeah. But I don't know what I'm dealing with yet." His voice is low, and it's as if he's talking more to himself than to me.

"Anything I can help with?"

He scratches his chin then lifts his glasses and rubs his eyes. He sets the black frames down and rests his elbows on the edge of the desk. "I have a feeling you're going to be very involved. But..." His voice trails off, and he fingers one of the file folders on his desk. He sighs. "I've found some errors. But the more I dig into it, the less I think it's an accidental error, and the more I suspect it could be purposeful manipulation of the numbers."

I sit down in the closest office chair and let my briefcase slide to the floor. I hope my wire is working. "What makes you think that?"

He looks at me, but it's a vacant stare as if he's looking through me. He shakes his head and exhales. "Look, it's late. I might be overthinking things. I might...I could be wrong. Let me do some more digging into this, and if I need to, since you're our new internal auditor, I'll come to you."

"What are you worried about?" Give me something.

"I'm worried I might have to fire someone. Have you ever done that? Had to let someone go?"

"No." Be honest when you can. Undercover 101. "But I've been in a situation where I found out someone had made mistakes. And I got them in trouble."

He leans back in his chair. His eyes glaze over again as if he's slipping back into his thoughts.

"Is this someone you care about?" I ask.

He inhales loudly, and his chest rises. "Not like what you may be thinking. But it's someone on my team. And...it could be a big fucking mess. You know South Fork Research?"

"Yeah."

"Like I said, I'm still digging into it. But if I'm right, there are some errors that could impact that deal. It could be some serious egg on BB&E's face."

"Are you worried about your job?"

For the first time since I've entered his office, he smirks. A touch of jovial Chase returns. "Nah. There are days I don't even know why I'm in this job." He raps the desk with his knuckle. "And today is one of those days." He exhales and rubs his forehead. "No. I'm worried about my team. But...I still don't know what I'm looking at. It's like maybe I've watched too many crime shows and my mind's off on a wild car chase."

"I'd love to be able to help you. Maybe a second set of eyes could help clear up things."

For a moment, I think he's going to hand me a folder, but instead he flattens his palm over the stack.

"No. Before I bring you in, I gave Garrick a chance to dig into it. If he's made careless errors, I want to give him the chance to discover it himself."

"If? You think there's a chance he made intentional errors?"

Chase's gaze falls over my right shoulder. His eyes close to slivers. He swallows then swivels his chair back to his monitor and puts on his black frame glasses.

"Ask me later in the week."

I'll take that as a yes. Chase Maitlin discovered what we've known existed, and he's now researching it himself. If I'm right, that means Chase Maitlin is not the guilty party. He has also effectively dismissed me.

"I'll see you tomorrow?" I rise, showing him I'm taking his hint and leaving his office.

He doesn't turn away from his monitor. "No. I've got meetings for some other clients down in Miami. Maybe Chicago later in the week. I should be back in the office on Friday."

I pause in the doorway. "You still thinking you'll make the wedding?"

"Yeah. Wheels in the air three p.m. Friday, so we'll need to leave the office by two."

I want to ask him more, but he's lost in the monitor. I have Anna's contact information, so I'll reach out to her.

When I get home, I pull out my FBI issued cell and text Hopkins.

Me: Maitlin digging into reports. Acting like he's discovering. Not acting like he's guilty.

Within seconds, Hopkins responds.

Hopkins: Think he's on to you? Could he be playing you?

His serious countenance comes to mind. All the pencils and the crazed hair.

Me: Unless he's a trained actor, no.

Hopkins: Be careful. Sound tape of Michell's and Tom's office from this morning is mostly inaudible. Tom berated Mitchell. Our interpretation is the anger was over you being at the club. Also possible Mitchell told Tom you're FBI. There's disagreement on the team on this point, but be careful. If you're right, and it's not Maitlin, any other suspects?

.   .   .

Me: Garrick Carlson. That's who Maitlin suspects. But Maitlin's comments hinted he thinks others are involved. Was wearing a wire. You can listen to the conversation. 8 p.m. in Maitlin's office.

Hopkins: Walters only wants to know who's responsible. Once we know that, we pull you. Cooper Grayson found the bugs in his office. He's BAU, but knows he's being monitored.

Cooper Grayson is the head of the Chicago Real Estate Development Group. That's not the account Maitlin's concerned about right now, nor the account that has piqued the SEC's interest. But the charity's purchases of property at highly inflated prices from Grayson's company all around Chicago are partially responsible for kicking off the investigation into McLoughlin. If these guys really are as integrated as we believe, then they know the pressure's on. And if Mitchell's in on it, then they all know I'm FBI.

Which means Maitlin could be playing me. Garrick could be the patsy. I haven't made any progress, because I still have no evidence.

I switch over to the notes app on my phone and tap the keys.

Maitlin in on it? Gut says no. Mitchell in on it? Gut says yes. To do: Spend more time with Garrick.

FIFTEEN

By the time Friday morning comes, I'm exhausted. I've spent the last three days in planes, conference rooms, client lunches and dinners, and even two rounds of golf. It would have been a normal week. Fun, even. I like business trips. But I spent my nights poring over numbers, reverting to my originals and the numbers in our portal.

There is absolutely no question. Garrick Carlson is manipulating and, in some cases, outright forging numbers. By my estimation, revenues to-date are off to the tune of $25 million. I've been wracking my brain, and I don't believe I've ever introduced him to either of the owners of South Fork Research. I could swear I remember John Fischer in my office and zero flashes of recognition between the two. Does that mean it could be Eileen Becker, Fischer's partner, asking him to inflate revenues? Possibly. Or maybe someone in the company I don't know.

Eileen Becker never travels. She has young kids and seems to have an agreement she primarily works from the office. The only time I've ever spent time with her was in Chicago, in meetings or lunches at the South Fork office building. But it's not my job to try to figure out who is paying Carlson to commit fraud.

The point is, BB&E has a big problem. I've pulled everything together to take Mitchell through it. When I think about the fallout from this...shit. I hate it for the man. Sometimes it sucks to be at the top.

We'll probably lose South Fork Research as a client, even if they've been paying Garrick to make the changes. Maybe we can work together to keep the issues private. It's not unheard of for a deal to fall through during due diligence. For BB&E's sake, I hope we can keep it out of the press.

"Morning, Mr. Traveling Man." Rhonda's smiling, holding out my cup of joe. My expression must be crap, because hers changes to concern. She follows me into my office.

"What's wrong?"

Rhonda's my confidante at the office for all things. But not this.

"Long week." I pull out my laptop and plug it in on my desk. "Did you get me in to meet with Mitchell and Bennett?"

"One today. It's only Evan Mitchell, and you have fifteen minutes."

"That works." Once he hears what I've discovered, he'll clear whatever he has at 1:15 and probably bring Tom Bennett in.

"I hope it's really an emergency. You know how Karen can be. She pushed hard but finally caved."

I shrug. His assistant can be a bit of a pit bull.

"Did you lose an account?" She's timid and sympathetic. It wouldn't matter if I screwed up all my accounts; Rhonda would still have my back.

I shake my head and focus on the laptop, willing her to go away. I'm sick to my stomach from this mess. The potential fallout from this scandal could rock so many lives. I've come to care about the employees here. So many good people. And it all happened under my watch.

"Wait." She points at me in alarm. "You're not wearing a t-shirt. You're in a pressed Oxford. What's going on? Are you resigning?"

"Rhonda. Chill. I'm leaving the office early today to head to my friend's wedding, remember? We land and head straight to a rehearsal dinner. I didn't know if I'd have time to change." That's part of the reason. If I'm honest, the shit hitting the fan today did make every single fun t-shirt feel wrong.

"That's right." She relaxes into one of my chairs. "Sydney mentioned the wedding."

She has this gleeful smirk on her face. I smile for probably the first time since Monday.

"Care to share anything?" She's so high school, it cracks me up.

"Ask me after the weekend." I know damn well that's not going to satisfy her, but it's really all I've got. I haven't had much time to think about what's going on with Sydney. Her words say she's just going as friends, that she liked my friends, and I'm not naive. I mean, who wouldn't want to take a free ride in a private jet? But, that kiss...

As if our conversation conjured her up, Sexy Sydney taps my doorframe.

"Morning, guys." She acknowledges Rhonda with a smile then turns to me. "How was your trip?"

"Good. Normal trip."

Rhonda pipes in. "Oh, you know. Golf, lunches, dinners." She's teasing, and I play along. She's not wrong. That pretty much summarizes my normal and may be part of the reason I've kept this job. I enjoy it. Thought I was good at it.

Rhonda glances between the two of us, smirks, and stands. "I'll let you two catch up." She's almost to the door when she adds, "Garrick Carlson's still out sick."

That news does not surprise me. It's better that way. It'll give Evan time to meet with the executive team and determine how to proceed. My guess is HR will get involved, and he'll be escorted out but told there'll be an investigation into potential criminal wrongdoing. I don't really know, though. It's not like I've ever been involved in anything like this.

Sydney sits down in the chair. She sits upright with her legs crossed, the picture of professionalism. All business.

"Is the plan to still leave at two?"

"Yes." She's dressed in a black dress pantsuit, but the silk top she's wearing is fire engine red. I'm sensing that singular dash of color is her way of dressing for the rehearsal dinner, crossing business wear to evening wear.

"Should I meet you in the lobby? You know, so people don't think anything?"

"If you'd like. I don't think it matters. We don't have a non-fraternization policy at BB&E." And I'm not sure how much longer I'll be employed here, but no need to go into those details.

"I know. I checked." I could be wrong, but I think her cheeks get pinker. "It's just, wouldn't you rather people didn't talk?"

"Sure thing." And now, I am smiling. Because she's thinking the same thing I am. This weekend, there's a chance we'll be giving them something to talk about. Today is going to suck balls, but this weekend may more than make up for it.

"Did you end up finding anything more on the reports you were looking into? I have time this morning if you want to go over it. I did go into South Fork Research, but I didn't find anything."

Based on what's in the portal, she wouldn't. I study her for a moment. I could bring her in, but there's no reason. I need to take this to the top boss and let him decide how to handle it. Sydney's new, and there's no reason to involve her in what will be a total shitstorm, unless Mitchell decides he's putting her on this.

"No, it's all good." I rap my knuckle on the desk, my cue it's time to get to work. "I've got a ton to do today. I'll meet you down in the lobby at two?"

Her face contorts. She gets up to leave, but before she heads down the hall, she tosses one last glance over her shoulder. Her dark, shiny bob swings as she does so. She looks almost sad.

The sick feeling in the pit of my stomach returns. That sad look reminds me of my ex. Always sad if I couldn't talk longer. Always wanting to spend more time together. Never understanding if I needed gym time or time to work on some of my projects. But nah, there's no way Sydney's another

Angela. She's too independent. She's probably thinking about me a fraction of the time I'm thinking about her. That whole following thing…I've just got to forget about it.

I get to work, going through emails, responding to clients, and working with my team. The hours fly by, and before I know it, it's time to gather my folders and meet with the big boss to upend his world. Karen sits outside Evan's office. His door is closed, and she asks me to wait a moment.

Tom Bennett, our CEO, opens his office door. "Maitlin." Two men I don't know exit his office, and as they're shaking hands, three additional men come down the hall and enter. It seems his assistant wasn't lying when she said he had back to back meetings today.

There's a stillness to this end of the floor that's unnerving. On my floor, across from my office, there are rows of open cubicles, and at any given moment there's a hum of activity, voices on phones, clicking keys on computers, sometimes you can hear the machine whir of the printer from down the hall. Up here on the executive floor, Karen sits in front of the executive offices by herself. A guard protecting the men who live behind closed doors. She swallows, and I can hear it.

Evan's thick wooden door opens, and music drifts through the empty space. If I was up here day in and day out with this level of reserve, I'd pump some music, too.

"Maitlin, come on in."

Evan's office boasts a solid wood desk slightly bigger than mine. The office has both a sitting area with a sofa, two club chairs, and a coffee table, and a small round table with four chairs. There's a great view of the city, and on a back shelf, there's one photo of his wife and kids. It's the same photo from a Christmas card he sent out a couple of years ago.

I automatically head to the round table so I can spread out my files and open my laptop to show him what I've got.

"Karen said you've got something important to share."

The music pumps. I don't know what he's listening to. It's got a heavy base and some crazy sounds as if he's got a bad connection and there's static mixed in. It's the low pounding base that's going to drive me nuts.

"I do. Do you mind if we turn down the music?" I glance for the source and see a small handheld radio with an antenna. Ah, that's why he's got static. "Dude, you know, there are way better options for music. If a device has an antenna, you shouldn't be using it."

Evan glances over at his vintage equipment. "It serves its purpose."

"I've found something very disturbing. You're going to want to turn the music off." I open my folder and gesture to the chair at his small table.

He shoves his hands in his pockets. He glances at the report I've laid out, but he's too far away to see it.

"Let's go up to the roof. I need some fresh air." He doesn't wait for me to respond. Simply turns and strides out of his office. As I'm gathering my folders and laptop, I hear him tell Karen we'll be up on the roof.

I catch up to him as he's approaching the red stairwell door.

"Karen said you only have fifteen minutes?"

"She was giving me time to eat. It's fine."

He opens the door and holds it for me to pass. The floor and stairs are smooth concrete. I've never been up to the roof, but

I know some of the smokers like to come up here on smoke breaks.

Evan passes me and ascends the steps. He reaches the top and pushes open the door. The stairwell fills with the sound of machines whirring. He holds the door for me, and I step out onto the roof. The view is stunning. Looking out, to the east you can see Jersey City, and to the north, the Empire State Building. We're surrounded by skyscrapers of varying heights. I'd bet at night the view is spectacular.

There's a low wall around the perimeter, with a wide, flat lip. Evan heads directly to the north side, away from the rooftop entrance. I circle, surveying the entire roof. We're the only two up here right now. Without all the walls and hallways of the lower floors, the space feels smaller than you'd think it would be.

"So, what've you got?" Evan leans his back against the wall, which is about chest high.

I have my folders and well-thought-out presentation, or explanation, pressed to my chest. Fuck it. I'll get to it when he asks for the details.

"Garrick Carlson has been manipulating data. Revenue and profit from both this year and last year have been falsely inflated. My guess is someone from South Fork Research must be paying him. It's the only thing that makes sense."

"You don't know who?"

"No. But I expect that would come out with a police investigation."

His dark, bushy eyebrows push so close together the man almost has a unibrow.

"Have you contacted the authorities?"

"No. Of course not. You're the first person I've told."

He places both hands on the edge of the wall, his back to me. There's a stainless-steel plate that runs along the edge, and he grips it.

"Is that the only account?"

"I haven't gotten into his other accounts yet. But after a cursory review, I'd say he's falsely inflated the revenue on Chicago Real Estate Group, Medical Supply, and Biohazard Waste. His only other account is a pro bono account, and I'll look into that next week."

Evan stares across the city, his back to me. He's a good foot taller than I am, with wide shoulders. In his dark suit, he's formidable. Apparently, back in the day, he was an avid lacrosse player. Soccer, that was my sport. But I've always thought it wouldn't be pleasant to see Evan crossing the field gunning toward you in soccer, lacrosse—any sport, really.

"Garrick is out sick today. Who do you want me to loop in? Human resources? Tom? Someone from legal?"

"Does Sydney know what you've found?"

I shake my head as he examines me. I get the sense he doesn't believe me.

"No. I didn't tell her. I wanted to tell you first. I can bring her in next. If you want, I can have her double-check my findings."

His eyes form chestnut slivers as he squints.

"You guys are close?" he asks.

"Close? I mean, you asked me to get her settled."

"And you're taking her to a wedding this weekend. And she was out with you last weekend. How settled did you get her?"

I take a step back, defensive anger rising. Confusion, too. What the fuck does it matter? And how is that his business? The guy who fucks other random women when his wife is home with his kids.

"It's all been kosher."

"You bang her?"

"We've got a huge PR issue, and your concern is where I'm putting my dick?"

He takes one step forward. "Yes or no? Are you fucking her or not?"

I take one step back for space. Then it clicks. "Wait? Are you fucking her? Is that what this is about? That's the reason she got the job, and maybe she's tired of being one of your many fuckbuddies, so you're jealous?"

His hand balls into a fist as he grinds his teeth, peering over the city. I can't fucking believe it. Mitchell and Sydney. The thought curls my stomach, but I push it back. Folks' jobs, their livelihoods, are at stake.

"No matter what's going on with the two of you, you need to get your head in the game. South Fork has been in the press a lot since the acquisition was announced." Does he not realize this? I barrel on. "Due diligence is coming. The stock price of the company buying them has shot up. That purchase can't happen. There are potentially so many levels of fraud here. That's where your head needs to be."

Those beady eyes glower at me, and, based on his angry

countenance, I halfway expect a balled fist is going to collide with my face. I stand tall, ready. Then he exhales, and a transformation occurs. His shoulders round, and he loses half a foot in height. He turns and grips the wall again.

"You're right. You're right." He rests his arms on the wall. "So, how'd you catch it?"

"I keep printouts of all the original files. Garrick did a good job of covering it all up. But if you go back far enough, four, five, six years back, his sloppiness shows. He changed figures that don't even match tax filings. You know, it's very likely Garrick isn't the only one who's complicit. How you handle this is going to be the difference between being an Arthur Anderson or being a Price Waterhouse."

Evan hauls himself up on the wall.

"Evan, it's not that bad, man."

He looks over at me and laughs. Maybe a few levels lower than Joker-demented-level laughing, but the crazed eyes and titled head land him several levels beyond sane.

"You think I'm gonna kill myself over this?"

I point. "You're on the edge of the roof."

He continues shaking his head, chuckling, producing an unnatural sound, and slings his legs over the other side. Yeah, that's right. The side with the street twenty-two floors below.

"Man, I'm serious." I step forward so I can launch myself and grab him if I need to.

His shoulders raise and lower, visibly breathing in gulps of air. The air is fresher than down on the sidewalks, but it's not exactly country fresh either. I take another step forward.

"You ever sat up here? Looked down?"

"Never been up here before. I don't smoke." He's nodding. *Keep him talking*. "You come up here a lot?"

He pats the wall beside him. "Come sit up here with me. It's freeing. It makes you realize these everyday problems aren't so big. Millions of people are going about their lives right now. They don't give a shit about our problems." He turns and looks me in the eye. "Come sit."

I step up to the wall. There's no way I can climb up on this thing without getting black shit on my shirt. It's the shirt I'm wearing out tonight. He smirks down at me.

"You need a leg lift?"

Fucking twat. "I think I'm good down here on the ground. Where you should be, by the way."

He points over at a brown plastic chair. Tons of cigarette butts are mixed in with the gravel roof. "Grab one of those chairs and step up here. Or are you scared?"

I am so sick of men who look down on the short guy. He's a fucking dumbass to even be sitting on that stupid wall.

I stomp over to the chairs and drag one back. The sound of the gravel and the hum of something, I suppose the air conditioning or ventilation system, are the only sounds. A lone passenger jet flies overhead in the distance, too far away to discern the logo.

I pull the chair up to the wall and step up on it. I peer down. I'm not scared of heights, but we're at a height that gives one pause. He pats the wall.

"Sit."

I'm right beside him. Can see everything he can see. Can grab him if he decides to bust the move of a 1920s stockbroker.

"I'm good."

"Sit. With. Me."

I stare at the wall. I stare down. We are high in the sky.

The heavy metal door opens, and two smokers join us on the roof. They each have an unlit cigarette in their fingers, and one has a lighter in his hand. They're far away from us. They hesitate, nod, and claim the far end of the roof.

My phone vibrates, and I pull it out.

Rhonda: Five minutes.

"I've got to run. I have a flight to catch. What do you want me to do?"

I take a step back, far enough away to show him I'm not sitting on that damn wall, and close enough I can still snatch his suit jacket if he lurches forward.

"Fuck." He slings his legs back over onto the roof and lands with a thud. "Is everything in those files?"

I pass them over to him and nod.

"I'll go over it with Tom. Give me the weekend to come up with a plan, okay?"

"I figured you'd want to look into it. Other than during the wedding, I can be reached at any point this weekend."

"Where are you off to, again?"

"Iowa."

"And Sydney's going with you?"

I lead the way to the elevator shaft, ready to get off this roof. His hand falls to my shoulder, and he spins me around when I don't answer.

"Yes, she's going with me. She met my friends last weekend, and they like her. Is that a problem?"

Even if he was with her before he hired her, it's hard for me to give two squats because the guy is married. With kids.

We step closer to the stairwell, and he lifts his shoulders, regaining his full height. And another transformation occurs. He loses the glower. The old Evan is back. The guy I know and respect. No trace of the crazed joker. He's calm as he squeezes my shoulder like we're buds.

"No. I don't have an issue with her. She's smart. She seems to be doing a good job, although I did ask her if she saw any issues with South Fork, and she said no." He raises an eyebrow in silent question.

"She wouldn't have seen anything." Everything on the portal, everything she has access to, has been altered. You need the original files, and prior years, to catch the adjustments and reclassifications.

"Well, can you do me a favor?"

The sound of the smokers laughing drifts through the air. They are far enough away we can't hear their conversation, but they look happy. I stop looking at them and face Evan. Raise my eyebrow, waiting for it.

"Can you not tell Sydney about this? Let me meet with Tom, HR, legal, and the board. I need some direction. So, you know, we handle it the right way. PR will need to get looped in." He runs his finger through his hair, sending his patch to Level 1 as he ticks off all the people he's got to involve.

"Do you need me to stay here this weekend?"

"Nah, you go. I've got your number if we need to loop you in." He lifts the folder. "I assume you've got a matching file you can reference?"

"Yes. And it's on the portal, too."

"Good. Well done, Maitlin. We're lucky we've got you on the team. Once we get through this, we'll have to look at how to reward you. A promotion is definitely in order."

SIXTEEN

Sᴀᴅɪᴇ

I step outside BB&E's building five minutes before schedule. The black sedan, a corporate car service, is parked on the curb in front of the building. I wheel my suitcase over to it, and the driver gets out and pops the trunk.

"Maitlin party?" he asks.

"Yes." I gesture to my wrist. "I think Chase is going to be a little late. Do you mind if I go get an iced coffee?"

"Not at all. I have water in the back of the car."

"Thanks, but I could use the caffeine. I'll be back in a minute."

While I'm paying the street vendor, my phone rings. I have an open view of BB&E. The coast is clear.

"Aaron?" He doesn't call often, and when he does, there's a part of me that expects him to be calling from a hospital. He's working a gang, and the risk level is high.

"Can you talk?"

"I wouldn't have answered if I couldn't."

"I'm coming to New York for the weekend. Send me your address."

"I won't be here. I'm going out of town."

"For work?" There's a mixture of disbelief and annoyance in his tone.

"Yes," I snap.

"This is what I meant. It doesn't work for us to both be UC."

"Aaron. Don't call me again. I do wish you all the best."

I hang up and slide my phone into the side pocket of my pocketbook and zip it closed. A mixture of emotions ricochet. Guilt. That was harsh. My rib cage expands as I take a deep inhale of the crisp fall air. Relief. I don't think I'll hear from him again. I'm ready to put him behind me. Aaron cared most about Aaron. If anything, he tore me down.

The sun beats down on the pavement, and I tilt my head back to absorb it. Aaron and I only worked because I had no expectations and never pressured him for more. I never imagined he'd have trouble letting go. But that's the thing. When you have few people in your life, your dependency on those few people strengthens, whether it's deserved or not. Aaron's been deep undercover for too long. I hope he gets a break soon. A real break, for a long time, so he can build a personal life. He's lost touch with himself, but it's not my problem. Maybe by refusing to be his crutch, I did him a favor.

The driver gets out of the car and leans against it, watching me as I slowly pace the concrete.

"I'm sorry about the wait."

"No problem at all. It's a gorgeous afternoon. But what time is your flight?"

I hesitate to tell him. If we were flying commercial, we'd be screwed. And, as it is, we might be forcing them to delay takeoff.

I pull out my cell to call Rhonda as Chase rushes through the revolving door. Within seconds, his small carry-on is tossed in the back of the car and we're both in the back seat.

"Let's go," he says, more to the driver than to me.

Chase is all business. He's tapping away on his phone. Presumably telling his friends we're on the way. Grim is how I'd describe his expression. His lips fall in a straight line, and tension runs across his brow.

"Everything okay?"

He holds up an index finger as a silent shush and continues texting. I shift in the seat to gaze out the window. Storefronts pass by as the car whizzes along Park Avenue.

I take the opportunity to look at Chase. He looks good in a suit; some would say handsome. He's a good-looking guy in a t-shirt, especially the tighter ones that fit snugly around his biceps. But in a well-fitted suit, he transforms into a respectable, driven, focused businessman.

When he's finished, he swipes up and flips it over, face down, resting it on his thigh.

"Hey, had to deal with some things. You ready to go to the middle of nowhere?"

"I don't think you can call Cedar Falls the middle of nowhere."

"Ever been there?"

"No. You?"

"No. But I've got a good idea of what to expect."

His brow is now relaxed, and he kicks back comfortably in the back seat of the car, crossing an ankle over his knee.

"You sure everything's okay? You've seemed really tense lately."

"You worried about me, Frost?"

"Well, yeah. You're throwing me off with the suit. Is it for the rehearsal dinner or something at work?"

"Rehearsal dinner. Did you and Evan Mitchell ever...date?"

"What? Why would you ask that?" The question is so left field. The man's married. I maneuver myself in the seat to better face him.

Chase opens his mouth like he's going to say more, then closes it. Then he slips his phone into his jacket pocket and reaches down to pull out his laptop.

"If you don't mind, I have a few emails I need to send before we reach the party plane."

"No problem. Did you figure everything out on South Fork?"

He pauses. "I did mention something about that to you, didn't I?"

I nod.

"I figured it out." Then his fingers fly over the keyboard.

While he works away, I pull out my personal phone and send a text to Agent Hopkins.

SF: Suspect Maitlin alerted Mitchell to fraud discovery earlier today.

We have so many rooms to listen to on this operation, it's important to alert the team when there are some offices that need priority surveillance. I slide my phone into my pocketbook with a discreet glance at Chase. His head is bowed, and all his focus is on the open laptop resting on his crisp, pressed trousers.

When we arrive, the Esprit jet sits on the tarmac, and our car drives up almost to it. Thanks in large part to our driver breaking speed limits and swerving through traffic, we made it here five minutes before three.

Chase takes my hand as we hurry to the ramp.

"Ready for the weekend?"

"I am. Are you?" I've only known the guy for a few weeks, but the apprehension radiating off Chase this week has been noticeable.

"I'm glad it's Friday. Ready for a drink."

We reach the steps, and I tug on his hand, forcing him to give me one more second before we're in with the group.

"Will you tell me what's going on?" I'm playing the role of a concerned friend, maybe even concerned love interest. Everything indicates the source of his stress is the key to my case.

"Yeah, Frost. When the time is right, I'll tell ya."

He steps aside and gestures for me to go up the stairs ahead of him.

The luxury private jet is by far the nicest plane I've ever been on in my life. Blonde leather seats and walnut tables lend a refined, luxurious design. The interior feels more like a posh den in someone's home rather than a plane for transport.

Each of the couples is grouped together. Olivia and Sam are sitting in two seats with a small table between them, Mason and Delilah are sitting on a wide sofa-like seat in the back, and Jackson and Anna are in two seats on the opposite side. I glance toward Sam. Sam the billionaire, with personal security and a lavish life. I lead the way toward the empty seats closest to the richest guy on the plane.

Operation Quagmire hasn't uncovered anything suspicious regarding Esprit Corp. Other than Maggie having worked for Senator McLoughlin, we haven't discovered any additional connections between this group of friends and McLoughlin's cronies. Agent Hopkins has instructed me to keep my ears open for any work discussions between Maitlin and Sam, but at this point, these guys aren't suspects.

For my part, I'm not entirely sure what to think of Maitlin. His net worth is eyebrow raising. This weekend, I hope to gain some additional insight into how he's accumulated over $12 million in his brokerage account as a mid-level employee living in one of the world's most expensive cities. My gut says he's not the guilty party, but I need answers.

The flight attendant offers beverages. I ask for sparkling water, since I'm on duty. But Olivia requests champagne for each of us to kick off the weekend, and to fit in, I accept a glass and automatically sip. The bubbly liquid goes down smooth. It's light, cool, and refreshing. Delicious. *As sober as possible is the goal.*

Once we all have glasses of bubbly, Olivia raises hers and says, "To Maggie and Jason, and to a fun weekend with friends."

We all lean toward the center of the plane to clink glasses. Chase finally sets his phone down and stops texting to join in the toast. I'm not sure who he's been texting so furiously and emailing before that, but if I get a chance to sneak onto his phone, I will.

After the toast, we're instructed to buckle our seats as we prepare for takeoff. I'm now facing Chase, and he has raised the small table that is between our two facing chairs. He rests his elbows on it, taking care to keep hold on the champagne. He has dark circles under his eyes, and when he exhales, his cheeks fill and push out. It's as if he's visibly breathing out stress.

In a low voice, meant for only me, he dips his head and says, "So, I forgot to tell you. We're sharing a room at the hotel. They were booked, but I did get them to switch me to a room with two queens. I promise I'll be a perfect gentleman. This isn't me expecting anything this weekend. It's just, it made sense for us to stay where everyone else is, and I know I should have talked to you about it, but it's been this insane week—"

"It's okay," I interject to stop his rambling. "Two beds are fine. Thank you."

He relaxes back against his chair. "Thanks for being cool about it."

"No problem." I smile to reassure him. My own room would have been better, but I can deal with this. I didn't carry a gun with me, and while I do have a wire tucked into my suitcase, should I decide I need to wear it, he wouldn't recognize it for what it is if he saw it.

As soon as the plane ascends and levels, discreet seatbelt lights go off, and the captain's voice comes on overhead. "Feel free to walk around the cabin. Our expected arrival time is 5:02 p.m. central. Lucinda, your flight attendant, will be available at any time. Should you need anything, simply press one of the call buttons. She will be distributing an afternoon snack for everyone in about an hour, but if you want anything to eat or drink before then, please let her know."

Olivia raises her voice to the group. "Why don't all of the girls sit together? I know Jackson and Sam have some business they wanted to go over on this flight, and Mason and Chase, you guys can continue one of your epic card games."

Chase mutters under his breath to me, "Of course she assumes I don't have any work to do." I understand his frustration. Without thinking, I reach out and squeeze his knee. He gives me a private smile then addresses Mason. "All right. Come on, man. Let's do it."

When I stand, I squeeze his shoulder before heading over to the girls. His muscles are like iron rods without any give. He's stressed, all right. We trade soft smiles before I head over to the sofa area for girl bonding time. I take Mason's spot on the sofa beside Delilah.

Jackson and Chase talk in hushed tones, then Jackson claps Chase on the back and pushes him toward Mason, who is already shuffling cards.

Delilah diverts my attention away from Chase with a touch on my wrist. I recognize her eager expression. Fear rises as I anticipate the round of twenty questions she's going to hurl my way. I know my backstory backward and forward, but still, this is my first UC op, and every day feels like a test. Only, if I screw up, I'm not going to get a briefing from an FBI trainer.

"So, you and Chase?"

I automatically glance back to see if he heard her. He's in the middle of shuffling cards and chatting with Mason. I don't think he's listening, but still, I give Delilah a shush-it look.

Anna and Olivia smirk.

"We're not a couple."

All three women lean in.

"So, you're just friends?" Delilah asks, her voice rising an octave.

"We're colleagues. And he's asked me out on a date. Look, there's a lot of pressure when you're going away with someone for a weekend. Please don't add more." Be honest when you can. And that right there is about as honest as a girl can be, and what someone in my shoes would say. I soften my words with a weak smile.

"We won't," Anna reassures me while throwing a pointed look to Delilah. "I'm so happy you came. I can tell he likes you." She holds up her hand defensively, probably in reaction to my visual response to her comment. "I know, it's all new. You work together, too. I get it. Even if nothing works out with you guys, I'm glad you came this weekend."

"Yes, please don't let us pressure you," Olivia adds. "We never see Chase with anyone, so we're excited. But, while we like him, we would never hold it against you if things didn't work out with him. Chase is, well…" Olivia turns to Anna as if asking her to complete her sentence.

"Chase is a close friend to all of us. But he can be a lot to take. I've known him for a long time. Like Olivia said, if it doesn't work out, we won't blame you."

"You know, I can hear you guys." Chase interjects. His voice rings with annoyance, but he's grinning as he shifts cards in his hand.

Anna lifts her shoulders as if to say, *whatever*.

"Where are you from originally?" Delilah asks. And here it goes, twenty questions.

"Virginia."

"Oh, really? Jackson's from Virginia, too. What part?" Jackson and Sam are engaged in conversation, and he doesn't turn when Anna offers up his past. I picked Virginia as my cover story because I've lived in DC, and I'm familiar with it, but I don't know if I'm prepared to deal with someone from the same supposed hometown. Shit. I should've spent more time reviewing the backgrounds of these people.

"Richmond." If memory serves, Jackson's not from the city, but if he is, Richmond is large enough it would be believable that we didn't know each other.

"Ah, Jackson's from Fredericksburg." Anna must not know much about Virginia, because she drops that line of questioning. "How are you liking New York? Are you getting settled in?"

In reality, I haven't been to my real apartment since starting this case. Since it's filled with boxes that need to be unpacked, I haven't felt the need. But I do miss having my stuff. The impersonal apartment the FBI has set up doesn't feel like home.

"I'm getting settled. You wouldn't know that if you saw my apartment, but I really like the gym Chase introduced me to, and I'm getting to know my neighborhood. I found a cleaners I like, a Starbucks… I'm building my collection of menus."

"She likes the gym because we go to the best gym in Manhattan," Chase offers with a grin.

The others must be used to him spouting off about the gym because they ignore him.

"Do you have family in the area?" For this assignment, we're keeping it simple.

"No. My parents live in London, and I don't have any siblings. What about you all? Do you have family in the area?"

This line of questioning does the trick of deflecting attention away from my story. Delilah is from New Orleans, Olivia is from Connecticut, and Anna is from Savannah. That discussion leads to updates on siblings. It sounds as if they know each other's family members. All the talk has me missing my sister and realizing it's been a long time since I saw my parents.

Throughout our conversation, which, truth be told, mostly consists of the other three ladies talking and laughing, I catch Chase watching us. He's quick to look away when we connect. Mason's a veterinarian, so I know there's no work talk going on between the two of them. From the bits of conversation I overhear, both are trash talking to each other. Well, Chase is about ninety percent of the trash talk, and Mason adds a ten percent sliver.

I can't hear anything from Sam and Jackson's table, but there's a printed contract on the table between them, and it appears Jackson is highlighting various points in the document. From what I understand, they work together closely, with Jackson as general counsel for the venture capital group Sam runs, so it's not surprising they are taking advantage of this time on the plane. Not once do they engage Chase in their discussion.

After we land, we exit in pairs. Sam and Olivia remain on the plane longer than the rest of us to speak to the crew. As we descend the steps to the tarmac, Chase wiggles his eyebrows with his signature I'm-a-troublemaker grin.

"Ready to dance?"

"As ready as I'll ever be."

SEVENTEEN

CHASE

The boutique hotel Maggie picked for out-of-town guests exceeds my expectations. As far as small-town hotels go, The Black Hawk in downtown Cedar Falls has a pretty hip vibe. We all agree to meet downstairs at Bar Winslow to check out the hyped stuffed olive martini bar after we drop off our bags in the room. The plan is to have a drink then head over to the rehearsal dinner, which is being catered in a private room somewhere in the hotel.

Sydney seems taken with the restored details in the hotel and points out the original penny tile on the lobby floor, prompting me to ask, "Are you into old homes? Restoration and stuff?"

Her face contorts as if I've asked a difficult question and she has to think about it. "I appreciate architecture. I love buildings that have been around for centuries. So much in the United States is contemporary. It's refreshing to find historic buildings here."

"Do you travel a lot outside of the U.S.?" I guide her up to the bar, and Sydney never answers me because Maggie comes out of nowhere and throws her arms around Sydney like they're best friends.

"I'm so glad you came," she squeals. "This weekend is really going to be all about friends. Nothing super fancy. I do hope you guys enjoy yourselves. Across the street is this place called Cup of Joe that I recommend you visit for breakfast. And I don't know if you noticed, but Main Street Cedar Falls is like a page out of a Norman Rockwell painting. We're supposed to have great weather this weekend, and there are tons of great bike trails all around. The concierge can help you rent bikes. If you're into that sort of thing, I highly recommend it."

Even I can't miss the bridal glow Maggie has. I've been to my fair share of weddings in New York, and I don't think I've seen this level of enthusiasm in a bride before. She's wearing a simple black sundress with tiny flowers on it. I scan the bar and spot Jason across the room, in a group of older adults. He's positioned so he doesn't lose sight of Maggie. I'm not really one to fawn over happy couples, but I have to admit these two are cute.

I excuse myself to order us drinks, and when I return, Maggie and Sydney are still talking. "Do you still keep in touch with Senator McLoughlin or anyone from your old company?" Sydney asks. I side-eye her because that's a weird question. Maybe they haven't had the easy stream of a conversation I thought they were having. Or maybe she has a bit of a fangirl crush. The senator splashes across my news and Twitter feed frequently. Rumors about affairs follow the guy, but nothing's ever been substantiated, I don't think. He doesn't do it for me, but maybe to the ladies he's a Casanova.

Jason steps up behind Maggie, and he answers for her. "No, she never had much to do with Senator McLoughlin, and thank goodness. That guy is a royal prick. Mark my words, it's going to come out that man is a crook. Worst kind of politician."

Maggie twists so she can better see Jason. "I don't know why you've never liked him. I mean, I know you're not a Republican, but he's not that bad."

Jason's head vibrates slightly up and down as he answers, "Yeah, he is." There's a ruddiness to his cheeks that tells me he's had more than one cocktail. "I looked over their books once for Maggie. Nothing added up. That charity is raising a lot of money, but he's not donating anything. I'd bet it comes out he's using funds from that charity to finance his campaigns. Mark my words. There's gonna be some kind of scandal around that guy." I read *Page Six* and *Vanity Fair*, and scandals already circle the guy, but I don't share the knowledge.

Maggie slaps him on the chest. "That's not true. He's done great things for Chicago. He's created places for families to stay when loved ones are in the hospital. And we, well, McLoughlin are one of the biggest donors for South Fork Research."

"My point exactly. South Fork Research routinely loses money on patents. And the other source of donations from his so-called charity is for a company that buys up rundown property."

"That's to build much-needed housing for families near hospitals." Maggie rolls her eyes and seems to vehemently disagree with Jason's assessment.

My heartrate picks up pace. That's another one of my fucking accounts at BB&E. It's pro bono, so I've never even looked over Garrick's work. Fuck. It never occurred to me to pay attention to a charity that raises money for cancer research.

"Isn't McLoughlin Charity one of your accounts?" Sydney asks.

Jason sips his drink and inspects me over the rim of his glass.

"Pro bono." Everyone looks at me like I'm speaking Greek. "They don't pay us. We handle whatever they need to be done at no charge."

"Do you do the work yourself?" Jason asks.

"No. Someone on my team."

"Look over it, man. I'm telling you. And right after Maggie showed me those books, she got a job offer to move here."

"You say that like it's all related. Don't be putting things in their heads. The non-profit world is a small world. Chicago was closer to family for me, so I was easy to recruit. You don't have to be so suspicious of everyone." He bends down and places a light kiss on her forehead.

She turns to us as he holds her tight against his side, and she explains. "He reads way too many John Grisham novels."

My phone vibrates in my pocket, and I excuse myself. I scan through a long list of texts that have come in from Cooper. It's all work-related. Questions he has. I suppose he must be wrapping up at the office before heading out for the weekend. There's nothing that needs an immediate response.

Rhonda also sent a text telling me I have six tickets for a show at a club on Tuesday night if I want them. It's not unusual for tickets to be floating around. I'm sure all the guys at the executive level decided they'd rather not go out on Tuesday night, so the tickets are moving down the totem pole. She's gone home for the day, so there's no need to respond to her either.

I return to the barroom and stand in the doorway. Sydney's now standing with Anna and Delilah. Tonight she's wearing low kitten heels that bring her to a few inches below my height. I haven't seen her wear low heels before, and I like it. Her silky ebony bob shifts as her head tilts while she talks. There's an elegance to her movement.

She glances over her shoulder and catches me watching her. I lift my drink in salute. Her glossy pink lips curve upwards, her only acknowledgment before she returns to her conversation with the girls.

"I can't believe it, but it seems the great Chase Man has it bad for someone." Jackson pops an olive into his mouth, smirking as he comes to stand beside me, angled so he too can watch the ladies.

"An appreciation of the female form is not the same thing as having it bad. And she's a colleague."

"What do you care if she's a colleague? You've been thinking about leaving that place for years. And given what you emailed me, I don't know why you're still working there." Yeah, neither do I.

"I don't think I'm her type."

Jackson thumps me on the chest. "Why would you say that? She's stealing glances at you. You guys are in that flirty phase."

"You think she's checking me out?"

He lifts his shoulders as if he's sifting through a file of observations. "Yeah, I'd say so. Anna thinks this could be the one for you."

"Christ, Anna thinks every woman I come across could be the one."

"No, that's not true. Anna thinks every woman you come across and introduce her to could be the one. If she doesn't get to meet them, she assumes they don't mean anything to you."

I look up at him. He's wearing this shit-eating grin. He's amused by this. 'This' being the prospect of me dating someone. I ignore him and return my gaze to Sydney.

"She's out of my league." I pop an olive in my mouth and watch her. "Class personified," I add.

"So? The ones that are too good for you are the best ones. Make you work to be a better man. And since when do you worry about punching above your weight?"

I can't hear what she's saying, but Anna's bending down to say something in Sydney's ear, and I'd bet money she's telling some classic "Chase story." All three of them look over here and giggle. The whole scene brings back that stifling sensation I used to get watching sorority girls who treated me like I was a kid brother, or worse, a total joke.

Jackson looks thoroughly amused, and I have this urge to shove my fist into his stomach and wipe that annoying-as-hell grin off his face. "Hey, when are you gonna get the balls to propose to Anna?"

The grin fades. *Boom.* He takes half a step backward and slides one of his hands into his pants pocket.

"I had planned on doing it this weekend. Found this scenic trail near here. But then I realized if we got engaged, we'd be taking the spotlight off Maggie and Jason, and I know Anna wouldn't want that."

"You've had that ring a long-ass time."

"I know." He huffs. "It's just now it's been so long. It needs to be perfect."

I'm about to tell him that I don't think Anna has grand expectations, and she'd be happy with him simply asking her, but we're interrupted by Maggie's father announcing it's time to make our way into the rehearsal dinner.

The room is set up with tables aligned to form a large rectangle. Sydney and I make our way around the rectangle, searching for the place cards with our names. In the center of the rectangle is a long table filled with candles of varying sizes. Low flower arrangements are set on all the tables. Sydney fingers me in the ribs and says she thinks the flowers are beautiful. I take another look at them to see what she likes. The colors are predominantly blue and some shade of pink. There's a lot of greenery mixed in too.

"Is that what you like?"

"Hmmm?" she asks.

"Are those flowers your favorite?"

"Oh, I don't know. I love flowers. These are Vanda orchids. Maggie said tomorrow at the wedding she's using tons of daisies."

"I could see that." I don't know a lot about flowers, but if I were to buy Maggie flowers, I'd probably go for something like a bunch of daisies.

We find our seats, and I pull Sydney's chair out for her. She sits gracefully, straight up, erect. She has a long, lithe neck and angular facial features. She's almost regal. If I were to buy her flowers, I think I'd look for white orchids. Yes, the same kind of potted arrangement my Mom crows over, so she could enjoy them for a long time.

We sit there at the table for hours. Waiters keep our wine glasses full, almost everyone sitting at the table gets up to make a speech, and this rather annoying photographer in black walks around the circumference of the table snapping photos. I'm certain she caught me mid-chew more than once.

Sydney's dark eyes glisten in the candlelight, as does her silky hair. She's enamored by the speeches. She seems almost entranced. At times, her shoulders shift forward, and the red silk chemise she's wearing slips forward too, revealing more of the curve of her round perfectly shaped breast and the edge of a black lace bra. I'm glad she's here because if I didn't have her to watch, I'd probably die of boredom.

At around ten p.m., the last of the speeches finally concludes, and it seems there are no more home videos of Maggie growing up to be shared. At one point, someone did say something about Jason's parents no longer being alive, and that Maggie's mom tried to pull together a video for him, but no one could locate photos. This person referred to it as being a shame, and all I could think was *thank god*. This dinner would have been twice as long. It was fun and all, in a "let's sit around for a really long dinner" kind of way, but it's after eleven on my internal time clock, and it's been one hell of a day. One hell of a week, for that matter.

We say our goodnights to everyone and make our way to our historic—meaning stuffy—room. Sydney loves it, so it's fine. And there are two queen beds, as promised. Exhaustion rolls over me. The countless glasses of wine and martinis take a toll.

We shift around each other in the bedroom the way friends would. I jump in the bathroom first, not to be rude, but out of necessity. I brush my teeth so she can take as long as she wants once I'm done.

When I exit the tiny bathroom, she carries a bundle of items and clothes in and closes the door. I quickly change out of my suit, slip on some pajama pants and a t-shirt, and slide into the cool, crisp sheets. We never discussed who was taking which bed, but I don't expect she'll care.

If I thought I actually had a chance with her, I'd probably stay up. Put on my A-game. But I've spent the entire night watching her, and I know without a doubt, that girl has no interest in me. And even if she did, if Jason's right regarding his suspicions, then everything is way more fucked than I realized. Sydney's the kind of girl who deserves a guy who can make her his sun and orbit around her, and my gut tells me that can't be me. I do not have a good feeling about what's coming down the pike. I see lawyers and conference rooms galore in my future.

EIGHTEEN

SADIE

I wake early like I always do. The shades are closed in the room, but bright sunlight leaks through the curtain edge. I roll onto my side and stretch. Chase's queen bed sits three or four feet away, and he's passed out, in almost the same position he was last night after I finished in the bathroom.

The barely perceptible lines around the corners of his eyes, lines I've only noticed this past week, have flattened out. If it wasn't for the dark scruff lining his jaw, he'd have a youthful appearance. The quilt has fallen to his waist, exposing...well, nothing. He's wearing a t-shirt, but below the thin cotton you can see the hills and valleys that define his pecs and lead down to a firm stomach. Even relaxed, in sleep mode, his biceps are thick. He acts like such a carefree playboy, but the evidence is there. He works hard.

Last night, I could feel his gaze. Maybe it's my FBI training kicking in, a heightened awareness we've cultivated through rigorous training programs. But I felt it, and my body reacted with a tingling sensation and temperature increase.

I didn't like it. The uncomfortable sensation in the pit of my stomach and a jittery nervousness I haven't felt since high school. I'm on assignment. Chase Maitlin is a suspect. I tend to believe he's innocent. When Jason shared his suspicions regarding McLoughlin Charity, Chase went pale. He didn't say anything, but he looked alarmed as if he was just now putting all the puzzle pieces together.

Listening to Maggie and Jason, it became clear to me that they aren't guilty. Everyone else on Operation Quagmire is doing far more to close out this case than I am by being at this wedding, but I'm still playing an important role on our team. At least, if you consider determining who is not guilty to be important.

Chase opens one eye, then the other one, and rubs his face hard. He rolls over on his side, facing me, and smiles. "Morning."

I return his smile.

"You been up long?" he asks.

"No. I woke up a few minutes ago." I sit up and kick my legs over the edge of the bed and stretch each arm up to the ceiling. "I normally wake earlier than this. I guess all that wine had me sleeping later."

Chase lifts his watch off the bedside table and frowns. "Seven in the morning is hardly late. The rest of the crew won't be up for quite a while."

"That place Maggie told us about, Cup of Joe, it opens at seven. You want to go with me, or you want to sleep in?"

"I'll go with you. I don't sleep late. Maybe we can look into renting bikes after breakfast. You hit the bathroom first. Won't take me long."

"You can go first. I'm not one of those women who take a long time to get ready." Men assume every single woman needs to primp.

"Nah. You go first." There's something about the way he says it, almost a discomfort, and I scan him, trying to decipher what's going on. Then I notice a telltale shape beneath the quilt and understand.

I don't say a word and stifle my prepubescent grin. What am I, twelve? He's a man. It happens. He simply wanted time to make adjustments before getting out from underneath the covers. I hope that's all he wanted, at least. I spend a few extra minutes brushing my teeth and applying moisturizer and sunblock. Then I pull my hair back into the short stub of a ponytail, knowing I'll shower later in the afternoon when getting ready for the wedding. I consider grabbing my wire, but it's outside the bathroom in my suitcase. We're going for coffee. It's not like it's essential. I wore it yesterday, and I'd be willing to bet the audio won't be useable, given the background noise.

Chase takes his turn in the bathroom and, true to his word, takes less time than I. He doesn't try to rub that fact in my face, and I appreciate it. He didn't shave and simply pulled a baseball cap over his bed head hair.

"Ready to go?" The dark circles below his eyes are gone, but he still has a look I'd describe as pre-coffee. Or maybe that's projection on my part.

The hotel lobby is quiet, as is Main Street. The shrill chirp of birds canvasses the street. I glance around but don't spot any birds and assume they must be perched in all the trees that line the sidewalk, contributing to the small-town flair.

Cup of Joe isn't what I anticipated. Chase opens the door for me, and the place is an assault on the senses. There's a 1950s design aesthetic, which is fine, but it's the splash of bright, vibrant colors everywhere that has me blinking. I had kind of anticipated an old school, vintage aesthetic that blended with the 1800s theme from our hotel, but this place pops.

The menu also stands out, filled with flavored roasts I've never heard of but would probably appeal to many. A young twenty-something barista with a bright nose ring and tattoos lining her arms awaits my order. I crave my Starbucks menu. "Do you just have regular coffee? Black?"

She tells me about a roast that sounds like what I'm looking for, and when I agree, she lifts a bright blue turquoise mug from a line of multi-colored ceramics then asks Chase what he wants.

"I'll have the same roast she's having, but I want milk and sugar." For some reason, his effeminate order makes me feel superior. Chase must pick up on my ego smirk, but he rolls his eyes and makes it clear he couldn't care less what I think of his coffee choice. He could have ordered the cake batter flavor. Thinking about that level of sweetness in coffee turns my stomach.

We sit down with our coffees, and I inhale the rich aroma. It's freshly ground and brewed, and the scent is strong, so much stronger than what I normally make at home. It's decadent, and I close my eyes for a moment to fully absorb it.

Chase pulls his phone out of his pocket. "I wonder if we can find some trails online."

"I'd imagine the place where we rent bikes will have suggestions."

The barista overhears us. "If you guys are looking for bike trails, I'd recommend you ride down Main Street and pick up the Cedar Valley Paddler's trail. If you're up for some miles, you could ride into Waterloo for lunch. It's a pretty scenic trail that passes some lakes, and it's easy going." Clear plastic containers with brochures of nearby attractions and local maps line the area beside the register.

Chase and I agree to the suggested plan with quick nods to each other, and he convenes with the barista so she can point on her folded trail map the recommended route.

As he confers with her, I check email. There's a coded email from Hopkins to call home. Chase seems to be engrossed in conversation with the hospitable barista, choosing to stand near the register and wait as she serves the random stray customer entering this early on a Saturday morning, so I head to the restroom in the back. It's a single bathroom. I lock the door and call Hopkins.

"All okay?" His deep timbre pierces the quiet of the tiny, clean bathroom.

"Yes. You have an update?"

"Wiretaps aren't getting anything on Mitchell and Bennett. They're acting like they know they're under surveillance."

"Which means Mitchell is in on it."

"I think so. When Maitlin gave Mitchell that update, he took him to the roof. It's unusual."

"Got it. Anything else?"

"Chicago DA is preparing indictments. It should be at the end of next week. Anything on Maitlin or the others you're with?"

"I don't think any of Maitlin's friends out here are involved. But his friend who worked at McLoughlin Charity did suspect fraud. I'll tell you more later. There are some angles we can investigate."

"Be alert."

"Will do."

Chase and I rent bikes and depart in comfortable silence, riding along scenic paved pathways, mostly with me leading the way. We attempted to ride side by side to start, but there are so many people out and about, walking and running and biking, that it's too difficult to pair up. Riding alone gives me a chance to unwind and meditate and breathe in the fresh midwest air.

We ride all the way to Waterloo, single file almost the entire ride. By the time we pedal into town, I'm relaxed and feeling like it's a vacation Saturday.

Chase waves me over to a small red and white hut. A large sign proclaims it's the Maid-Rite. It's one of the places the barista recommended. It's a little early for lunch, but I'm famished, and we both go for cheeseburgers, fries, and milkshakes. As I down the cheeseburger in under three minutes, I realize we've got about a ninety-minute ride back to town on our bikes in front of us. I push the fries away and stir the straw in my vanilla shake.

Chase hasn't eaten any fries yet, but he's about to open the wrapper on his second cheeseburger. He pushes it away, the same way I pushed my fries away, then twists off the cap to his water bottle and chugs.

"So, did everything go okay with Mitchell yesterday?"

He sets the water bottle on the table, and his mouth opens. He pauses then says, "That's a little out of the blue."

I shrug. No one said I'm a pro-UC agent. "You seemed stressed. Rhonda told me you were in with him. You barely said two words until we were with everyone, and then it took a card game and alcohol to relax you."

"Fair enough. I told him I found out Garrick has falsified data on an account that's going through an acquisition. South Fork Research. It was purchased based on inflated revenues. It's gonna get ugly. The stock price on the company purchasing them went through the roof. And as for whether or not he took it well, I don't know." He scratches his head, then along his jaw where he has the beginnings of a trimmed beard. One day of not shaving, and he's turning into a lumberjack.

"You know it was Garrick?" I ask, cursing myself for not putting on a wire before heading out this morning, or before we climbed on bikes.

"He's the only one who handles those books. Next week I'm going to dig through all his accounts. McLoughlin Charity, that Jason was going on about last night? That's also his." He balls up a napkin and tosses it on his uneaten cheeseburger.

"What did Mitchell say?"

"He's taking it to Tom, HR, PR, legal. You know, the works. They haven't had to deal with anything like this before. He's gonna let me know what they decide to do on Monday. I'm guessing it's a hellish weekend for him."

"Did he just take your word for it, or did you show him proof?"

"I had a folder with everything in it, but we didn't go through it in detail." He half closes his eyelids and frowns, then jerks his head up. "You can't tell anyone, Sydney. No one."

"I won't. I promise."

"I shouldn't have told you, but..." He trails off, half closing his eyelids again.

"But what?" I prompt.

He exhales. "I don't know how much I trust Mitchell."

"What do you mean?"

"I mean, he said the right things, but I didn't get good vibes. I've been debating leaving that company for a while. I only stayed because it was fun. But mark my words, it's about to become a shit show. I know you just got there, but as your friend, I recommend you think seriously about whether you want to stay. You might be better off leaving and never placing BB&E on your resume."

"You think it's gonna get that bad?"

"I do." He looks me directly in the eye without any hint of deception.

"You worried about the company?"

"I'm worried about my team. They're good people. Rhonda, she needs the money. I mean, I can hire Rhonda over at one of my companies. But I can't hire the others. They don't have the right skill sets. My other companies are real estate and Internet. I don't need full-time CPAs."

"What exactly do your other companies do?"

"Well, real estate. I buy properties for rental income. And then, you ever heard the term 'domainer'?"

"You buy up domains?"

"Yep. Started in high school. Maitlin Incorporated. Everything I earned as a waiter, I put into domains. By college, it generated some big money. Used that to invest in real estate. Really, all domains are is virtual real estate. So, I turned to physical real estate. Bought some beat-up places near campus, fixed 'em up, flipped 'em. When I moved to New York, I invested in an apartment building with eight rentals. Just kept reinvesting." He rolls his finger around for emphasis. "Then I added mailbox money."

"Mailbox?"

"Anytime I hear of a restaurant needing money, especially bars, I invest. They send me checks each month. To the mailbox."

"And you reinvest?"

"Yep. Take my earnings, re-invest. I probably reached the point a few years ago where I started seriously questioning why I was working at BB&E. Then they kept promoting me. A lot of my job is playing golf and going out to bars."

"Like the gentleman's club?"

He lifts his shoulders and loudly inhales. "No. That club started as networking for me. Networking with the domainers."

"Networking? You're sticking with that?" I smirk, keeping it light, although there's a part of me that can't stop thinking about that place, wondering if that's the real Chase and what he wants in a woman.

"Well, one of my buddies, a fellow domainer, took me. I'll grant you, that place is on the edge. But the domain industry, I mean, it's a lot of youngish guys. The ones who do well have money to blow. And contacts. I can't emphasize how much it helps to know people in that industry. It's small. Incestuous. Then, like I said, I ran up with the bigwigs there. Mitchell and Bennett introduced me to their friends. Cooper Grayson. EJ They asked for me to be on their accounts. It snowballed. Fun times." He raps the wooden picnic table. "Nothing gold can stay."

"You know, I'm not sure Robert Frost had this scenario in mind when he wrote that."

"Robert Frost? That's *The Outsiders*."

"It's…" He's laughing at me, so I drop it and point to the bikes. "I'm going to the restroom, and then you want to head back? We've got a long ride in front of us."

The restroom is tiny and not the kind of place I want to spend much time, but I pull out my phone from my backpack and dial Hopkins. He doesn't answer, but I send a text.

Me: Garrick Carlson is our guy. Not Maitlin. Mitchell TBD. Told Maitlin he'd be working this weekend on biz plan for handling South Fork fraud.

I drop my phone into my backpack and head back out to meet Chase. He's already cleaned up our table. He heads to take his turn in the restroom, and when he returns, we're off.

"You want to lead? I don't mind following."

He grins and shakes his head. "Nah. I like the view."

More people are out now, and our return trek is slower. Passing pedestrians isn't as safe with so many people, especially kids, out. But the sky is blue, all the leaves still hold on to a strong green hue, and there's this feeling in the air that fall is coming, and we should enjoy one of these last perfect summer days.

"Sydney!" Chase shouts from behind me.

I look over my shoulder at him.

"I need to take a call. Let's take a break."

He breaks away onto the grass, and I follow him, lifting off the bike seat as the bike bounces up and down over the uneven meadow. Chase drops his bike on the ground, and the back wheel spins, suspended in air, while he heads away from me, to the shade of a large silver maple.

I pull to a stop beside his bike and gingerly lean my rental onto the grass. Chase holds his thumb up to me as he talks on the phone, and I give him a thumbs-up back. It's curious he doesn't want to have his conversation near me. He's so far away I can't hear him, and out here in the open there's no way I can get close enough to him without looking like I'm trying to hear.

I pull out my phone and see a message from Hopkins to call him. There's another large tree, far enough away from Chase that he won't be able to come up to me without me having plenty of time to hang up the phone, so I head over to the shade.

"How do you know it's Garrick?" Hopkins cuts to the chase.

"Chase told me. That's what he discovered. Informed Mitchell of what he learned right before coming here. Mitchell said he'd discuss with PR, legal, and Tom Bennett."

"Office is quiet this weekend, but that doesn't mean they can't all be working from home. All signs are pointing to Mitchell being dirty. And Garrick's still MIA. Be careful."

"It's still white-collar. If anything, they'll be contacting lawyers and coming up with a plan for proclaiming innocence." He sounds so serious, but none of this is dangerous.

"Heat's on. They know it. I don't expect they'd come after an FBI agent. My guess is they are planning to frame Maitlin."

"What makes you say that?"

"His accounts. He was our obvious suspect. But we'll see. One thing I can guarantee you. They have some kind of plan, and lawyers are Plan B."

"Okay. One more thing. Maitlin's income is legitimate."

"We know. Team verified everything last week."

"He'll testify if we need him to. I'm sure of it. He's not loyal to the company, only to his team."

"He won't have a choice about testifying. When you get back Sunday, check in. There's a good chance we'll pull you off UC, and you won't be going back into BB&E on Monday. I'm not sure what else we gain by having you there."

"Will do."

When we return to the hotel room, gritty from hours on a bike, Chase insists I shower first. When I exit the bathroom with a towel wrapped around my torso, his gaze travels over my entire body.

"It's steamy in there. The fan isn't working. I need to get dressed out here."

He closes his eyes, and when he reopens them, it's a different Chase. He avoids looking at me as he gathers his toiletries.

"You doing work?" His laptop lies open on the bed.

"Preparation for the worst."

He pulls the door closed, and I block it with my hand.

"The worst?" I ask.

"I'm lawyering up. If they plan on scapegoating me, I want to be prepared. Always gotta prepare for the worst."

He pulls the door while averting his eyes.

I smile to myself. This guy, who goes to raunchy voyeur clubs and watches people have sex on stage, felt self-conscious looking at me wrapped in a towel.

I slip into my sundress, blow out my hair, and dab on some make-up. It doesn't take me long to get ready. It's one of the benefits of a shorter hairstyle. I don't want to be taller than Chase at the wedding, so I pull on the sandals I packed.

He steps out of the bathroom, freshly shaven, with a towel wrapped around his waist. Shameless, I appreciate his form. His broad shoulders, well-defined pecs, his hard-earned six-pack, and the smattering of dark curls.

"Like what you see?"

"Yeah, I do." I don't look away. My body responds. Increased heartrate, elevated temperature, it's more difficult to swallow. Without a doubt, I am physically attracted to him. I squeeze my thighs together and suck air in.

He breaks the moment by looking away and gathering his clothes. I blink, and guilt rears its ugly head. I'm still on a job.

As soon as the bathroom door closes, I fumble in my suitcase with the wire, toying with the device. It doesn't seem to be functioning. I wiggle the wire connecting the transmitter and the battery pack. It's tiny and should fit inside my bra, but the wire connecting the small battery pack is loose. I need tools to fix it. The shower turns off.

I text Hopkins to tell him the device is broken. He doesn't respond, but he won't care. He already told me he doesn't think I need to be on the case.

The door handle jiggles. I toss it under my intimates and close the suitcase as the door opens.

"The mirrors are too foggy to see. I'll tie it when it clears out."

He's wearing dress pants, another dress shirt, and a tie hangs loosely around his neck.

I step forward and straighten the tie beneath his collar. In my flats, the top of my head reaches his nose. I look up at him and loop the silky material into the perfect knot. I rest my fingers along his chest and let them venture along his muscles.

I raise my gaze from his tie. Dark, chestnut eyes take me in, stealing my breath. His head drops, and his lips press to mine. Timid at first, and then I open up. His tongue strokes mine, and he aligns my body to his.

Thoughts circle. I shouldn't be doing this. The room blurs, and I lean into him, lightheaded. He's not a suspect. But I shouldn't be doing this.

He cups my ass, pulling me closer, eliminating any distance. My breasts press painfully against his hard curves. I wrap my arms around him and skim the tips of my fingers through his thick, dark hair. He tastes of mint, and he feels hard, strong.

Don't Stop Believing, by Journey, Chase's ringtone, sounds through the room, and Chase pulls back. We're both breathing heavily, our skin flushed. In all my life, I've never been so turned on by a man's kiss. It's probably due to the adrenaline pumping from doing something I know I shouldn't do. It's the only reasonable explanation.

His chest rises and falls. He grasps my hips, holding me close with his hands and his heated gaze. He shakes his head once, then twice, and steps away to answer the call.

NINETEEN

CHASE

Maggie's folks' home reminds me of the house from *Father of the Bride*, a movie I saw ages ago when my mother and sister tag teamed and forced me to watch a *classic*. It's a two-story, white clapboard home, with a black asphalt driveway on the side. A basketball goal rests at the end of the driveway. Cars are parked all along the street, and little signs direct us to the back yard.

I don't miss our friends' reaction to me holding Sydney's hand. Smiles and smirks. Yes, I've been telling them there's nothing between us, but that was when I didn't think Sydney had any interest in me. I still think she's way out of my league, but that kiss. It was even better than the one at the club.

Damn. If we didn't have a prior commitment, we would still be in that room.

And after? I felt like I scored a home run and the stands erupted in applause. Like I scored the winning goal in the last two minutes of a soccer game. Like I made the shot from the three-point line. That kiss showed me I have a chance with Sydney Frost. From here on out, I'm putting on my A-game, and I'm going for it.

We follow Sam and Olivia into the back yard. White foldable rental chairs are lined up on each side of the aisle. There's a wedding arch set up at the end of the chair-created aisle, wrapped in sheer white fabric with a green and white flower arrangement looped through the curve of the arch. Buckets of daisies mark the end of each row of chairs.

Sam leads us to the groom's side, and our crew fills up an entire row of chairs. Sam disappears to find the rest of the wedding party, as he and his brother Ollie are both groomsmen. Even though they're groomsmen, their matching ties are the only indication. I told Sam he's a lucky bastard. When I think back on some of the weddings I've participated in, where I had to wear the penguin suit and be in attendance hours before the ceremony, I just shake my head. Maggie is one low maintenance bride.

The afternoon sun is setting lower, beginning to duck beneath the canopy of trees, but it's still strong enough to make me wish I wasn't wearing a suit jacket and tie. There are times when the ladies don't know how good they have it. But when I look at the bombshell seated next to me, I don't mind the suit so much. A-game, after all.

I sit back, relaxing my arm possessively around the back of Sydney's chair. She leans into me as she and the ladies chat about the flowers and how beautiful they think the back yard looks. I keep my cool, but I want to reach over to Jackson and tap him and say, *Do you see this? She digs me!*

The acoustic guitar is joined by additional musicians, the music transitions, and the groomsmen walk down the aisle. They're followed by Yara, Maggie's old roommate, a pretty cool chick I've hung out with several times, and Zoe, Maggie's sister. Zoe holds her daughter's hand but drops it midway down the aisle when the toddler insists on scattering some daisies along the way.

The music transitions into a tune I recognize from my childhood. It's *Somewhere Over the Rainbow.* I've heard this played at a wedding or two before. Sydney holds her fingers over her lips when Maggie exits the back door. She's wearing a simple white dress and has flowers in her hair. I lean down and press a kiss to the back of Sydney's head. I do it without thinking and freeze when I realize what I did and how it might come off. But she burrows against me and reaches for my hand, as if it's the most natural thing. We've gone from a kiss to touching each other, leaning against each other, and linking hands.

Sam's father, Mr. Duke, is serving as the officiant. He speaks of love and what love means. I've never put a lot of stock into the concept of love. I've never been one to really listen during wedding ceremonies. But today, I listen. I even chuckle when Jason dips in for a kiss before it's time and he's reprimanded by Mr. Duke.

Jason and Maggie have been through so much. I know most of their story. Best friends turned lovers. Her first love was his best friend. He died. They moved from college to New York together. In some ways, grew up together, if you consider you're still growing up in your twenties. There's a lot there that's evident in all the emotion going on in their words. As I watch them, for the first time during a wedding, I find myself thinking, *I want that. I want what they have. I*

want someone to look at me the way Maggie looks at Jason.
The single life I've clung to feels hollow.

After the service, we all stand and slowly disperse farther into
the back yard. They've set up a small bar to the side, but
there's also a table with pre-filled iced tea and iced water in
mason jars. The bridal party has gathered at the end of the
yard, and a photographer is snapping photos and shouting
orders. The DJ takes over the music, and the photographer's
direction intermixes with the hum of conversation and the
acoustic numbers I'd guess Maggie hand-selected.

I leave Sydney to discuss the wedding with the ladies and
head over to get us both some iced water. When I return with
her glass, the others comment they want one too and drift
away from us to the beverages.

"What did you think?" I ask her, stepping close.

"It was beautiful. Touching."

"Are you glad you came?"

"Very." She looks me in the eyes when she says it, and vibra-
tions flow up and down my spine. A part of me resets, like a
software program with an update. For all my hype about
being the single guy, I'm absolutely okay with putting those
days behind me. It's life altering to come to that realization,
to know I'm okay with handing in my single card.

I strum my fingers along Sydney's back, and she steps closer,
wrapping her arm around my waist. I place a kiss against her
silky hair, and this time, it's right. She feels right. It's way too
early in the game to call it, to say Sydney's the one. But
there's a possibility. And I've always been intrigued by possibilities.

Maggie's father steps up to the microphone. He thanks everyone for coming and informs us that Maggie and Jason are about to take the floor for the first dance, and they would appreciate everyone joining in.

The Luckiest from Ben Folds Five streams through large black speakers, and Maggie and Jason take their place beneath a canopy of twinkling lights.

Sydney watches with a tender smile.

"May I have this dance?"

Her smile widens, and I take her water glass and deposit it on the edge of a nearby cocktail table, then lead her to join others already dancing. I'm not a particularly mushy guy, but all sorts of things are going on in my chest and my brain.

"I'll always remember this," I share.

"What?"

We're almost eye to eye. She's several inches shorter than I am in her flats, and I hold her close as we sway to the song, her cheek close to mine.

"I'll remember our first dance, to a song called *The Luckiest*. And I'll remember the feeling I have right now, that I'm the luckiest guy in the world." I lean down and place my lips on hers. A soft peck to share my emotions. I keep it appropriate to show her respect. And I hold her as close as I dare.

"You barely know me."

"Yes. But I like what I know. You're intelligent. Independent. A good person."

She steps back, not out of my arms, but creates some separation between our bodies, which I suppose is appropriate.

"I like what I know about you, too."

"Tell me some things I don't know about you, Sydney."

She doesn't say anything, just gazes up at me. I don't know if she's lost in the music or debating what to share.

I prompt her by asking, "What's something about you that would shock me to learn?"

"I'm a skilled marksman."

"Marksman. You mean like with a gun?"

She giggles. It's the first time I've ever heard her make that sound, and I dig it.

"Yeah. With a gun. But I'm not bad with a bow and arrow either."

"Not gonna lie. Didn't see that coming."

"You don't like guns?" My expressions sometimes do give me away.

"City boy, right here. We tend to frown on guns. Mass shootings, school shootings. We view those as bad things. Thugs have guns. Where did you say you grew up?"

"My dad likes guns."

"Does he hunt?"

Lines ripple across her forehead then flatten as she answers, "Yes. What about you, what would surprise me to learn about you?"

I twirl her around to buy me some time to think about what I want to share.

"I played soccer at the University of Minnesota."

"Really?"

I nod. The ladies love the sports shit. Well, some do. Some want the always successful guy, the leader, the MVP. I don't stand out as any of those things.

"When I was younger, like elementary and middle, my goal was basketball. My knees are mangled with scars."

"From basketball?"

"Yeah, it's a tough sport for the short kid. I can't even count the times I went sailing across the asphalt, arriving home with bloody knees."

She makes a giggly sound again, a light laugh, enough to let me know I'm entertaining her. I inch closer, holding her in my arms as we slowly step back and forth to the music playing in the background. Her hands lightly rest on my back, and I feel every place she touches me, my skin sensitized. The lights overhead grow brighter as the sun sets over the fields that Maggie's parents' back yard backs onto, and we're one of maybe three other couples swaying to the music.

The music transitions to another acoustic song, and before she can ask, I twirl her around and pull her back to me, careful to keep several inches between us, mindful others might be watching us, and not wanting to embarrass Sydney in any way. After all, the median age of most of the onlookers, sitting in chairs watching the dance floor, I'd guess is sixty-plus.

"So, you wanted to be a basketball player but ended up a soccer player. And I'd guess you were pretty good if you played college."

Here goes. "I only played my freshman year. I wasn't there on a sports scholarship, so it didn't matter to my parents if I played or not. And I wanted a normal college experience, you know? When you play college sports, it's still college. Your team becomes your family, and you get great experiences, don't get me wrong. But I wanted the experiences of a normal college kid." The overhead lights reflect on her dark mahogany irises, creating a shimmering effect. She's gorgeous.

"Didn't like getting up at five in the morning?" she teases.

"Nailed it." I grin. She did and she didn't. But if she wants to tease, that works.

Her fingers graze the back of my neck, and goosebumps spread all across my body. I inch closer, close enough that if I leaned forward, our cheeks might collide.

"I understand." Her fingers venture higher, into my hair, forcing me to close my eyes to rein in my body's reaction. "I wanted a normal experience at university, too."

"Did you not have one?" There's a sadness to her tone that prompts my question, a glimmer of a past experience she's considering sharing, and then a wall rises. Teasing Sydney returns so quickly I can't be certain if she ever left.

"Completely normal. So, what else, Mr. Wannabe Basketball Player? Anything else that would surprise me?"

"I'm learning Mandarin." Languages come easily to me. I didn't go to school on a sports scholarship, but I did go on an academic scholarship. Being fluent in three languages out of high school definitely helps. Fluent if you consider scoring a three, or professional level, to be fluent.

Her right eyebrow raises, and I know I made an impression. Maybe a bigger impression than when I shared my athletic prowess.

"Your turn, Ms. Frost. Tell me more about you. What was little girl Frost like?"

The corners of her full glossy lips lift, maybe in amusement. What I would like to do with those lips.

"She was pretty determined. Focused."

"No. I don't believe it. You? Serious?"

She steps forward, closing the distance between us, close enough her curves brush my chest. We are aligned, and her lips are close enough to my ear that when she speaks, our cheeks brush and the warmth of her breath tingles.

"I always knew what I wanted to be, and I had a singular focus."

"And what did you want to be?"

She takes a step back, and I miss her warmth. She removes her hands from my back and places them lightly on my shoulders, assuming a more distant position.

"Come on, it can't be that bad. What did you want to be? A singer? An actress?"

"I am what I want to be." There's an edge to her tone I don't quite understand.

"Wait? You're telling me you wanted to be an accountant when you were a kid?" Now that shit does not add up. I've never met anyone who wanted to...unless? "Were your parents accountants?"

"My dad. I wanted to be like my dad."

"Ah. Do you ever thank him?"

This time she laughs. A full-on belly laugh. The song ends, and Maggie's cousin announces dinner is now ready. We're having a buffet dinner outside by candlelight, augmented with white Christmas lights hung almost anywhere they could find. There's a tree line that backs up along the end of her parents' property, and then there's a large field that goes on, almost as far as the eye can see. It's not her parents' property, but they know the owners and received permission to use the edge of the field tonight.

The centerpieces on the tables in the reception mimic the daisies in glass mason jars, wrapped with tiny golden lights. We've fallen in line behind pretty much every other person. I'm not in a rush. I have Sydney to myself like this. The people in front of us in line are strangers. I reach for her hand and place a kiss on her knuckle.

There's surprise in her expression, and I lift my shoulders and search for something to distract her from my impromptu action.

"Are you one of those girls who thought about what kind of wedding she wanted when she grew up?"

"No." She shakes her head slowly as she draws out the word. "You?"

"I was never a little girl," I point out.

"No, I mean, when you were a little boy, did you think about what kind of wedding you wanted?"

"Oddly enough, I guess yes, to some degree. My family tends to throw big weddings. Cocktail hour. Menu options. The second round of desserts sometimes late at night. Groom's cakes. I guess to some degree I'd think about what I liked at a wedding and what I didn't. I'm a big fan of groom's cakes."

The light melody of her laugh wraps around me. It's a sound I like. A lot. I've always been the jokester. Laughter pumps me up. Her laugh…it's captivating.

"I don't think Jason has a groom's cake," she says, a tease in her expression.

"No. I wouldn't think so. I'm pretty sure he chopped off his balls in exchange for Maggie wearing his ring."

She rolls her eyes as we step forward onto opposite sides of the buffet table. I load my plate with lemon chicken that's doused in a creamy sauce, white rice, long french string beans that I suspect have seeped in butter, and I lift a buttery roll from the basket on the end. I bypass the cheesy vegetarian pasta option and the salad. I plan on leaving plenty of room for cake. I've already seen the cake, and it's not one of those perfectly crafted cakes that looks gorgeous but you know the icing's gonna taste like sugar cardboard. No, you can almost see the knife marks from where the icing was spread on this one. It's gonna be moist and taste like it came out of someone's grandma's kitchen and will be worth every single calorie.

Sydney's plate, meanwhile, is half salad and a small scoop of cheesy pasta and a large helping of green beans. I make a mental note to be sure I grab her slice of cake. Otherwise, she'll probably grab the thinnest slice they cut.

Seats at the tables are first come first serve, and Sydney and I end up seated at a table of Maggie's family. All our friends are interspersed among the tables. There's a low hum of conversation, and the sound of crickets chirping rises to a staccato, competing with the acoustic music in the background.

Uncle Theodore and Aunt Dottie introduce themselves as they are sitting at our end of the table. A younger kid, maybe fifteen, nods but centers his focus on his phone that's lying flat on the table, his posture and attitude making it clear he'd rather not be here tonight. I don't blame the kid; I've been in his shoes.

We learn from Uncle Theodore that Maggie's parents bought this land over thirty years ago for almost nothing. Over the years, a neighborhood sprung up around them, and everyone fears the farmland supplying our dinnertime view will one day be sold. Theodore and Dottie's home is about a mile away, but it also backs onto parcels of this same tract of farmland. Some years they use it for corn. This year they planted soybeans.

The music shifts, and I immediately recognize what's about to happen. Miley Cyrus shrieks through the speakers, far louder than the acoustic beats from before, and the younger ladies all rise.

"Sydney, come on," Anna calls from a few feet away. And this is the part of the night where I need a refill and to find a good spot to sit and watch.

I say my goodbyes to Uncle Theodore and Aunt Dottie, clear our plates, and join the growing line in front of the bar table. Jackson nods and, without my saying a word, passes me an ice-cold glass beer bottle, dripping in condensation. It must have been lifted from a watery cooler.

We find a little section beside the makeshift dance floor and stand like middle school boys watching the action. The girls sing out the lyrics, forming their own circle beneath the trees. We leave the chairs for the older guests.

Of all the women, Sydney glows. Maybe it's the long-ass bike ride we took earlier today, but she has a healthy sheen, flushed smooth skin, and her lustrous dark hair swings around like a veil of silk as she dances. She's in a demure sundress, not meaning at all to be sexy. But she is. The light fabric drapes against her curves, leaving room for the imagination to roam. And boy, does mine gallop away as I watch her for what feels like hours.

All of us stand there gawking as we make mindless jokes and jabs. Every now and then Jason steps forward and whisks his bride into his arms. When a slow song rotates through, all the men step forward to hold their women. And yes, I hold Sydney. Every. Chance. I. Get.

Not long after the cake is cut, people trickle out. Jason and Maggie become busy as each guest attempts to hug them and wish them well. After the buffet dinner has been cleaned up, I join Jackson in helping some of Maggie's cousins fold chairs and stack them for the rental company to pick up in the morning.

"You boys don't need to do this. We have help coming. You all must be so tired. Traveling from so far away. And it's late in your time zone." She pats us while simultaneously urging us to, well, head on back to the hotel. It's pushing nine, so not that late, but I expect she's probably exhausted.

"Thank you for having us. It was a beautiful wedding." Maggie's mom is an older version of our friend. She reaches out and makes a point to touch each of us. Her dad looks on, watching his wife. He's had an emotional night. No one missed his tears during the father-daughter dance.

All the guys say something similar in thanks, and then Sydney joins me. Her fingers slide into mine, and when we gaze at each other, awareness rises. We're going back to the hotel together. And things are going to happen. Things I want to happen are going to happen.

We're all quiet as we ride back in the back of the limousine. I wrap my arm around Sydney as she absentmindedly toys with my fingers in my lap. I have an urge to brush a kiss across her cheek, but Anna's gaze on us stops me. She's resting her head on Jackson's chest, observing us, as he places a soft kiss on the top of her head. She's an old friend, and I know without a doubt she's going to have a lot of questions—or, well, her version of hazing—after this weekend.

When we arrive at the hotel, Sam's words jolt me out of my stupor.

"You need help, man?" he asks.

I scan the back of the limo then laugh. Delilah is passed out, mouth open, emitting a slight snoring sound, as her head rests on Mason's chest, her blonde hair flowing all over him. She's using him like a BarcaLounger. The man looks down on her with so much love even I can see it. Word on the street is he proposed and she said no, yet you'd never know it looking at the two of them. Not sure I'd be able to still be with a woman if she declined my marriage proposal. I don't totally get them, but different strokes and all that. And his kid is super cute. I'm rooting for the three of them.

"No, everyone, gather near them. Don't wake her up. I want photos." Olivia instructs us all, and we gather on both sides, crowding in awkwardly. Her phone flashes, and Delilah covers her eyes with one hand, and Mason leans over her, protective.

Sydney and I are the first to exit the limousine. Main Street, Cedar Falls, is quiet, especially compared to New York City.

Most businesses are closed, including Cup of Joe across the street. A few restaurants and bars remain open, and golden lights from those locations flood onto the street. We all slowly file into the hotel, coupled up.

"Anyone up for a martini?" Sam calls.

I don't slow. I barely glance back to see who's going to join him.

"I'm tired. You?" Sydney matches my pace step for step as we make our way to the elevator. In reality, tired is not an accurate descriptor. With each step, I become more and more awake. Energy radiates through every muscle, an awareness I'm about to have this gorgeous woman alone, in our hotel room. And this time, we're not just friends. She kissed me, and we've been touching all night.

And now I want to kiss her. All over. The elevator door closes, blocking out the rest of the world. I press our floor number and step forward, crowding her up against the wall, my body pressed to hers, like I wanted to do all night. This woman is intoxicating. I have the smallest of tastes, dipping my tongue, testing the waters, before the elevator jolts and the doors open.

We stumble out together, laughing, but by the time I'm turning the key in our door, there's no humor between us. No, we both know what's coming. There's been a current of energy between us the whole night, with every soft touch, every glance.

It's on the tip of my tongue to reassure her that we can go at her speed. To tell her I don't have any expectations, just because we're sharing a bedroom. To tell her I don't want to do anything that makes her uncomfortable when she closes the distance between us.

Our lips smash together, and she pushes my jacket off my shoulders. Our kiss is manic, hot, an explosion of all the energy that's been simmering between us. She backs me toward a bed, ripping at my shirt, pulling it out of my pants. It's a fucking dream.

Her hands are on my belt buckle as I grip her ass, rubbing her against my wicked hard erection, when she pauses to ask, "Do you have a condom?"

Hell, yes. I always do. It's the way of the Boy Scout.

I grip her dress and lift it. She understands and raises her arms. I toss the dress across the room and sit back on the bed, my pants unbuckled and unzipped, my cock standing at attention through my boxers.

Sydney stands before me in a black lace silk bra and the sexiest matching black thong I've ever seen. Her stomach is flat, taut, and her breasts curve, round and erect. I fist them, dipping my head to suck and nip, making her moan. Her palms press hard against my chest, and she shoves me back on the bed. I lift onto my elbows to watch as she grips my trousers and boxers and pulls them off. They get stuck on my damn dress shoes, but it's not a problem because within seconds she's slipped them off and I'm naked except for black dress socks. She climbs up on the bed, straddling me, and she's looking at me like I'm the slice of cake she refused to eat but really wanted at the reception tonight. And I like it. I like every single thing about this.

She falls on top of me, mouth on mine, frantic, hungry. Her slender fingers grip my cock with a strength that has me grunting and flipping her over. I love that she wants this, but if I don't take control, this is gonna be over before I've had a chance to slip inside that tight pussy.

She bounces slightly on the mattress and lights up.

"You like it rough?'

She smiles then reaches between us for my cock.

"I want this."

"Oh, you'll get it. I promise. But we're gonna take this slow."

I swear…she huffs.

I lower my body onto her, cradling my arousal between her legs, against her center. Her thin lace panties are the only separation between us, and fuck if it doesn't feel good when she thrusts her hips up over and over. She's seeking friction, and I'll give it to her. But first, I need to explore.

"Patience," I command.

With one twist of my fingers, I unsnap her bra, slip it off, and send it sailing. I close my mouth over one of her perky, dusky rose nipples and suck hard, then bite.

"Fuck, yes," she cries as her nails dig into my back, urging more. This woman is on fire.

I glide down her body, kissing and savoring as I go, then drag the thin black material to the side and venture further, tasting her. She grips my hair, directing me to continue.

"Right there. Yes, harder."

I find her clit and hammer my tongue against it as she mewls her approval, then ease two fingers into her wet channel and lightly bite. Her whole body rises forward as she orgasms, whimpering. It's the knife's edge of pleasure, and I just discovered a pleasure point.

I trail kisses along her hip, and her belly, and over her breasts. She's quivering below me.

She kisses me. Deeply. It's as if she's tasting herself, and it's a flavor she likes. I pull back, breaking our kiss, breathing heavily, and look at her, long and hard, eye to eye.

Her long legs wrap around my waist, and her hips rise, welcoming me. I'm on the verge of sliding home when I remember.

"Fuck, condom."

I jump off her and hunt around the room for my pants and my wallet. Two in my wallet, more in my suitcase. Not that I was hopeful, but I'm always prepared. Like a good Boy Scout.

When I climb back onto the bed, Sydney takes the condom from me and rips it open with her teeth. *Holy. Fuck.* She's aggressive, and it's hot as all get-out. She slides the condom on, pushes me back onto the bed, straddles me, positions the tip of my cock between her folds, and slides down, taking me in, tilting her head back, looking to the ceiling, moaning. Her breasts are perky and bounce as she moves up and down, using me to take what she wants. I caress and massage her breasts, loving the tight feel of her around me, watching in awe as she rides me to bring herself closer to another climax. She's in complete control, and it's hot, and she's close, but she's gazing up, and I don't know where her mind is, and the first time she comes with me inside her, I want to know she's thinking of me.

I flip her onto her back once more and claim her, the sounds of my body slamming against hers and our loud gasps for air the only sounds in the room.

"You want to fuck me, huh?"

"Yes, yes."

"Look at me. I want you to look at me when you come. Are you coming now?"

I slam against her, then slow and rise, using my thumb to stroke her clit, to bring her to the edge with our gazes locked on each other. She moans and arches her back. "Right. There."

A thin layer of perspiration coats her skin, glistening in the streetlight through the window.

"Are you coming?"

And then she breaks with a quiver, milking my cock, and I let it go, never breaking my gaze, memorizing her face as it distorts in ecstasy, her lips open, whimpering.

I collapse onto her and kiss her, enveloped in her warmth. It's a slow kiss, a grateful kiss. I'm in awe. For it being our first time, and for us barely knowing each other, sex with Sydney was pretty fucking stellar.

"Please tell me you want to do that again."

And there's that sound again. Her giggle. Giggle might not be the right word. It's light. It's real. It's the sound of her coming out of that frosty shell. And I fucking love that sound.

TWENTY

SADIE

A heavy, warm body presses on top of mine, comforting and cozy. I snuggle back against the heat source. A hotel room, Cedar Falls, the wedding, last night. Chase. I'm not wearing clothes, and while my naked back is to his front, without visual proof, there's strong evidence he's not wearing any clothes either.

The pleasant warmth his body emanates increases to the intensity of a furnace. I inch forward to separate us.

Bright golden light breaks through the edges of the drapes, providing little hint as to time. We're all supposed to meet downstairs at ten for breakfast, then we'll head home at, I suppose, whatever time we make it to the tarmac. The hotel room's digital clock can't be seen from the pillow level, but I always wake early. We should have plenty of time before we need to meet the others.

I lie still on my pillow, not wanting to wake Chase. One arm is draped over my waist, keeping me near. This warm intimacy is what I've been craving for a long while. Not just physical intimacy, but someone to depend on, to be close to.

When I completed my paperwork for my apartment lease, it asked for an emergency contact. Why, I'm not sure. I suppose they need a number to call if they find a body. I listed my sister's number, and the twenty-three-year-old squinted and said, "That's international." She pushed the paper back to me. "It's much smarter to have someone local."

Yes, I moved to a new city, and most people in my situation wouldn't have a local emergency contact either. But here's the thing. I lived in D.C. for years and had one person I counted as a friend I could use as an emergency contact. One.

Is that what last night was about? Me being lonely? Did all it take is some alcohol and a sweet wedding for me to throw my inhibitions out the door and forget I'm on an assignment? Once my carefully constructed wall came down, I practically threw myself at Chase.

He doesn't know my real name. There's a good chance I'll be off the case tomorrow, or at least off UC, and then what? I admit to my boss I let myself get involved with the prime suspect? My heartrate quickens as the reality of what I've done bears down on me.

Yes, we cleared him. And he's a good guy. But I'm on a job. He's not even my type. I tend to surround myself with rule followers, Type A competitive leaders. Not t-shirt wearing nonconformists.

Chase's top priority is to enjoy life, and I have to admit, it's a draw and completely different from anyone I've known, but that doesn't make any of this right. *Breathe. It doesn't matter.*

Chase is not something I need to wrap my head around. Chase's priority is to enjoy life, and as such, he'll be on to his next conquest within a week. When I don't show up at the office, he probably won't notice because he'll be actively avoiding me after our hook-up. At least, that's the behavior I predict, if I know his type. And I think I do.

Last night was fun. A release that I needed. The sexual tension between Chase and me had been escalating, and that back yard wedding was so lovely. I bet every couple there got back home and did...well, things. Probably more than once, just like Chase and me.

I hope this hotel washes the comforters that lie on these beds between guests because ours needs a good wash. And these sheets, let's just say there's UV light evidence that we rejoined during the night, making love. Making love? It might've felt like that, but it can't be that when he doesn't even know my name.

Chase's thumb brushes my nipple, and the areola swells. Gentle kisses trail my shoulder.

"Morning, sexy."

Goosebumps rise on my arms, and my spine tingles. He presses his back against mine, and a certain part of his anatomy I came to know last night presses against me, letting me know he's now fully awake. One last time...tempting but probably not smart.

I push myself up and sling my legs over the side of the bed. The blaring red numbers of the digital clock on the bedside table read 9:02.

"It's nine." Shocking. Never do I ever sleep that late.

Chase leans back on the pillow, hands behind his head, smug. "We didn't sleep much last night." He reaches out for me, trailing his fingers along my back. "Why don't you slip back in bed, sexy?" I have this vision of him using an adaptation of that line on one of the scantily clad women at his sex club, and I shiver. There's something about the way he says it that makes me feel like it's a line he's used a thousand times.

My mouth feels rancid, and a dull pain resides in my frontal lobe. I need water, toothpaste, and a shower, stat. My dress from last night hangs from a lampshade on the dresser, his pants are flung over a chair across from the bed, and his shirt lies in a crumpled pile on the floor. I reach for it, as it's closest, then change my mind. He's seen everything.

Naked, I walk with determination to the bathroom. "I need a shower."

"Would you like company?"

The shower is a narrow bathtub with an overhead nozzle and a plastic shower curtain with a hint of mildew along the bottom edge. I almost fell yesterday on the slick porcelain surface. Two people would be flat out dangerous.

"No, thanks. I won't be long." That's what I say, but it's almost thirty minutes later when I emerge, fully scrubbed clean. He's sleeping peacefully on his back, and the comforter rests along his waist. I stop and stare at his athletic chest and his abs and the dark curly hair scattered over his pecs and the narrow happy trail leading down.

"Come back to bed?"

His deep voice startles me, and I almost drop the towel. I breathe a calming exhale, then head with purpose to my suitcase.

"Shower's yours," I say with my back to him and my head down, busy pulling out my outfit for the day.

The bathroom door shuts, and the sound of the lock clicks.

I dress quickly in case he comes back out, run a brush through my hair, and peer into the dresser mirror to swipe on some blush and cream eyeshadow. I've repacked my suitcase, except for my toothbrush I left in the bathroom. He has yet to turn on the shower.

I gather his clothes from around the room, fold them neatly on the edge of the bed, and toss the throw pillows back in place. The toilet flushes, then the sink runs. He's probably brushing his teeth. He's been in there ten minutes and has yet to turn on the shower. We're going to be late meeting everyone.

I sit in a chair and open my handbag. I check my BB&E phone and have zero emails. The shower finally sounds, and I pull out my personal cell. My finger hovers over Jemma's name, my DC emergency contact. We met during basic field training, then went our separate ways. She went on to be an intelligence analyst. With my MBA and CPA, I could have gone on to be a forensic accountant. Could have skipped basic field training. But that wasn't my dream. No, I wanted special agent. And here I am.

Chase's voice sounds from the shower as he sings a song I don't recognize. *He sings in the shower.* I tap Jemma's name.

She answers, out of breath, huffing loudly into the phone. "Hotshot!" she screams. Back at Quantico, some of the guys came up with the name, but she's the only one who still uses it.

"Squirrel," I say back, mainly because I know she hates her Quantico nickname, and it's my passive-aggressive way of punching her back.

"How's New York?" She's still huffing into the phone.

"Why are you breathing so hard?"

"Sunday morning long run. Thank god you interrupted it." I smile. Jemma and I bonded during the physical training at Quantico. It's safe to say we both run out of necessity. The shower drones on, but I know I don't have much time.

"I screwed up."

"What do you mean?"

"I had sex with a suspect."

"You're UC?" Her tone drops an octave, and I imagine she's separated herself from any other humans on her jogging path, possibly standing away from the trail near trees.

"Yes. For this assignment."

"Is he gonna do jail time?"

"No. We've cleared him. He's no longer a suspect. But he doesn't know—"

"That you're FBI?"

"Right."

"Well, he'll be shocked when you tell him, but then after that, he's just gonna think you're a badass."

"Jemma, I don't know what I'm doing." I stare at the two queen beds, one rumpled and half-done, one well made.

"You sound like you're referring to more than a guy you hooked up with."

"I am."

"Special Agent not cracked up to be what you thought it would be?"

"It is, but it isn't."

"How long have you been UC?"

"A couple of weeks."

"You realize you moved to a new city and went undercover, all at the same time. I'm gonna guess you're feeling lonely."

"Yeah." I sigh. "And hence the bad decisions."

"Was the sex bad?"

I grin, reflecting on my multiple Os. "No. It was good. Bangin', as my university roommate used to say."

"Then not a bad decision."

The water turns off, but Chase continues belting out the song I've never heard before.

"I gotta go."

"Hey, remember, there are lots of career options within the FBI. UC might not be your thing. Call me tonight, okay?"

I end the call. Leave it to Jemma to focus solely on work. Is work what has me down? Is she right? Is it the drain of being UC twenty-four-seven for the last couple of weeks that's affecting me? Or is that I am on assignment and did some-thing that's unthinkable? My chest tightens. When I get home, I'll call Hopkins. I'll probably be off the case. This will be a mistake no one needs to know about.

I zip the interior pocket of my pocketbook, effectively hiding my personal phone, just as the lock clicks and the bathroom door opens. A freshly shaven, baby-faced Chase greets me with a white bathroom towel wrapped below his trim six pack.

He points an index finger at his mouth. "Freshly brushed, minty fresh. Get over here."

He wiggles his index finger, telling me to come to him. I shake my head, more at me because instead of telling him last night shouldn't have happened, like I should do, I rise and in three steps stand before him.

He bends and gives me a good morning kiss that has me pressing against his crotch and lifting my ankle in the air like some starlet in a 1940s film. A part of me does want to throw him back on the bed for a repeat of last night, but no.

"We're supposed to meet everyone in five minutes." I point at my wrist to emphasize and scold.

He tilts his head, smirks, and wiggles his thick eyebrows. "We can be late." He pinches me. "I can be quick."

I laugh. "I don't do late. Hurry." I push him to his suitcase and slip into the bathroom to grab my toiletries and commence the search for any lost items before zipping up my suitcase.

Within three minutes, he's dressed, and his suitcase is zipped. I open the door to the hotel room, and he wraps an arm around me and pulls me back for another kiss. It's a slow, sweet, minty kiss.

"What was that?"

"I just like kissing you." He opens the door wide for me.

When I reach down for my suitcase, he swats my ass playfully and says, "I've got it. Go, Miss Punctual."

We're the first ones down and have almost completely finished eating before anyone else joins us. The situation does not go unnoticed by Chase.

The jet ride back is quiet, almost subdued. We're coupled off the whole way back, and somehow, I fall asleep only to be woken by a soft kiss.

"We're home."

He's been sweet and thoughtful all morning. Not the way I would've thought he'd be after a conquest. I shrug it off as him being around all his friends, and there not being any other single ladies in the vicinity. I've gone with the flow and held his hand, and snuggled against him on the plane, enjoying his touch and proximity, with full knowledge it will come screeching to a halt soon. Either I'll never see him again because I'll be pulled off the case, or he's going to put distance between us at the office so I don't mistake what's going on between us as more. I recognize his behavioral traits, or in FBI speak, his profile. His friends already said as much.

When the car service pulls up to my apartment, Chase jumps out before the driver and picks up my suitcase and meets me on the sidewalk. He follows me to my apartment building's door and brushes his thumb across my lower lip. The way he looks at me, the way he touches me, everything says he's genuinely into me. He could win an Oscar.

"I had a good time this weekend. A great time."

"I did, too." It's the truth.

"I have tickets to a show Tuesday night. Would you like to go with me?"

"What kind of show?"

"It's a DJ. Tickets came through work, so it's possible some clients might be with us. But I have extras. Thought I might ask some of this crew too if you're up for it. If you like hanging with them." He pulls me close, running his fingers through my short hair before tucking it behind my ear. "I like hanging with you. I want to see you again. Soon."

It's ridiculous, but my heart speeds along as if this is real. And this is where it's all confusing and probably why I have up and down emotions whirling inside because when I tell him I want to see him, too, it's the truth.

TWENTY-ONE

CHASE

"Good morning, Sunshine!" Rhonda flashes her pearly whites and follows me into my office with a steaming cup of joe.

"Wow. What a difference a weekend can make." My assistant extraordinaire places the BB&E branded mug on my desk and takes a step back, dramatically looking me up and down.

I glance down. I'm wearing my green hedgehog shirt. *Hedgehogs. Why can't they just share the hedge?* It's not stained.

"What?"

"Friday when you left, you looked like you were about to have to let ten percent of the department go, and this morning you look like you're going to announce raises." She grins, and I know that grin that's spreading across her face. It's the one that says *something happened and I want to know all about it*. "You and Sydney? This weekend?" She's shaking her head up and down, grinning like a banshee.

Now, if Rhonda were a dude, I might be willing to share. I've been known to let it rip about one or two sexcapades in the past. But it's not like I'm gonna spill to Rhonda.

I wave my hand in the air, signaling for her to get out as I bring my laptop to life.

"Oh, no. I'm not leaving. You've gotta give me something. Are you guys together now? Did it happen during the wedding? I swear, weddings are the best place for hookups."

"Rhonda, I—"

Tap, tap, tap.

Rhonda and I both look to the doorway. Evan fills the entrance, but I can see Tom behind him in the hall.

"Tom and I are heading over to Berkley's Diner for breakfast. You free to join us?"

"Of course. I've got to be back by ten."

"Shouldn't be a problem. We don't have long."

Berkley's Diner is a joint across the street that specializes in greasy griddle food. It's my go-to place when I'm hungover. Lots of BB&E employees go, but it's after nine, so there won't be many employees there now. I have an idea what they want to talk about, and it's probably best no one overhears.

I grab my backpack, which has my folders and notes still in it, toss it over my shoulder, and follow the bosses out. So much for my great morning, because following the two suits to the elevator sure does blow all the shit going on all over me. It feels like I'm the zookeeper who just got blasted by the elephant.

Rhonda tugs on my elbow as I pass her cubicle. "When you get back…" She wiggles her eyebrows and beams like a gossipy teenager.

Tom Bennett glances back at us. The guy definitely heard her. *Smooth, Rhonda.*

Tom and Evan lead the way to the diner, side by side. They're both easily half a foot taller than I am, and I can't help but feel a bit like the kid following the two adults. They're each wearing custom made suits, sporting expensive-ass watches, and wearing shoes I know damn well hurt their feet. I'm wearing somewhat wrinkled khakis because the wash and fold on my block is, by some standards, subpar, running shoes, and a sports jacket I snatched up off the rack on sale for three hundred bucks. Sometimes I think I should invest in my wardrobe, but then I remember the guys who spend thousands on a suit are often pretty much pricks.

The two of them lead the way down the narrow aisle, past the bar with shiny aluminum stools, all the way to the last booth along the wall of windows. The two of them slide into one side, leaving the other side open for me. There's a giant rip in the middle of the pleather, so I sit to one side in the booth and cover the unsightly jagged foam with my backpack.

We all order coffee and an omelet with hash browns. The hash browns here are around twelve hundred calories per order but so fucking worth it. I order mine with cheese.

No one else occupies a booth, and there's one old guy sitting at the far end of the bar sipping on coffee and eating pancakes swimming in syrup. The waitress leaves, and Evan glances behind him. It's only restrooms back there. He's not wearing a hat, but he should be wearing a fedora and trench coat the way he's posturing and looking all secretive. But, to be fair, this is some serious shit.

A television set playing on the wall behind their heads shows Senator McLoughlin speaking at a news conference. The subtext scrolls, and he's talking about healthcare. One more bill the senate struck down because ultimately it would hurt insurance companies.

The waitress returns to our booth with the coffee and fills our mugs. An awkward silence fills the table. Evan and Tom both stare. At me.

After the waitress is back in the kitchen, Tom leans forward, resting his forearms on the table. "We've worked all weekend on this. Since you're the one who brought it to us, we wanted to fill you in. Evan and I are flying out to Chicago to meet with executives from South Fork to bring them up to speed. We'll explain to them what's happened."

"You know chances are they are in on it, right? Possibly paying Garrick?" Tom lifts his arms and rests his forearms in an identical position to Evan, only his fingers wrap tightly around the base of a fork. "I'm not trying to make you angry. I know you go way back with them, but it's inconceivable they didn't know revenues were inflated."

"Do you have any idea what's it like to run a business? CEOs don't sit there calculating each sale. We look at spreadsheets. We trust the numbers put before us."

I shift, spreading my arm across the back of the bench. Tom is one pissed off man.

"Maybe you're correct." I placate him. "But what if I am? What are you going to do then?"

"That's not for us to decide. Our responsibility is to provide corrected financials and to notify the client. At this point, it is not a criminal investigation." Evan's deep voice has a commanding edge to it, and he looks back and forth between Tom and me as if he's waiting to see if one of us will argue, waiting to see who he needs to pummel.

The waitress arrives with our food, and Tom and Evan both back off the table, unroll the paper napkin tightly rolled around their utensils, and place it in their laps. Their movement appears coordinated, and it's almost comical.

I focus on my fiduciary responsibility. "I'll provide you the corrected P&L, and corrected earnings statements. The correction will be based on the original data we received from South Fork, but you need to realize a full audit must occur. We have clear evidence information was altered by a BB&E employee, but I have no way of knowing if what they've been sharing with us all along is correct. You get that, right?"

"I've known the founders of South Fork, John and Eileen, since college. We both have. They aren't criminals." Tom grits his teeth and adjusts his spectacles, pushing them farther up the bridge of his nose. "The point is, by the middle of the week, we'll have answers about how South Fork wants to handle this. We'll follow their lead, but we also are following the letter of the law. We meet with our General Counsel before getting on a plane this afternoon. He's had the whole legal department outlining exactly what we need to do in order to meet our fiduciary obligations."

"I'll get everything to you by Wednesday." Tom gives a short nod. "And I'll also have a notarized letter documenting what I found."

"Are you receiving legal advice?" Tom's face contorts as he asks the question. His hands are under the table, but I'd bet dollars to doughnuts those hands are balled in angry fists.

"Yes."

"You promised me you wouldn't tell anyone." Evan sounds shocked, but it's the way he cowers under Tom's glare that's noteworthy. It's pretty clear who's the alpha at this table. And it is not my man Evan Mitchell.

Tom shoves the table an inch my way, then rests his forearms on the surface, his tight fists hovering over his plate. "Who all have you told? Does Rhonda know? Anyone else on your team?"

"Evan asked me not to tell anyone. I haven't."

"Except your lawyer?" Evan questions.

I nod.

"No friends?" Tom doesn't believe me. It's clear he's done with this conversation when he pulls out his wallet and lays cash on the table.

"I know it's a serious situation. I told my lawyer for personal protection. It's going to get ugly. You know it. I know it. Believe it or not, this isn't a fun topic to laugh about with my friends. I am taking this seriously. And I'm glad to see the two of you are, too. I'll be interested in hearing how John and Eileen take the news."

It's going to blow the acquisition right off the table, an acquisition that, if the papers are right, would make each of them very wealthy. These two are fools to think John and Eileen are innocent. But here's the thing, and the real reason I brought in my own law firm. Chances are Tom and Evan are in on in it too, and I'll be damned if I'm going down as the patsy.

Tom rubs the side of his head, and it's like he's giving his right eye a massage as he does so. Yeah, I'd imagine he could easily have a migraine. The tension radiating between all of us is bringing on my own headache.

"Who's your lawyer?"

I'm using my buddy Jackson's law firm. Well, his old law firm, the one where he worked before he went over as a partner in a VC firm. It took him all of three minutes listening to me before he told me I needed the best, and he hooked me up. Not that I'm about to share any of that with these two.

"You've probably never heard of him."

"Give me the name."

I glare at him. Two can glare. For good measure, I rest my fist on the table.

"I want all the information before we fly out to Chicago." Tom sounds defeated.

"Dan Brown." Yeah, it's clear from the look he's giving me he recognizes the name. Whatever. It's the first name that popped in my head. I toss my used napkin on the plate. "Told you you wouldn't've heard of him. He's a buddy of mine."

The walk back to the office is ice cold, and not because of the outside temperature.

TWENTY-TWO

Sydney

Chase: All ok?

My phone's lying flat on the round table, and Hopkins reads the incoming text at the same time I do.

"Someone's worried about you, huh?"

"I'm sure he assumes I have a doctor's appointment or something."

Hopkins's cell rings, and he answers. I sink back and wait. This is the call we've been waiting for all morning. A decision from Bill Walters, the lead prosecuting attorney, on whether he still wants me working undercover. At this point in time, we've got so many cooks in the kitchen, in both New York and Chicago, I don't envy the agent in charge of managing Operation Quagmire.

Over the weekend, surveillance picked up phone conversations that implicate Elijah Mason, known simply as EJ, and Joseph McGurn. Joe is someone who's been on our home terrorism and mafia watch lists for some time. He didn't attend Stanford, and he doesn't seem to be in that clique of friends, but he piqued the team's interest when he went to a strip club with Chase. His only clear connection to this crew was Biohazard Waste Disposal's use of BB&E as an accounting firm. South Fork Research is also a client. But after we picked up phone conversations between him and Cooper Grayson from the real estate development firm, it's clear there's a deeper connection.

We're preparing to deliver indictments Wednesday or Thursday of this week to Senator McLoughlin, Cooper Grayson, John Fischer, and Eileen Becker. A sitting senator and CEOs from two of Chicago's most esteemed corporations. The team is now hoping when we bring them in, we'll get more evidence against Elijah Mason and Joseph McGurn, bringing down two more companies, and hopefully stockpiling testimony against the senator.

We have surveillance ready to go in Chicago. We know Chase can provide us with all the evidence we need to prosecute Garrick Carlson, but we don't have a great amount of evidence against Tom Bennett or Evan Mitchell. They've been careful in conversations both on the phone and in the office. One could argue they've been too careful. The conversation in the diner with Chase felt planned.

One thing we do know, all those conversations they said happened with legal and PR didn't happen in the office. It's not enough to indict, but it's enough to indicate they may be doing what they can to buy time and keep Chase Maitlin quiet.

When I joined this team and agreed to UC, I thought I was homing in on white-collar crime. Penalties to the criminals caught would be minimum security prison or fines.

In the last few weeks, Operation Quagmire has exploded. It now involves members from the SEC, homeland security, the financial action task force, and organized crime in addition to public corruption, where it all started. Hopkins was right. This has become a career case.

That alone would be enough to give a UC rookie like me a case of nerves. But trainee nerves aren't why I'm nervous. Hopkins updated me on everything the team learned over the weekend this morning, and we listened to some of the audio picked up in the diner breakfast meeting.

I suspect they are stalling to keep Chase quiet on what he's found. But why? Are they planning to set him up to make him look like the guilty party? Did Tad really die in a drunk driving accident, or was he the first employee to stumble on to what's going on? It's a stretch, but if it's true, could they be buying time to arrange for Chase to have his own accident? If Joe McGurn is involved, then that means they have ties to the Chicago mafia. And that's the way the wealthy would commit a murder. Hire the hit. Make it look like an accident. Be absolutely certain the crime can't get traced to the source.

Garrick Carlson hasn't been into the office seen since Chase Maitlin let him know he'd discovered something wrong. His car is still in the parking garage. He could be holed up in his apartment, or he could have ordered a car service out of Manhattan. If he's on the run, a hired car would be smarter than driving his own car with a traceable license plate through the bevy of tolls one must pass through to get out of the city and out of the state. Or it's possible he's already been eliminated.

Hopkins doesn't think that's the case, though. He believes he's laying low to avoid being brought in for questioning. He suspects they're all buying time to lay a trap to make Chase Maitlin the patsy. He's probably right, and I'm overthinking all of this. The simplest explanation is usually the most likely.

"Got it." Hopkins studies me, staring me up and down as he speaks into his phone. "She can go back to the office after Bennett and Michell leave for the airport." There's a pause. "She'll be armed."

Hopkins hangs up and sets the phone down. He turns his chair so he's facing me and takes on an interrogation pose.

"Walters wants you in BB&E's office until we distribute indictments. You're to keep an eye out for anyone looking worried or acting unusual. You said your office is near Chase Maitlin's, right?"

"Yes. It's just down the hall from his. Are we going to bring him in and tell him what's going on?"

"Indictments go out Wednesday morning. Walters wants you to bring him in to FBI offices early that morning. We'll read him in, and that's when we'll interview him and let him know he'll be one of our witnesses. Walters doesn't want to risk anything getting in the way of his indictment against McLoughlin."

"Why not indict him today?"

"He wants to wait and see what happens in Chicago with Bennett and Michell. Right now, the heat's on. He wants to see who they go to and if they make some mistakes." It's an opportunity to gather more evidence. Once the indictments go out, any undiscovered guilty parties run a significant chance of remaining undiscovered.

"What about Maitlin's safety?"

"That's another reason to keep you UC. You can keep an eye out for anything unusual. We're going to put a detail outside his apartment at night." That's good. It seems far more likely they'd try something when he's outside or in his apartment at night, as opposed to in a corporate office building.

Hopkins chews on the corner of his lower lip and narrows his eyes. "You and Maitlin. Anything I need to know?"

He's not a suspect. Not now. And even if he was, I wouldn't be the first agent to have sexual relations with a suspect while undercover. That's what I've been telling myself. I also have no desire to come clean to Hopkins, or to a team of over forty agents, but surveillance is so heavy at this point. I'll need to wear a gun and have my wire on. If I stay on two more days, there's a good chance Chase will say something that will make it clear something happened between us.

"Things between us escalated over the weekend," I admit. "But not until after we determined he's innocent. And not until after I thought I'd be off the case once I returned." My stomach curls, but I force myself to face Hopkins head on. It feels like he's my supervisor, or my judge and jury, even though he's not. He's a teammate.

"Are you planning on seeing him after this operation concludes?"

"I wasn't." I shift in the hot seat and swallow. I don't even know if he'll want to see me this week. More than that, I don't know if he'll want to see me once he learns the truth. "Would it be frowned upon?"

He exhales loud enough for me to hear him. "My job is to keep you safe while you're undercover. Not to provide career counseling."

I stare at his polished black shoes.

"Look, I expected something might happen between the two of you."

"You did?"

He shrugs. "It happens. You've been playing a role, pretending to be someone else, and getting close to him. Doing your job. After weeks of getting to know him, you went away with him for a weekend. You won't be the first person to get close to someone during an operation. What I need to know is, can you do your job for the next forty-eight hours? The accounting piece, it's not sexy, but—"

"It's how we prosecute the criminals." Everyone knows this. "I can be the eyes and ears in the office. It won't be a problem."

"It's important that you not share anything with Chase until you have the go-ahead. I don't need to remind you that you don't know how he'll take the information. He could say or do something that would endanger this case."

"I understand. My number one priority is this case. My job. FBI first."

His bottom lip sticks out, and his head jerks up and down twice, then he straightens in his chair.

"Keep your eyes open. It's crunch time."

"Will do." I bend to pick up my briefcase, the one I've been carrying into BB&E. The one I hadn't expected to use again, as I expected to be out of the role as of this morning. "One more thing. Chase invited me to a club Tuesday night. It's a DJ or band, something he got tickets to through work. He's invited several friends to go with us."

Hopkins lifts his pen and scribbles in his notebook. "Which friends?" he asks without glancing up.

"Jackson and Anna, Sam, and Olivia. Also Delilah and Mason, but they've already said no. They have a daughter."

"No one from work?"

"I don't think so. He asked Rhonda, his assistant, but she laughed and told him he knew better than to ask her to go out on a school night."

He taps his pen on the paper and studies it the way he was studying me earlier.

"Is Jackson the lawyer?"

"Yes." He has profiles on every person listed, but at this point, we have profiles on hundreds of people from different corporations related to this case.

"You think he's the lawyer Chase went to?"

"Would make sense. He's an old friend. Unless he has a lawyer on retainer for his other businesses."

"See if you can get Chase to tell you more. I'd like to know who all he's shared his findings with."

"If we brought him in today, you'd get that info."

"Decision's been made. We're not bringing Maitlin into an FBI building until those indictments are out."

"I could talk to him in his office."

"We might not be the only ones tapping his office. You know that."

"I could tell him in my apartment. No one's tapping my FBI apartment, other than the FBI."

He scratches his head. "I'll run it by the team. Unless you hear otherwise from me, he's not to be read in."

"Got it."

My phone vibrates on the table, and the screen lights up.

Chase: This isn't you freaking out, is it?

Hopkins points at my phone. "You better get back in the office. Someone's wondering if you're getting *emotional*."

I check the time. "Bennett and Mitchell won't be leaving for Chicago for a few more hours."

"I don't expect either of them to aim to cross paths with you before they go."

He's right. Mitchell knows I'm FBI. If he's guilty like we suspect, he's going to continue to play his cards to look as innocent as possible, knowing full well the FBI is investigating his firm. He doesn't have any idea of the extent of this operation, or what we're really investigating, and that's the one reason we're optimistic he might lead us to additional evidence when he's in Chicago. That and the fact mistakes are often made when the pressure is on.

My hand shakes as I reach for the doorknob, and I glance back quickly to see if Hopkins noticed. He's staring at his laptop. I've got to get it under control. My portion of this case is still a simple job. Now I'm looking out for suspicious behavior, and if any one were to decide to come after Chase, I'd be there. But that's highly unlikely.

If I hadn't allowed myself more with Chase, I probably wouldn't be thinking twice about this assignment. And that's the rub. I feel like a girl who had a good weekend with a guy and doesn't know for sure if he's going to call her again. It's the butterfly effect of not knowing that I've never liked. It was one of the things I liked about Aaron. I wasn't that into him, so I never had to deal with these nauseating nerves.

Chase is texting me. He's asked me out on a date. Rationally, I have no reason to suspect he doesn't want to keep seeing me. But will he once he knows I've lied about so much?

When I return to the office, Chase's door is closed, as are the blinds to his window. Abnormal behavior for the office social coordinator.

"There you are." Rhonda pops up from her seat at her cubicle, and I jump back in surprise. She laughs. "I didn't mean to scare you. Chase must've asked me half a dozen times if you were back yet."

I nod and continue down the hall. She wants to ask me about this weekend, I can tell, and I am not ready to talk to her. She falls in step behind me. Chase and I did not coordinate our cover story, something I didn't think about because I didn't expect I'd be here.

She stands in my doorway, angled so she can see down the hall and into my office.

"Chase said he had a good time this weekend," she prompts with a grin.

I flip open my laptop and turn it on.

"I did, too."

"He's going to be upset he missed you."

I look up from the lights on my screen as it boots up. "What do you mean?"

"Well, he had me going to find out if you called in sick or what happened. I had to go up to HR and use my—"

"No, I mean, what do you mean by missed me? Is he gone for the day?"

"Yes, he has meetings outside the office for the rest of the day."

That's not unusual for Chase.

"Golf?" I ask. It's Monday, so golf might not be the best guess since a lot of courses are closed on Monday.

"Business meetings." I can't tell if she's covering for him right now or if he really does have meetings outside of the office. "But I'm gonna text him and let him know you're back. He was concerned. Is everything okay?" She adds the last part in a rush, as if it just occurred to her she should ask.

"Everything's fine. I had an annual check-up."

"I knew it was something like that. Well, it should be quiet for the rest of this week. Lots of people are out of the office."

Interesting.

"I guess Garrick is still sick?"

She nods. "Yes, it sounds like it's the worst. Tested negative for the flu but it sure sounds like the flu to me. He's gone into pneumonia."

"You've spoken to him?"

"Oh, yes. He calls in every morning. Sounds so sick."

I nod, taking this information in. So much for my elimination theory. I really am getting too nervous, too on edge. Too emotional.

The sound of a phone ringing echoes down the hall, and with a wave, she's off to answer it.

I pull out my personal phone and send a quick text to Hopkins, alerting him that Rhonda has been speaking with Garrick each morning. Evidence of life. I also text Chase.

Sydney: I'm back in the office. Where are you?

Within minutes, three dots appear.

Chase: Meetings. See you tomorrow?

Sydney: Y

Then I text Hopkins to update him. Chase is out of the office at an unknown location. I don't like it, but worry is unproductive. I have a job to do. I take a notepad and walk through all the floors except the executive floor, making a note of every employee not in the office, or cubicle, today. The information doesn't mean anything, but if we need to weed through potentially guilty BB&E employees, it might be useful information. I can do it tomorrow, too.

The hum of activity on every floor bears distinct normalcy. It's quiet, but not empty quiet. Phones ring, people talk, keyboards click as people type. Every now and then copying machines or printers add to the office symphony. I don't see anyone bent over on a phone, whispering. No one pays any attention to me at all as I roam the corridors. One receptionist on the eighth floor pauses and opens her mouth, presumably to ask if I need help, but closes it and returns to her computer screen when she sees the ID badge hanging around my neck.

When I return to my office, I get lost roaming through reports on the portal. What I'd love to see is personal email, but supposedly BB&E email is not monitored, and HR doesn't have a way to easily allow me access. It's fine. Once indictments are out, we'll get a subpoena.

The hours fly by, and the sounds of the end of day exodus commence. "Have a good night" and "See you tomorrow" ring through the hall.

Chase never came back to the office. I went to the gym and spent two and a half hours there, hanging out, keeping an eye on the weight room, doing stretches and spending time on the treadmill and Stairmaster, trying to not look conspicuous.

I'm curious about where Chase is and what could possibly keep him from the gym, but I don't want to seem like a nagging girlfriend and text him too much. After all, I got busted following him. I need to play this cool. And the reality is if we were dating for real, I just saw him yesterday and have a date with him tomorrow. It's not like we have to see each other every day. And if it were real—and judging by my nerves, whether I want it to be real or not, my mind thinks it's real—not seeing him or knowing where he is is normal. And I need to be okay with that. I shouldn't be nervous not knowing where he is.

We don't have a tail on him, so the team won't know where he went either. And that's okay. I'm sure he's fine. Garrick hasn't been eliminated.

We had expected he'd be in the office and I'd be the one keeping track of him. Night detail is planned. As a precaution. Only a precaution. If the team felt he was in danger, he wouldn't even be walking the streets. We'd put him in protective custody. No one believes he's in danger. If he doesn't come home, Hopkins will notify me.

I turn the corner on King Street, lost on my runaway thought train, and stop. Sitting on the stoop to my apartment, oblivious to his surroundings, engrossed in his phone, is none other than Chase Maitlin.

TWENTY-THREE

CHASE

A running shoe kicks against mine, snapping me out of the email vacuum. Sydney stands before me, post-gym, hair pulled back into that tight little tail, tight black leggings, a jog bra, and a drapey sweater that covers her arms and back but leaves her flat midriff exposed. Christ, she walked home from the gym looking like this?

I jump to my feet, and my thighs and butt cheeks tingle from sitting on concrete steps for so long. I shake each leg vigorously, one at a time.

"What're you doing?" she shrieks.

"My legs fell asleep." I move to the side to let her by, hoping she'll calm down if I get out of her way.

"No, what are you doing here?"

I don't really quite know why I'm here. I had a shit day. An overwhelming day. I didn't want to go home. Or even the gym. I wanted to see Sydney. But you can't share that kind of shit when you're in a new relationship.

"Chase, are you okay?" She touches my arm. I exhale the day's exhaust. All the bullshit seeps away. Does she know the effect she has when she touches me?

"Can we go inside?"

"Yeah, sure." Her head turns left and right as she takes the steps up to the apartment building door. I look up and down the street, like she does, but don't see anything unusual. There's a homeless person leaning against a trash can at the end of the block. He or she has been pretty still. Hasn't moved since I got here. And there's a guy sitting in a car down the street. He's parked illegally, so I figure he's waiting for a spot to open up. Finding free street parking in Manhattan is not for amateurs.

I follow her inside. It's my first time inside her apartment building. The black and white tile floor bears the standard New York grunge look. The grout between the tile is black, but there are spots of lighter gray grout, proof that a long-ass time ago all the grout was white. There's a metal mailbox with slots for all the residents. She opens one of the narrow doors with a tiny key. There are a few fliers inside. Her mail slot is the only one in the row without a name below the number. She glances at the fliers and tosses them in the round blue recycling bin placed conveniently by the mailboxes.

There are stairs leading up, but she bypasses those, and we walk down a narrow hall to an elevator. She presses the number four, and we wait. And wait.

"It takes forever. Want to just take the stairs?" she asks.

"Sure."

I follow her up, sort of hating the cardigan wrap sweater thing she's wearing, as it falls midthigh, completely hiding that firm, perfectly shaped butt of hers. Not that I've spent a lot of time looking at it, but we do go to the same gym. And I did get a chance to have my hands all over it, all over her, this past weekend.

If I'm honest, I'm hoping to get to reacquaint myself with all her body parts again tonight. It's been a long time since I wanted to see a woman immediately after a hook-up, or a date. But Sydney's not a random hook-up. There's depth to her. She's intelligent. Driven. She holds back from sharing too much in a way that reminds me of myself. I'd bet she's been hurt before.

Hell, it would be smarter to walk the other way given we work together, but I'm drawn to her. I like being around her. My life is a shitstorm, and for some reason, I find myself clinging to her as if she's a life raft. Instead of going home, I came to her place and sat on her doorstep. During that wedding, foreign emotions were piping up. What I'm feeling is more than lust.

The timing sucks, though. Never in my life have I been involved in anything this fucked up. It's unnerving. Jackson has me taking enormous steps to protect myself. He's convinced they're setting me up as the fall guy, and he says even if they aren't, I'll be a suspect. Me, a suspect. The worst I've ever done is buy some ganja from a guy who knows a guy.

Inside, I'm a fucking ball of nerves. On edge. I should be having dinner with Anna and Jackson. Hanging with friends. Letting them tell me it's all going to be all right. But I'm here. Climbing four flights of stairs to be near Sydney. My friend? Girlfriend? Are we going there?

She unlocks the door to her apartment, and from behind her I push it open. As soon as she's inside, I follow, closing the door and flipping the deadbolt with a click.

"Are you okay? Is something wrong?" Her fingers caress my jaw, and that's it. I snap.

My lips fall to hers, and I back her against the wall. She's slow to respond at first, caressing my back. I grind into her, and within seconds, her legs wrap around me, welcoming me into her core. And fuck, this right here is what I need. I need to sink into her right now. If only she was wearing a skirt. But no, she's in full-on workout gear.

"Bedroom?" I grunt, teasing her nipple through the thick material. She returns the favor, massaging the outline of my erection through my khakis, and I know we're on the same page.

"Down the hall."

I break from the kiss and hoist her higher around my waist. For the first time, I glance around her apartment. It's a standard nothing one bedroom. We're standing in her den, there's a kitchen behind me, a short hall and a door at the end of it. That's where we're going.

She kisses along my neck, sucking on my earlobe, driving me fucking crazy as I charge toward her bed. I don't bother with the light. I set her down on the comforter and toss off my jacket, then pull my t-shirt over my head. She's still at first, watching me, then she springs to action, removing her sweater. She performs arm stretches to spring herself free of that jog bra. There's no way to get a woman out of one of those things easily. I would've taken her with it on. But damn if seeing those breasts doesn't make my already hard erection harder. All blood heads south, and I have no thought other than slamming into her.

I undo my buckle, kick off my sneakers, and drop my slacks as she rises on the bed to wiggle out of those Lycra leggings. She pushes the leggings and her panties down those long, lean legs where they crowd her ankles. I reach for her feet and drag off each shoe. She's naked before me, but I'm mesmerized by those dark, hungry, alert eyes of hers. She wants me as much as I want her, and damn if that isn't one powerful aphrodisiac.

She crawls backward on her elbows, pushing those round, perfect breasts out toward me, with a sexy as all get out, come hither look. I bend down, lift a condom out of my wallet, fist it, then crawl up the bed to her.

She spreads her legs, making room for me, as I trail kisses along her smooth inner thighs. My plan had been to take her hard and fast. But she's offering herself up. And we've slowed down.

Sydney waxes. I stop, hovering over her core, placing kisses, then take in her smell. I love her sexual scent.

She wiggles and tugs on my arm, attempting to pull me up to her.

"I've been at the gym. You don't want to do that."

I lick my lower lip. She thinks a little sweat's going to bother me? Oh, no. It's like a salty dessert. I slide my tongue inside her, and she moans, spreading her legs further. Yeah, baby likes that. I find the precious little button that will send her over the top and coax it with my tongue, as I finger her. Her back curves up off the mattress. She's so close, I can feel it. I'm learning her body, her tells.

"I want you. Now. Fuck me, Chase."

Fuck. I rip open the condom, slide it on, and place myself at her entrance. I pause, but baby doesn't want to wait. She lifts her hips to meet me. I look in her eyes and slide straight home.

"Fuck, you feel so good. So tight."

"No, you, Chase, right there." She's thrusting up to me with her hips, guiding me. Fuck, she's perfect.

Then she flips me over onto my back and takes over.

"Holy shit. Yes. However you want," I tell her, and I mean it because there is nothing like watching her take charge, owning it. If she wants to use me for an orgasm, I'll let her any day. The only problem I have as I pinch her nipples and make her moan, as I raise my hips to pound into her, is that she feels so fucking good I'm going to come, and I have to stop staring at her to make it last. The moment she stills and angles forward, groaning, I let go. And fuck, that release.

She collapses onto my chest, and I hold her. This, this is what I needed. Sydney, naked in my arms, spent. All the fucking worry of the day gone.

I kiss her. Run my fingers through her hair, slide off the band holding it back so it spills forward.

She rolls off me onto her side, and I slip out of her.

"My hair." she mutters, running her fingers through it and pushing if off her face, behind an ear.

"You're gorgeous. Always." I place a kiss between her breasts and climb off the bed to take care of the condom. "Stay here."

When I return to the room, feeling a whole lot fucking better, she's under the covers, leaning back on pillows. I join her beneath the covers and pull her delectable tight body to my side. She positions herself so she can play with my chest hairs, strumming her fingers lightly through them. It feels fucking amazing. She's amazing. I kiss her forehead.

"So, where were you today?"

I groan. "You wouldn't believe me if I told you."

"Try me."

Ah, fuck. I suppose getting all this off my chest is the other reason I came over here.

"I was in the FBI headquarters."

"What?" She lifts her head off my chest to stare at me. I want her cuddled against me, so I maneuver her back down.

"Yeah, remember how I told you if I were you, I'd leave BB&E?"

"Yes." She's tentative, drawing the word out as she answers.

"Well, I've pulled in lawyers like I told you. As a precaution. I might be being paranoid, but the whole thing doesn't sit right with me. I told Jackson. Now, he's a lawyer, so you know the type. Super cautious. But he hooked me up with some defense lawyers from his old firm. Next thing I know, they've got me sitting in a room at New York FBI head-quarters."

"Who'd you meet with?"

"FBI agents. Real fucking agents. With guns. Real guns. Like, you wouldn't believe it. But not as cool as in the movies. A lot of them weren't even in great shape, you know, pudgy."

She lifts her head again off my chest. "Which department did you meet with?"

"General? My lawyer set up the meeting. They took the information as a tip. Said they'd look into it. Asked me if I'd be willing to testify if it came to it, and I said yeah. Have to tell you, I do feel a bit like a weasel. But I did tell them BB&E might do the right thing. I mean, I can't imagine they'd go to the FBI, but there could be a press release about errors in reporting, and it could all be handled on the up and up. My legal team, the guys Jackson set me up with, insisted I do this. Said it's better if I go to the FBI myself, rather than wait until I'm a suspect. They said if I'm right about BB&E, what I've done is confidential, and the FBI probably won't even open it up as a case. But if they have plans of shipping me down the river, letting me take the fall as the corrupt employee, then, I've covered my bases."

She rests her head back down on my chest. "Smart lawyer."

"Yeah. Never thought I'd be a whistleblower. Anyway, hopefully nothing's going to come from it."

"Let's hope." She places a kiss on my chest and holds me close. This right here, her naked body against mine, it's the most perfect sensation.

My vision adjusts to the dim light of her bedroom. Her bedroom's in the back of the building, and there's another building not far away. Light from one of the units across the way spills into her bedroom window. It must be a cloudy night, because there's not much additional light. The walls in the room are bare, painted primer white. There are no photos anywhere. She has one bedside table with a white ceramic lamp. There are no magazines, no books. Our hotel room this past weekend had more character than this room.

"Where's all your stuff?"

"Hmmm?"

"This room is barren. Do you still have boxes to unpack?" I didn't really take time to look around when I came in earlier, but I don't remember seeing any packing boxes.

"Yes, I still have stuff to unpack."

She places her lips on mine. Soft. Plump. Lips I'm building an addiction for.

"Maybe I can help you?" I don't like the idea of her living in a shell of a place like this. She's new to New York, and I want her to get settled in. I want her to stay awhile.

She squirms, and I kiss her. Her thigh slides along mine, and my dick twitches. I roll her over onto her back and kiss her until she's breathless, massaging her breasts because I can.

"Maybe you can help me…" Damn that seductive smile. This right here, this is what I've needed.

TWENTY-FOUR

Sydney

The dark shadow of a male figure rummaging in my bedside table sends me from drowsy to high alert within two seconds. Not wanting to alert the intruder that I'm now awake, I lie perfectly still, muscles tense, ready to pounce. He reaches into the drawer, where I keep one of my handguns. I crouch, weight on my knees and the palms of my hands, ready to leap onto him if he clutches the gun and gain the element of surprise.

He picks up a ballpoint pen. My eyesight adjusts. Details fill in of the sub-six-foot male. "Chase. Holy shit, you scared me."

"Sorry. I was trying not to wake you, but I wanted to leave you a note. You have no paper anywhere. I should've just texted you. I'll see you at the office, okay?"

"What time is it?"

"A little after five a.m. I need to get in a run this morning. Shhh. Go back to sleep, sexy. I'll see you later. And don't forget, we have plans after work. We'll go straight from there, okay?"

He pulls the comforter back up around my shoulders, kisses my forehead, and I watch his shadow depart. I close my eyes and try to drift back to sleep, but it doesn't happen. Too much adrenaline pumped through me when I thought a bad guy was rifling through my drawer, searching for my handgun.

I stretch, put on my workout clothes and running shoes, and head out for a run. New York City never sleeps, it's true, but there are times of day when it's sleepy and slow. 5:30 a.m. qualifies. The people who are out and about are mostly delivering goods to bodegas or stores, or setting up their sidewalk food carts. The city cacophony, the humankind, rises as the sun does, and beams of light bend around buildings in sharp rays. I round out my run by jumping over the spray of a man's water hose as he squirts the stretch of sidewalk in front of his deli. He smiles as I do so, and for one brief second, we acknowledge each other. I run on, and he continues, whistling as he sprays.

When I return to the apartment, I check my personal phone before going back for a shower. Sweat pours down my neck, along my chest. My shirt's drenched. There's nothing better than the post-run high, the feeling I'm checking everything off my list today, crushing every goal.

I have one text from Hopkins, sent around 11 p.m. last night, telling me to call him. Shit. I press his name, and he answers on the second ring.

"Morning."

"You alone?"

"Yeeesss."

"Maitlin didn't stay at his apartment last night."

"I know." I run my fingers through the sweat-drenched hair at the base of my neck and wait.

"Wondered if you'd cop to it."

"He's not a suspect."

"And he's given us everything we need. He came in through tips."

"He told me. Did he meet with anyone from Operation Quagmire?"

"No. He and his legal team were long gone before Tips connected his info to us. Unless you want him to end up in WITSEC, you may want to find a way to encourage him to keep his mouth shut."

"WITSEC? What's happened?"

"You'll get a full debriefing tomorrow. So far, everything we're uncovering is in Chicago. Did you notice anyone or anything suspicious yesterday?"

"No. I walked around on every floor except the executive floor. No one looked at me suspiciously. I didn't see anyone acting strangely. Have you located Garrick?"

"No. At this point, we're pretty sure he's flown the coop."

"What about his sick calls to the office?"

"He's probably making them from the Caymans or some tropical locale without extradition. We've got an indictment for him, but he's the one guy I don't expect to locate tomorrow.

Anyway, today's your last day UC. So, one more day to keep an eye on your lover boy."

"Ha." He's ribbing me. I deserve it. Don't have a defense. Getting involved with someone while UC doesn't look good. Hopkins, as my handler, could be making a much bigger deal about this.

"Keep an eye out today for anyone packing up files. Anyone watching you. Indictments go out tomorrow, and I want you here, in our offices, got it?"

"Yeah. Are Bennett and Mitchell still in Chicago?"

"Yes."

"Has surveillance picked up on any of their meetings?"

"No. They're acting like people who are fully aware they're being monitored. It doesn't matter. This case was never about BB&E, anyway. They were more of a piece to understand how everything was happening. Maitlin gave us everything we need yesterday, although we suspect additional businesses may be implicated, so we'll be bringing him back in. He agreed to testify. His lawyer basically agreed to him doing anything at all to help our case."

"In exchange for indemnity?"

"Of course. He's got a damn good defense team already lined up. If we hadn't already determined he was innocent, I'd be suspicious."

"He's not a party to any criminal activity."

"I know. How's he gonna take it when he finds out you're FBI?"

"Crossing the line, Hopkins." He chuckles, but a sinking sensation in the pit of my stomach tanks my runner's high.

"Did you already tell him you're FBI?" The question bears no semblance of the earlier friendliness. I understand. This is mission-critical.

"No. I would not jeopardize the operation." I pronounce each word with care, slow and precise.

Hopkins is on the phone, but I can visualize his shoulders relaxing as his business-as-usual voice returns across the line. "Well, my advice is you wait. See if you still feel the same about him after you're not seeing him every day."

"I won't tell him until I get clearance." I tell Hopkins what he needs to know, and nothing more. He's a good colleague, but that doesn't mean I want his relationship advice.

After we end our call, I drop the phone on the kitchen table, and it clatters, the sound ricocheting through the barren white-walled apartment. *How is Chase going to take finding out I'm UC?* I shake the thought out of my head. It's my job, my career. He can't be mad at me for doing my job.

Last night, the early-in-the-dating-process nerves dissipated. He wouldn't have been sitting on my doorstep waiting for me if he didn't feel something. But Hopkins is right to a degree. There's no guarantee we'll still work when I'm not seeing him every day, and when we're struggling to find time to see each other at all. I've tried to be as honest as I can with him, but I wouldn't blame him if he decides I've told too many lies.

By the time I'm dressed to go to the office, I have an entirely different set of disconcerting emotions rolling through me. That's another reason I shouldn't date when on the case. I'm not good with relationship emotions, and I prefer to not have them. I'm also nervous about Chase's safety, and I don't feel like I can express that to Hopkins without him thinking it's because I have feelings. It's all a mess.

Frustrated with myself for putting myself in this situation, I focus on my gun options. The gleam of the metal has a calming effect. My slim Smith and Wesson M&P Shield calls to me. it's too bulky to fit in the suit jacket unnoticed, and I don't treasure the idea of it resting all day on my inner thigh.

Since we're going to a club tonight, I choose a black sheath dress and a black suit jacket. Kitten heels for the office, and black stilettos for night. The outfit works for going from work to a club, but it's not great for concealing a gun.

Yesterday was the first day I carried into BB&E's office. Maybe that's why I'm on edge. We're close to issuing indictments, which always generates a whir of excitement and nerves. I don't see any of these guys, almost all of whom are dads with pictures of kids on their office desks, attempting to off an FBI agent, but you never really know how someone will react when they're facing incarceration. It's a piece of training they drill into us.

It's doubtful they'd have Chase followed. Highly doubtful. His suspicion they might plan to use him as the fall guy is probably spot on. But if it occurred to them a lawyer might encourage him to step forward as a preemptive measure, well, it's not an inconceivable scenario they'd want to track who he was talking to. If they saw him enter the FBI building, then at the very least, Chase dialed up the heat yesterday.

If only he could've waited until later in the week to play the role of an informant. I don't like running through possible scenarios, but I can't shut my mind down. And if they're aware he's talked to the FBI, then that would foil their plan. But the team has probably already thought of this. If they thought Chase was in danger, they'd pull him off the street, and he'd be in WITSEC right now.

I hold the slim graphite gun, the metal cool on my palm. It's not my favorite weapon, but it's discreet. I slip it into my briefcase, in the interior side zipper compartment with my FBI issued cell. That will work for the day. It's better than having it between my thighs all day. The bag will be sufficient. Better to have the safety than to end the day in regret.

TWENTY-FIVE

Chase

"Anna. Why?" Whine mode has gone full throttle. Getting Anna to cave is typically within the realm of possibilities.

"I'm sorry. It's just Jackson has some research he wants to focus on tonight, and I need to brainstorm some fresh concepts. Work's been too busy lately. It stifles the creative flow."

Yeah, I have a feeling I know the kind of work Jackson and Anna want to focus on tonight.

"And it's a Tuesday night. Why are you so hot on going out on a Tuesday?" Now she's whining.

"I'm curious about this Calvin Harris. Aren't you? I mean how do you become a *celebrity* DJ?"

"By dating Taylor Swift?" she asks.

"No. He was big before her. And, besides, who turns down tickets to a sold-out show at The Velvet Room? I'll tell you who. A lame-ass, that's who."

"I'm sorry, I really am. But we're gonna pass on this one."

I huff, but I don't hold it against Anna. I should be taking a pass on this one, too. I have several more accounts I should be reviewing, but at the same time, I'm ready for a release. All day I've been going over spreadsheets with a fine-tooth comb, and I'm ready to let it go for a night.

"Sam and Olivia are still in. And Sydney's still going, right?" Anna asks.

"Yeah." I tell her, not missing her slick little segue.

"I like her."

"I do, too."

"I can tell. Chase, I'm happy for you." I can hear the smile in her words. I have a full-on visual of the way Anna must look right now with her goofy grin. She probably thinks her little buddy has grown up and fallen in love. And all signs point to her being correct. Last night, after an intense, stressful day, there was definitely only one place I wanted to be.

Rhonda taps on the door. It's the end of the workday, and she always stops by before heading out to catch her train.

"I gotta run. Maybe this weekend we can all get together?" I say to Anna.

"I'd love that. Have fun tonight." Yeah, yeah. I've got eight tickets in a VIP booth, and we're going with four people. I hang up.

"Rhonda, you sure you don't want to come tonight? VIP booth. That's, like, five grand." I asked her over the weekend, and she shot me down, but I didn't do the hard sell.

"Wouldn't Ronnie like a night out?" Yeah, Rhonda and Ronnie. High school lovers. I keep asking her to bring in her yearbook so I can check out their dated hairstyles. In current times, Rhonda sports tall black bangs that are more eighties Halloween than anything you'd see in a magazine.

"He'd love it, but there's no way I can get a sitter. And besides, I told you, soccer practice. No can do. But have fun. You'll have to let me know if this Calvin Harris is worth the money."

"Which client did we get these tickets for, anyway?" I really should have taken these tickets and invited clients, not all my friends. But my head's not in the BB&E game these days.

"I have no idea," she answers as she backs out into the hall. "But I know why they ended up in your lap."

"Because I'm the best?"

"No. Because it's a Tuesday! No one else wants them," she shouts as she waves goodnight.

I check the time. We're not meeting up with Sam and Olivia until after eight. Even that's early, but it'll be fine. It might be Tuesday, but it's sold out, so it'll be packed when we arrive. I'm in the mood to blow off some steam. But, truth be told, I'm a little jealous of Jackson and Anna. I wouldn't mind sitting back with a glass of wine and unwinding in the quiet of my apartment with Sydney instead of going to a packed club. I've spent so long taking free tickets, always being on the go, it didn't even occur to me to turn the damn tickets down.

I unplug my laptop and slide it into my backpack, spinning my office chair as I do so. I freeze. Several filing cabinet drawers are ajar.

The tall metal cabinets are to my back when I sit at my desk, so on a normal day, I don't pay them much attention. I scrutinize the uneven drawers. *Don't freak.*

Rhonda may have been in a hurry when she was filing. I open the slim drawer in my desk and lift the tiny silver keys. The locks on these cabinets are so small, it's hard to imagine they'd keep anyone out who wanted in. I push the drawers closed and lock them, my shoulders and neck muscles tense. Then I step outside to the cabinets that line the wall near Rhonda's cube. Methodically, one by one, I lock them all.

"What are you doing?" Sydney's standing at Rhonda's cubicle entrance wearing sky-high fuck-me heels that put her maybe an inch taller than I am. I don't remember what she was wearing earlier today, but it wasn't those heels, because if she'd been wearing them, I would've been thinking of her in those heels and nothing else all fucking day. I want to slide my hand up her thigh and find out if those silky sheer hose adorning those long lean legs are thigh highs, but in my peripheral vision, I spy Trey, a guy on my team, still working at his cubicle. We are not alone.

"Closing up. You ready to go?" *Please say yes.*

"Yeah. Where are we meeting up with everyone?"

"Well, Jackson and Anna bailed, and Sam and Olivia are meeting us at The Velvet Room, so we're on our own for dinner."

"Jackson and Anna aren't coming?" She sounds disappointed, which gives me a perverse shot of pleasure. I want her to like my friends.

"No. Can't say I'm surprised. Those two bail with relative frequency." That wasn't like Anna before she moved in with

Jackson, but she's gradually been upping her cancellation rate.

"So, it's just us and Sam and Olivia?" I like how she says "us." I drop the file keys into my slacks pocket and enter my office to grab my backpack.

"Unless you have someone you want to invite? We have four extra tickets." I should've asked her earlier. I'd like to get to know her friends.

"New here." She lifts her shoulders, raising her hemline as she does so, exposing more thigh. "What about your friends at the gym? You want to invite any of them?"

"Any particular friend of mine you want me to invite?" She wouldn't be the first girl I dated to harbor a crush on one of my friends.

"Chase," she scolds, "I didn't mean for me, you big goof. I was just thinking you spend a lot of time there, talking to those guys. You might want to invite one of them." Two things strike me from her comments. One, she applied the word *big* to me. I like that. Second thing, she's been watching me at the gym.

"That's a negative, Ghost Rider. I'm not bringing along competition on our date." Those glossy, delectable lips lift into a sexy as fuck smile, and Trey be damned, I pull her to me for a kiss. I press her slim tight body to mine, and I know she can feel the outline of my growing erection against her. She moans, which is hot, then pushes me away, which is still hot, but not as desirable.

"Let's get out of here. Let me get my briefcase, and we can leave."

I follow her out, close enough that I can rub my palm posses-sively against the curve of her buttocks. When we arrive at her office, I see the briefcase in her chair, and I step past her, chivalrous. I lift her briefcase, and it's heavier than my backpack.

"What're you carrying in here?"

She reaches for it. "You don't have to carry it. I'll get it."

"Nope." I brush her hands away. "I've got it. But, man, you don't pack light, do you?" I ask as we head down the hall, side by side, for the elevators.

"Where do you want to go for dinner?" she asks, changing the subject.

"It's just the two of us. What're you in the mood for?"

She gives me a look that goes right to my crotch.

"You want to skip dinner? I can be down with that."

She responds with a laugh, and it's pretty fucking adorable.

"No. Come on, big goof. Let's walk around and check menus. See what we find."

"Big goof? Is that your new name for me?"

She wrinkles her nose. "I guess? Does it bother you?"

"No. I never mind being called big."

She giggles again.

"I'll be your big goof," I tell her then sneak a kiss on her cheek.

All in all, I could get used to this. My girl working down the hall from me, us leaving the office together, scouting for food. Who would've thought it? Of course, on the flip side, this is the second day in a row I've skipped my evening gym routine.

"Tomorrow after work, we gotta hit the gym, okay?" I ask, but it's as much to reassure myself. Sydney's hot as fuck, and she's smart, easy to talk to, gets along with my friends. More than any of that, I want to be with her. But I'll be damned if I'm going to be one of those people who slips into a relationship and does a personality one-eighty.

She doesn't answer me, and it might be my imagination, but I think her grip on my hand tightens as we walk. I take it as a sign she likes talking about future plans.

"You up for Italian?" She wrinkles her nose. We had reservations at a snazzy place near The Velvet Lounge, but they were for six, and I'm not really in the mood for fancy. Of course, this is a date.

"You want sushi?" I prompt.

"Sure. Sushi sounds good."

I whip out my phone, press some numbers, confirm we can get a table, and have us in the back of a taxi in less than three minutes. I am a master at winging it.

We'll have to be seated at the sushi bar instead of a table, but it's all good. When we arrive, I offer our bags to the coat check. Syd reaches out for her briefcase. "That's okay. I don't need to check my bag."

I look over to the bar. There will be some space below our feet, but not much. Whatever. I check my bag, and we're seated in front of the two vacant stools. Kassandra, the hostess here, winks at me, and I thank her and ask about the design competition she's prepping for at Pratt Design School.

It pays to pay attention to all the people, and this is one of my regular restaurants.

After she leaves, I prepare to take a crucial step forward in my relationship with Sydney. Sushi ordering. Either we can do this together, or it's gonna be a bust.

"What kind of sushi do you like?" I'm all nonchalant, playing it casual, like I'm totally cool with whatever she says. If she tells me she only eats California rolls, I'll play it cool.

"Well, I eat almost anything, but I tend to prefer sashimi. But if you want to split a roll, I can do that." She rushes to reassure me, but all I want to do is fall on my knees and worship her.

"Sashimi it is." I wave the guy over and order a platter. It's the purest way to enjoy the fish and by far the healthiest. Of course, no fun makes for a dull boy. I point at my favorite menu item. "You open for some tuna nachos to start?"

We order and get our drinks. We talk about work. She asks me questions about some of the different players on my team, about some of the accounts. It's all the kind of stuff you'd talk about if you started a new job and were planning on staying. But she's gotta get out of BB&E.

"Do you need help finding another job?" Why didn't I think of that earlier? She might think it's too hard to get a job somewhere else, and that's why she's ignoring my advice to jump ship.

"No."

I roll my wrist so she can see the time on my watch. "We've spent over an hour talking about that place. Why do you care?" Her gaze falls, maybe to the wasabi remnants on her plate. Guilt strikes. I'm such an ass. "Look, I've told you more than I should have. But I did that because I care about you. Trust me. You don't want to stay there. I can help you find a new gig. I bet Sam can find a position for you. And if not, he's got contacts. We can talk with him about it tonight."

Her suit jacket hangs on a nearby hook on the wall, and I reach for the bare skin on the base of her neck, below her straight, angular bob. Goosebumps rise along her arms as the rough pads of my fingers trace the delicate skin.

She runs her fingers along my jaw, then slides off the stool in slow motion. She presses her voluptuous lips to mine. I trail my fingers along her thigh, up below the hemline, and hold back a whimper. Thigh highs. More than anything, I want to go back to my place right the fuck now.

"I'll be back."

Huh?

"Restroom. Then we've got to get going, right?"

Oh, yes. She slips past me to the back of the restaurant, and I watch her. The swing of her hair, counterbalancing the swing of her hips, the way her black dress curves around the lines of her tight, firm ass.

"Hot date?" Jin, one of the sushi chefs I've chatted with on occasion, asks as he delivers the billfold while wiggling his thin black eyebrows.

"Yes, Jin. Hot date," I tell him as I slide my credit card into the billfold. She's so fucking hot she has me wanting more, and this from a guy who days ago was adamant he didn't do "more." They always say you don't know it's coming, and when it hits you, you're unaware until the damage is done. Well, the damage is done. I am knocked out. The single game holds zero appeal now, all thanks to Sydney. Mom might tell me it's too early. And maybe it is. But you know what, it's like tapping melons, searching for the best fruit. When you know, you know. And yeah, she is way out of my league. But right now she seems to see something in me. I'd be a nutjob not to go for it.

When we arrive at The Velvet Lounge, a line has formed from the entrance and around the block. We slide out of the cab, and within moments, the driver's door of the black Tesla parked on the curb opens, and Wes, Sam's security guy, gets out wearing jeans and a t-shirt. He opens the back passenger door. Olivia exits the car, followed by Sam.

"Hey, guys," Olivia greets us, hugging Sydney first, then me. Sam and I shake hands.

"Wes's parking the car, then he's going to meet us inside."

"Oh, do you mind if I keep my briefcase in your car? Does that work?" She looks at me. "I'd feel better about that than checking it."

I look to Sam, and the trunk pops open. I drop both my backpack and her briefcase in. I trust bag check, but given some of the files in my backpack, storing it in Sam's car is probably a smart move.

"Why don't we wait outside for Wes? He might have a hard time getting in without us," I say as we approach the entrance.

"Wes's already spoken to the bouncer. He won't have any trouble." Dismissing me, Sam turns his megawatt cowboy smile on the ladies. "You ladies ready and rarin' to go?"

We step up to the red velvet rope, and one of the bouncers nods to Sam, lifting the brass hook to let us in. They haven't opened the doors to a general audience yet. VIP booths are allowed in whenever we arrive. And that's the way it should be, given the price tag for a booth. We also have a specially assigned cocktail waitress who will be there to assist us throughout the night. I offer up our tickets to the bouncer, who barely looks at them.

Music pulses, a techno beat, and multi-colored strobe lights flash in coordination with the bass. A smoky haze fills the air. Shiny gold accents the edges of booths and stair railings. Black reigns supreme, covering the walls and floors, and even the countertop on the bar.

The ladies follow a hostess through the bar and into the club area. Sam and I follow close behind. My curiosity has me asking him about the whole door admission thing.

"So, why'd you talk to the bouncer ahead of time? I had the tickets."

"Wes is my security. He's got a concealed weapon. He likes to give bouncers a heads up. Sometimes he won't carry, but most places like this don't mind. They tend to welcome the augmented security. They just want to know who's who."

We slide into the booth. There's a dance area behind us and one before us. Our booth is on an elevated platform. It's in a short line of VIP booths. We can see everything, and the crowd can't get too close as we're in our own little area, cordoned off from the regular joes. Worth five grand? I think not. A nice little way to wine and dine some clients, if you have some that are into this kind of thing? Sure.

Our booth is a semicircle, and the ladies slide in first, leaving Sam and me on the outside of the booth. It's large. After all, it's designed to seat eight. The music is pumping loudly. We have to shout to be heard.

We order our drinks, and I yell over the table to Sam, "Security go with you everywhere?"

I could swear I remember Jackson telling me Sam hated security. And there was this whole thing he went through with a stalker. Crazy shit, but it's hard to feel bad for a guy for drumming up too much attention after being named one of New York's most eligible bachelors. Yeah, when I think of all the pussy that guy must've been getting, I don't feel bad for him. Not at all.

"Not everywhere. But Wes's been with me for a long time. He's more than security."

Right about then, Wes enters the room and stands to the back. He's wearing a black sports coat over his black t-shirt. It's my kind of outfit. He and Sam exchange nods.

"You want him to sit with us? I don't mind."

Sydney glances over her shoulder, connecting the dots between our conversation and Wes.

"He wouldn't want to. He's not going to drink on the job, and he'd say he has a better view of the area standing back there. He came in earlier and decided where he'd stand. He's not the only security here tonight. They're expecting quite a few celebrities."

"Isn't it someone's birthday? That's why Calvin is doing this show?"

"I think it's some model's birthday. One he's friends with."

Olivia looks skeptical. "He's not into celebrities anymore."

"Do you know him?"

She smiles. "No. I read it in *People*."

Of course, this entire conversation is done while shouting and leaning across the table. It's one of the reasons I usually only hit nightclubs when I'm looking to score. These are not the kinds of places one comes to have a conversation. My throat burns from the shouting.

I lean back on the booth, spreading my arm across the back. Sydney sidles up next to me, and the feeling is fucking incredible. I'll behave myself with my friends sitting at the table, but as soon as Sam and Olivia give the signal, we're out of here. I can't wait to take this bombshell home.

Sydney pushes her black handbag toward the center of the table, so it rests beside Olivia's. Women are funny. So many bags.

Sydney and Olivia both order electric blue martinis. Sam goes for a bourbon, and I get an ice-cold beer.

We tap our drinks together to cheer the beginning of the night. The dance floor fills with people, to the point it's wall to wall bodies. A swarm of people pack around the circular central bar, the one that separates the entrance from the dance floor. Blue and white strobe lights flash over the bumping and grinding patrons.

Someone comes out and announces Calvin will be out soon. The lights transition to multiple colors and the beat intensifies, pulsing louder. On the second level, a raw wood balcony circles the open room. People gather above, looking down into the crowd. I've never been here before, but it looks like the club must extend farther back on the second floor. The balcony floor is an unfinished metal grid, an industrial design. The whole place has a steampunk feel.

A big muscle-bound guy with a shaved head stands in one corner. His muscles and the shine of his head draw my attention. The throbbing light highlights his enraged expression. I shift, looking over my shoulder to get a better look. I'm not gay or anything, but I notice muscles, and that guy's got muscles of the Mr. Clean variety.

Right about then, Wes comes running out of nowhere, screaming, "Get! Down! Get down!"

Sam shoves Olivia down. Wes leaps over the booth wall. He lands on his side. *Bam*. On our table.

"Get! Down!"

Time slows. He's sideways on our table. Shouting. He holds a silver gun. His fist grips my shoulder. Pain lances. I duck. Below the table.

Olivia and Sam crouch. It's dark.

Screams cut the pulsing beat.

Sydney crawls. On her knees.

Firecracker sounds erupt above us. *Pop. Pop. Pop*.

Screams. Lights.

Beyond Sydney, on the dance floor, Wes crouches. On one knee, he lifts a pistol.

In the next second, he's flat on the ground. Sprawled out. *Pop. Pop*. Rapid fire. All around. Above us. Beside us. Behind us.

Screams rise. The base beats a rhythm. The booth cushion slices open. Right behind Sam's head. Bright white stuffing breaks through vinyl.

The top of our table rings. *Pop. Pop. Pop*. Firecrackers. Noisemakers. Shrill screams.

Fucking chaos.

Lights alternate colors. Blue. Pink. Yellow.

The techno beat pounds with bass punctuated with human screams. Cries for help.

A woman lies flat on her back on the dance floor, sprawled in an unnatural way, her legs open wide.

Olivia yells, "Sydney! Wait. Don't."

My head hits the top of the table as I half rise, blinking through smoke.

I find her. Leaning over Wes's body. Two fingers on his neck.

She leans over him. *Is he dead?*

Her hand covers his.

I blink.

She lifts his gun.

Pop. Pop. Gunshots. Bullets.

The music pounds.

I blink.

The blue light of a phone screen shines through the dark.

Sydney casts one glance to our shelter. Knees up to our chins. Hunkered down below a table.

She raises onto one knee. Arms out. Gun in the air. "F.B.I.!"

TWENTY-SIX

Sydney

Phone lights shine in the darkness. People are videoing this massacre. Welcome to the social media age.

From the dance floor, I'm a sitting duck. I took out one shooter on the balcony. There could be more. I scan the area. It's pitch black a few feet beyond the balcony rail. The disco lights continue to flash, as does the music.

I need the lights on. The music off. Most everyone has taken cover below tables or against walls. I rush to the bar, gun poised. Ready to take out any additional shooters.

One of the bartenders half rises. Bodies are packed behind the bar, huddled together.

"Can you turn on the lights? Turn off the music?" I shout.

He picks up his phone. Within seconds, overhead white lights flood the place, and the music stops. Muffled weeping fills the silence.

I can now see from the balcony to the back wall. There are two sets of closed double doors on the back wall.

"Police!" New York's finest stream in, guns high. My gun is in the air, and the first one through the door heads straight to me, cautious and slow.

"FBI," I shout. It echoes. I lower my voice. "Off duty. No ID. Shooter on balcony. I hit him. He had a long gun. Automatic." I point my handgun in the direction of the assailant. "Area has not been cleared."

He looks me up and down. I'm in stilettos and a little black dress. And I'm gripping a Glock 22.

"We need an ambulance. Three are down. Probably more."

He lifts a handset to his mouth and radios back. "Assailant down. Shooters possibly still at large."

Police officers in the back have already started the process of clearing out anyone near the exit door.

He backs up and talks to one of the other armed police officers. His partner approaches me.

"Come with me."

"I can help sweep. I was Top Gun." He might not know what that means, but in a nutshell, it means I have better aim than any of these guys. Not that these men would want to hear that.

"You're off duty. SWAT arrived. They'll take over. We need you outside."

I hesitate. Shooters could still be at large, and I left Chase under a table inside. But I need to do my part so no one else gets hurt and we can get medical attention for Wes. He had a pulse, but it wasn't strong.

As we exit the club, officers in bulletproof vests file in, on alert, guns raised. Ambulances line the street, as do cop cars. The whole street is blocked off. Maybe living in the age of social media isn't so bad after all.

"She says she's FBI. Off duty."

The officer in charge steps right up to me.

"Agent Keating," I tell him. "I need to call in."

"FBI is on its way. What do you know?"

"Club scene. Fire from the top right balcony. Automatic assault weapon. Six-foot-plus white male. Private security for one of the customers saw the assailant before he started shooting. He shouted for everyone to take cover. Then the assailant shot into the crowd. Security returned fire." I pause, as a vision of Wes on the floor, with two visible hits, comes to mind. "He needs a medic. I took his gun and shot back. Hit him between the eyes. The balcony has two exit points. I don't know where they lead. If there are additional assailants, I'd expect that's where they are."

The officer in charge, a SWAT team member, and a few other agents who had crowded around, agree on strategy. Tactical SWAT is currently in the process of securing the location. Patrons are filing out, guided by SWAT. Farther down the street, on both sides of the barricade, both east and west, media vans can be seen.

The muscles in my palm and fingers cramp around the Glock.

"All clear. Location secure," is announced nearby.

The medics pour into the building. First responders on a mission to save lives.

The officer in charge surveys, shouts commands, and listens, seemingly simultaneously. I return to his side and wait. After a moment, he peers down at me.

"This isn't my weapon. It's the one I used to shoot the assailant."

He nods and directs me to a van. "Give it to Officer Carlton. Tell him it needs to be tagged."

Sam, Olivia, and Chase exit the building, closely following a gurney. There are no signs of injury on the three of them as they exit. My chest muscles relax. They are safe. Chase is safe.

I float toward my friends. Warmth clasps around my elbow.

"Keating? You okay?" Agent Hopkins stands before me, his FBI badge prominently displayed on his jacket.

The lights, the noise, the crying, all the action slows. I recognize what's going on. In training, I experienced a version of this. I'm coming off the adrenaline high. All my senses blend. I shot. I killed. A shot between the eyes. No one survives it. I aimed. I pulled. I took him out.

Agent Hopkins squeezes my arm. Hard. A slight pain. Not enough to bruise. Enough to bring me back.

"I'm fine." I hold out the pistol. "I shot the assailant. Someone else's gun. Need to deliver it to evidence."

"What happened? Was the shooter there for Chase?" Hopkins asks me, but a NYPD officer pauses. I follow his gaze to my gun.

"Bag this as evidence." The uniformed officer surveys me, and without saying a word, I can read him loud and clear. *Who the fuck are you?*

Agent Hopkins answers for me. "She's FBI. Undercover. She shot the assailant. It's not a government-issued gun."

Officer Carlton slips on blue rubber gloves and lifts the gun with care. Swarms of officers and paramedics flood the street. An army of first responders swirl about. My breathing slows.

I flex my hand, stretching my fingers out, then tightening them into a fist, in and out. The whir of tonight. The spray of bullets.

"I'd like to talk to Wes. He's private security. He alerted everyone before the shooting began. I want to know what he saw. I didn't see the shooter. Not until after the shooting started. He used a military assault rifle. He came there planning to kill many."

"Most recent count I heard is nine dead, eight in critical," one officer states.

Officer Carlton speaks up. "I heard three shooters."

I glance at him. He looks like he wants my confirmation. No one is a good source of information at this point.

"Can we go in? Check out the scene?"

Hopkins gives a brief nod, and I follow his lead, his badge. "You wore your wire. But you didn't carry?"

"No. My gun's in Sam's trunk."

As we approach the doors, two more agents I don't recognize in blue jackets with giant yellow FBI letters emblazoned on the back greet us. Hopkins introduces them, says they're working on Operation Quagmire.

When we step inside, it's a completely different scene from this evening. Dead bodies remain where they fell. Investigators assail the place. A cluster of men stands up on the balcony. They're checking out the dead assailant. Searching for clues. Unfortunately, the dead don't always provide reliable answers.

Without the lights and music, the place has the aesthetic of an abandoned dive bar. The walls are painted flat black. Dark matter, blood, mars the floor. Footprints abound where people traipsed through it. Bloody streaks line the floor, as if the injured were dragged or crawled.

I center myself on the dance floor. Breathe in and out. Close my eyelids and replay the event. I raise them. I scan the bullet holes. Search for a pattern among the holes riddled along the floor and tables and the backs of booths.

I hurry up the metal stairs, to the balcony, sidestepping the throng of men, so I can double-check my theory. Hopkins follows me. I point.

"You can't say he was aiming for us, specifically. But look. Every single bullet is on the left side, where we were. And we'd need to count, but does it not look like more bullets were sent to our table?"

Hopkins surveys the area then waves at our FBI counterparts to join us on the balcony. As we discuss the bullet hole patterns, one of the officers hovering over the assailant's body interrupts us.

"His tats say he's gang. We don't know who all was here tonight. It's possible this is gang-related."

Great. Now Operation Quagmire encompasses gang-related crime.

Hopkins taps me. "What're you thinking?"

"I'm thinking we've got a shitload of chefs in the kitchen. I don't know what we'll find about this guy, but my gut tells me those bullets were meant to take out Chase and me. Jackson, his lawyer, was supposed to be here tonight, too. The tickets Maitlin was magically gifted came from BB&E. If Sam hadn't brought his security with him, inside, every single one of us sitting at that table would probably be dead."

One of the other officers speaks up. "Twelve dead."

"Do you believe in coincidences?" I ask Hopkins.

He shakes his head.

I don't either. But I'm skeptical we'll be able to connect this to BB&E. Especially if that officer is right and the assailant is gang.

I peer over a crouched officer. The assailant has a shaved head. He's extremely muscular. A bodybuilder. Mid-fifties. Tats decorate most available skin. Hundreds of man-hours will be spent investigating him. Once we know who he is, we'll check his bank accounts. His family's bank accounts. We'll look for any signs he was paid off. But there won't be any.

These guys are too good. The media will play it out as yet another madman. In my gut, I know there's a connection. Because I don't believe in coincidences. Regardless of what I believe, a jury needs more than my gut and coincidences.

I killed someone tonight. I memorize his features. Then snap out of it and focus.

"Hopkins, if I'm right, how long before they realize they didn't hit their targets?" My fingers visibly vibrate, and I ball them up. No one seems to notice.

"I sent a protective detail with Maitlin to the hospital." Hopkins is thinking ahead of me. That's why we're a part of a team.

It's three a.m. before Hopkins nudges me and tells me to go home. I've told my story to countless officers, both FBI and NYPD. I've filled out paperwork. I've gone play by play over every single detail I remember. I've drunk two bottles of room temperature water and gone to the bathroom in a bodega a few doors down that's offered restroom access to officers. I have nothing more to add to this case.

A metallic taste fills my mouth, and mild nausea circulates. I've seen every single DOA body, including my first kill. Seventeen dead. More in critical condition. For the rest of my life, I will wonder if there is something I could have done to prevent this massacre.

I don't go home. I head to the hospital. Wes is out of surgery. He's in recovery. Sam and Olivia sit together in the waiting area. They tell me they sent Chase home a while ago. Neither of them questions me about my status as an FBI agent. They treat me like a friend.

"Sam, my briefcase is still in your car. I don't need it now, but I will."

"I'll get it to you. Are you going back to your apartment, or to Chase's?" He has his phone out, ready to send directions into the ether.

"You can send it to Chase's."

FBI headquarters as a delivery location might make more sense, but the last letters I want to utter to Sam and Olivia are F, B, and I. I want to be their friend. I don't want to throw up my undercover role between us.

Two men with FBI badges stand at the far end of the waiting room. I approach them. "Detail accompanied Maitlin home, right?"

One of the men nods. I can tell he recognizes me. He's not familiar to me, but I haven't spent much time in our New York offices yet.

"Two men."

I thank them and leave. My feet ache. Throb. I'm exhausted. I should go home so I can rest before returning to the office. I should, but I choose to shelve the "should."

TWENTY-SEVEN

Chase

The hot water pounds on my back and swirls in circles around the drain. The skin around my toes is sponge-like. It's time to get out of the shower. I rotate and let the water pour directly on my face and down my body.

Even with my eyes closed, I can't escape. The bodies. The blood. Muffled crying. The bright lights. The eerie silence that followed before sirens sounded. The faint, acrid smell of gunfire. The fear Sam wore, unchecked, as he held Wes's hand. "You're gonna be okay. Stay with us."

I brusquely wipe water droplets off my face and wrap a towel around my waist. Condensation covers the mirror. I swipe a clear path with my palm. The person who stares back at me is foreign. I don't want to be the guy in the reflection.

"Did you know Sydney's in the FBI?" It was the first question Olivia asked when we jumped in a cab to head to the hospital, close behind Wes and Sam in the ambulance.

I didn't know. Anything. Talk about being played. Who knew undercover agents would fuck suspects to get close to them? Because that's what it had to be. Right? She wouldn't work at both BB&E and the FBI. Someone might have a full career and "help" the CIA, but the FBI is a full-time gig. So, she had to have been undercover. I suppose it's possible she wasn't investigating me. She was investigating Garrick or BB&E overall, and she didn't expect to fall for my charms. *Yeah, right.* She's a real-life Bond girl. I got played.

And it doesn't even matter. One thing about death, it puts everything in perspective. All over the city tonight, phone calls and texts, maybe social media posts, are being shared, forever altering someone's world. The person they spoke to earlier today is no more. The person they planned to see this weekend won't be arriving. So, I was a pawn in an FBI undercover operation. Big. Fucking. Deal. Other people *died*.

I get dressed and stare at my bed. A designer decked out my whole place. I let her do whatever she wanted. Told her I wanted the HGTV reveal experience. Zero effort on my part. White paint with a fancy name on the walls and ceiling. Patterned black and white spread, with two muted tribal throw pillows. Then she had me buy this brown and white cowhide throw. All the framed images are black and white. Some photos, some art.

I'll give it to her. You can photograph the shit out of this place. But there's not a damn thing here to take cover from this hell I'm in. I shuffle out of the bedroom. I don't want to close my eyes. I'd rather stare at the white walls and my sparse modern furnishings than see what I'll see if I lie down.

The buzzer sounds, alerting me that someone's outside. Who the hell would be coming here at four a.m.? A coldness infiltrates. Shit. Olivia might want to tell me in person if Wes didn't make it. When I left, he was out of surgery. I thought he was out of the woods.

I bow my head and press the intercom button to allow her in. I'd speak, but it doesn't work. The intercom relays static, and that's about it. Side effect of living in an old building. I'd loved this renovated loft and the street, Hudson Square. Now, it comes across as disjointed. Alien.

I hold open the door, standing one foot in the hall in boxers and a t-shirt, barefoot. There are two other units on my floor, but no one's going to be coming out into the hall at this hour. The rickety elevator creaks up to my floor, and the single panel door folds open.

Sydney steps out into the hall.

Not who I was expecting. She's got two colleagues parked on the street. Protective detail, they said. I wonder if she's aware. But of course she is. She's FBI. They know every fucking thing.

"I hope I didn't wake you." She's tentative. Fiddling with her fingers. Wearing the same little black dress and high heels. Pink, verging on red, skin mars the area where skin meets shoe on her feet. Her hair still falls in a perfect straight bob. If it wasn't for the feet, I'd say this is just another day in the life for Agent Frost.

I lean against the doorjamb and let the door fall against my left side.

"What do you need?"

She pushes her hair behind her right ear and looks me in the eye. "Can I come in?"

Fuck her. But whatever. I kick the door open and walk into my apartment. The three windows in my living area open onto the building across the street. No one's lights are on, a reminder of the hour.

I hear the door click close.

"You want something to drink?" I ask as my bare feet pound the wood floor.

"I'd love some water." She slides onto the barstool that faces the kitchen area, and I push a glass over the Corian block countertop, another design feature courtesy of someone else's taste.

I stare at her. She squirms on the stool. I'm fully aware she's had a tough day, too. Hell, she killed someone today. But unfamiliar emotions roll through me, and my brain's not fully activated. I don't even know who the fuck she is.

"I have some explaining to do." She crosses her long legs and folds her hands in her lap.

"I'm all ears." I cross my arms and wait.

She twists off the barstool and limps over to the sofa, barefoot. My sofa is this modern, low back, cool-looking but not particularly comfortable, light brown suede piece with some throw pillows on it to soften it up. It'll do, but when my butt hits the ultra-firm seat, for about the thousandth time, I wish I'd requested a comfortable ugly plush sofa that a person can crash on.

I lean forward, elbows on my thighs, forehead against my palms. My eyes burn, my throat's sore, and my muscles ache. I lift my head and exhale.

"Let's get this over with," I tell her.

She pulls her feet up under her and cradles a throw pillow in her lap.

"I work for the FBI."

"I kinda got that."

"I'm a new team member to a larger operation. The task force suspected BB&E was engaged in illegal activities. As a new member, with my background, I was chosen to participate in an undercover role. I am a CPA, and forensic accounting is my specialty. It was supposed to be a quick assignment."

"So, did you catch the bad guys?"

"I can't talk about specifics in an ongoing case. I've probably already said too much."

A bug or something nips below my eye, and I rub it hard, then press up and down in vicious swipes on the right half of my face. If she can't talk about an ongoing case, what the fuck else can she say?

We stare at each other.

"If you don't have anything else to say, I'm sure you'd like to try to get some sleep." I gesture to the door.

"Chase, I'm sorry. I never meant to hurt you."

"Who says I'm hurt?"

"I was going to tell you everything tomorrow, or I mean today. As soon as I had the approval to do so."

"And when you told me everything, was there more you were going to say, or did you just cover all the points you wanted to cover?"

"My real name is Sadie. Sadie Keating. I chose the name Sydney Frost as my cover name. I thought it was a good play on my real name. I've never been an undercover agent, and I was nervous about it. It's not the role I want to play in the FBI moving forward. I might not have known that before this operation, but I know now. It's too hard for me to pretend to be someone else, to disassociate. The only way I could pull it off was to be as close to the real me as possible."

I swallow and grind my teeth as I absorb her statement. "And who is the real you?"

"Sadie—"

"Not your fucking name. A name is a name. I'm called by many of them. Women often choose 'asshole.' But that doesn't make me one. Who the fuck are you?"

"I'm an agent who got close to someone while on an under-cover assignment. At least, I thought we were becoming close." She squeezes the pillow to her chest like it's a life raft. "I've grown closer to you than I have anyone else in a long time."

She's staring down at the suede. There's a shitload of questions to ask her, but my throat's closing, and exhaustion is setting in. Only one thing really matters.

"When you were with me, when we spent time together, just the two of us? Iowa. Last night. Was that real?"

"Yes. I promise. I swear." She slowly lifts her gaze to meet mine.

My eyes burn. My emotion levels are sky high, yet in a state of paradox. I'm numb. I stand. Her dark eyes glisten in the moonlight cascading through the window. "I can't promise anything. I've got a shitload to think through...sort through.

And a shit ton of questions. But it's late. I just want to crash. End this day." She nods, and the light catches on a stray tear. "And I want to hold you in my arms. Thank the gods you're okay and that fucker didn't shoot you before you shot him." Tears sting. I rub my eyes and walk away.

She follows me into my bedroom, and I close the shades. She pulls off her dress and snaps off her bra, letting them both fall in a heap on the floor.

"Go. Get in the shower. Wash today off. Then we'll sleep."

She follows my directions and steps into my shower. The water pours down over her, and the steam builds. I hold out a towel for her, waiting. I watch her through the glass as she tilts her face into the water. Her shoulders shake as emotion rocks through her.

I drop the towel, open the glass door, and step in behind her. I hold her to me as she cries it out. Once her sobs settle down, I place soap on a sponge and wash her all over. I massage shampoo into her scalp, then finger conditioner through her strands.

I wrap a towel around her then drop my soaked sweatpants onto the shower floor, to be dealt with tomorrow.

I get into bed behind her, pulling her against me, spooning her, holding her tight. Filled with gratitude that I can. I don't have any idea what tomorrow will hold. How I'll feel. How angry I'll be. But one thing is crystal clear. When the world's thrown into utter chaos, you've got to focus on what matters. Names don't matter. Material shit doesn't matter. People. Those you love. At the end of the day, that's all there is. I could kick her out. But after the carnage of today, no way. She's my people. I'm holding on.

TWENTY-EIGHT

Sᴀᴅɪᴇ

I'm headed into the office. I don't have my phone with me. It's still in Sam's car. I believe he's having it delivered to your apartment today. Do not go into BB&E today. If you can, stay home. Call me when you wake up, and I'll bring lunch. -S

I spent minutes staring at that note, waffling on the signature. I have so much to explain, but how do you do that in a note? I opted for saying what absolutely had to be said. It felt a little formal, but sharing feelings isn't my personal strength. In closing, I finally decided on simply 'S,' as it has the added benefit of not throwing it in his face that he didn't know my real name until sometime early this morning. I thought about signing with love, or I love you, but we haven't said those words yet, and again…you don't pop that in a note. When he wakes, he could take this so many ways. The whole relationship built on lies thing…my gut says that's where our conversation, when we finally have one, could net out.

Chalk it up to one more reason you're not supposed to get involved when you're undercover. The guy you fall for will have to forgive you once he learns the truth, and he may not be able to. Of course, there are so many other reasons, too. Emotion adds a layer of complexity. Emotion can put the entire mission at risk. I hear my instructor's voice as I scold myself, but the reality is I didn't get involved with Chase until after we determined he wasn't a suspect. This piece of the case will provide supportive evidence, but it's not critical. We have a strong case against Senator McLoughlin and three successful CEOs, and evidence against one BB&E employee.

As I enter 26 Federal Plaza, I alternate between reprimanding myself for what I've done and defending what I've done. It's almost 11 a.m., and televisions in the main area and in the office are on, covering the mass shooting. On the screen, a woman in her mid-twenties cries, and the caption below reads *Shooter Girlfriend Unaware of His Plans*.

"There she is." Hopkins is the first to notice my entrance.

"Didn't think we'd see you today, Keating." Hopkins told me last night I didn't have to come in. It's a big day for Operation Quagmire, but all the activity is going on in Chicago.

White letters scrolling on the bottom of the screen catch my attention. *Sen. McLoughlin charged with bribery, extortion, and fraud.*

"Wanted to be here on the big day. Have all the indictments been delivered?"

"Everyone except Garrick Carlson. Still can't locate him. The Chicago team is interrogating Eileen Becker as we speak. She's agreed to fully cooperate, and she has evidence tying Tom Bennett and Evan Mitchell to the entire scheme. Apparently, she's been taping their meetings for a while now, as she didn't trust them."

"That's not surprising. She's the one member of that group who didn't socialize with the Stanford crew. She has two young children, too."

"We should be ready to deliver indictments to Tom Bennett and Evan Mitchell tomorrow."

"Is the organized crime unit still investigating Joe McGurn?"

"Yes, they asked us to leave him in play for now. Heat's on, and they want to see what he does."

"What about the SEC?"

"Oh, they're all over South Fork Research. There will be a trickle effect of charges to several they suspect were involved in insider trading."

"Any news on the shooter? Any connections to this case?"

"No. If it was a hit, it was done well. There are no ties we can find connecting him to any of the Stanford Six, or their businesses. The shooter has a history with gangs, but nothing that ties to McGurn's mafia connections. We haven't found any suspicious payments. He wasn't a social media guy, so there's little to go on there. His girlfriend came forward this morning."

The news replays the same segment of her crying in front of a microphone as he mentions her.

"She's got to be twenty years younger than him."

Hopkin's face contorts, and I can tell there are things he wants to say that won't be appropriate.

A caption below the girlfriend reads "McLoughlin Claims Witch Hunt." *Of course he does.*

"What do you need me to do?" It's my first day back in the New York office, but I spent one day in a conference room before I was nominated for the undercover role, so I need direction.

"I need you to get an appointment with psych. Standard protocol. You need to be cleared before you can resume field duty."

There are at least twelve men gathered in the office. Most of them are watching the television, keen to hear what the media is saying. There's a news conference scheduled in fifteen minutes with the Illinois DA's office. The New York DA's office will hold a news conference later in the week on our case. Right now, the sole focus of the New York media is last night's mass shooting. For that matter, the mass shooting is greatly overshadowing news of the Illinois senator's indictment. At the end of the day, one more politician charged with using funds from a charity inappropriately isn't remotely eyebrow raising. The ticker tape on the bottom of the screen announces that Senator McLoughlin will hold a press conference this afternoon.

Hopkins puts his hand on my shoulder and waits until he has my attention before speaking. "We'll be getting reports from the Chicago team all day. Not sure if you're aware, but video of you shooting the assailant last night has surfaced. It's all over the Internet. There's one video, in particular, that you can be seen clearly. You might be identified on the street."

One of the other agents adds, "You're gonna be a celebrity."

"You couldn't get the footage taken down?" I ask the question, but I know the answer.

He shakes his head. "So much footage is out there. There's no point. Our communications group is attempting to take charge of the conversation and focus on safety procedures. It's clear from the footage that taking cover was important for survival."

"Homeland's staying on this, right? They aren't going to give up? The coincidence is too great. They've got to look into the shooter's medical records. Maybe he had a terminal illness, so he agreed to this? Maybe he had a ton of debt, or someone he's close to did? Maybe he never expected to die, and something went wrong with his plan? Maybe—"

"The investigation is ongoing. There may be a connection. Homeland is on it. This isn't your case, you know that, right?" Hopkins squeezes my shoulder. "By now, everyone's seen you, and you'd be recognized as the person who shot him. It wouldn't be safe for you to interview his friends and family."

"I know. I just need for it to be investigated. Seventeen people are dead. If it's a for-hire situation, then at least one, if not all, of the Stanford Six should go down for murder."

"Hey, Sadie, you're on TV," one of the agents in the front of the room says.

On the screen, in amateur video shot by a shaky hand, an image of me fills the screen, as the videographer zooms in. I'm leaning over Wes, checking his pulse, crouched down, partially hidden from the shooter above by the lower level of the dance floor and the raised booth platform.

When Wes jumped over our table, he was seeking cover, as well as alerting us to take shelter. From the angle of the video, you can't see where I got the gun from, but it's clear I brace myself on one knee and raise the gun, two-handed for maximum stability. The video does not capture the assailant being hit, but that image will forever be seared in my brain.

The caption scrolling in white letters reads "Off-duty FBI agent killed shooter."

"Are you going to share my name?"

"It's gonna come out, Sadie. No more undercover work for you in New York, or maybe in the U.S., at least for a while."

"UC's not for me, anyway," I say, eyes trained on the TV monitor, like all the other agents in the room.

A commercial breaks in, and the agent in charge approaches Hopkins to ask, "Can you get her situated at her new desk?" Then to me, he says, "We shuffled some things around. You've got paperwork to do, just some repeat stuff on what happened last night. Get in with psych, then get outta here. We'll see you in the morning."

"What about Chase Maitlin? Are you keeping a detail on him?"

"For now. But Eileen Becker's testimony is far more damning to the Stanford Six than Maitlin's. We'll regroup later, but there's a good chance we'll pull it. Is he in the office?"

"No. I told him not to go in."

"They don't have anything to gain by going after him. I expect we'll drop his detail."

"What about Garrick Carlson?" My lips go numb as my heart rate increases.

"You think he's a threat?"

I think back on my interaction with Garrick Carlson. He's scrawny, not a physical threat based on size. But he's intelligent.

"Is the only evidence we have against Garrick Carlson from Maitlin? I haven't seen what Maitlin provided the FBI. I still haven't watched the tape of him coming forward."

Hopkins tugs on his chin, staring off in the distance. He's seen everything from Maitlin. I've been on my one little piece of this case for weeks, but there are so many pieces of this puzzle to consider. I suspect he's running through all scenarios. He scratches along his jaw.

"That's a good point. Maybe we should keep a detail on Maitlin until we locate Carlson. We suspect he's out of the country. We got a warrant and searched his apartment this morning when he didn't answer to receive the indictment. It doesn't look like anyone's lived there for weeks."

Our SPIC and Hopkins nod in silent agreement to discuss this point further, then Hopkins leads me to a desk that's in the bullpen. There's a desk phone on one side with a red light blinking behind a plastic square.

"You've got a message. Did you lose your FBI issued cell?"

"It took a bullet last night. Had it in my purse on the center of the table. My personal cell is in my briefcase, which was in Sam Duke's car. I'll get that back today."

"Did you hand your FBI phone over to evidence?"

"Yeah."

"Well, put in for a new one before you leave today. It takes a while to process."

I strum my fingers on the desk. Hopkins stands beside me, observing me.

"To be safe, should Maitlin go into WITSEC?" I ask. Going into witness protection isn't something to take lightly, but if last night's shooting was meant to take Chase out, then it would be our safest option.

"I expect we're going to end up with a wealth of additional evidence after we meet with all the individuals we've just charged. And once we indict Bennett and Mitchell, possibly more. Maitlin's a small piece in this. That's my opinion. But the team will give careful consideration to whether or not any of our witnesses need protection. We always do."

He leaves me to return to the conference room. A television on the far wall shows the footage of me raising the gun. The news is on loop. A newscaster starts in with, "This is what we know."

I drop into my desk chair and enter my code to listen to my voicemail. It's from Chase. "Hey, I'm up. Happy to follow your orders and stay home today. Your briefcase is here. Since you don't have your phone with you, here's my number if you need to reach me. Wait. You're the FBI. I'm sure you have my number. You probably know my last credit card charge too." The message ends, and I smile. He's probably half-joking. Hollywood portrays the FBI as all-knowing. We can find a lot of information, but it's not as easy as a computer whiz clicking a few keys on a computer. Joking or not, he didn't sound angry, and that's a good start.

I take care of the few things I need to and leave. I have an appointment with psychology tomorrow afternoon. They'll want to know how I'm handling my first kill. It's a good thing the appointment is tomorrow because right now I'm numb. I couldn't really tell her anything about how I'm handling it.

The cab drops me off on the corner of Charlton and Varick. I see the officers in the car across from Chase's building. The other vehicles parked along the narrow street sit empty. A bike messenger whizzes by on the sidewalk across the street as I press Chase's apartment number. He doesn't even speak into the microphone before buzzing me in. *Not safe at all, Chase.*

When the elevator arrives at his floor, he's standing at the door barefoot in jeans and a t-shirt. His hair is damp. He hasn't shaved, and the skin below his eyes bears a shadow.

"It's not safe to buzz someone in without checking to see who it is."

"Well, good afternoon to you, too."

I squeeze past him into his apartment. He kicks the door closed, grabs my hips, spins me around, and presses me against the wall. "You left without saying goodbye. Don't do that again." He pins me against the wall with his body and a smoldering, reprimanding glare.

"Yes, sir."

He smirks at my jest and pauses, gently running a thumb across my cheek in a caress. He swallows hard and closes his eyes as he pushes away from the wall.

"You brought lunch?"

I lift the white paper bag in response and step past him into the kitchen.

"Deli sandwiches. Hope you don't mind. I would have called to ask what you wanted, but I still don't have my phone."

"A deli sandwich is the food of kings. That's good enough for me. Your bag is over there. Sam had it delivered this morning."

I finish setting out our Reubens on plates and lick the thousand island dressing from my finger as I skirt past Chase to the kitchen table where he set down my briefcase.

"He let a random courier carry our bags?"

The sound of the icemaker fills the room as Chase prepares our glasses, picking up where I left off preparing our lunch. The contents of my briefcase are the same as I left them, the same papers, and my laptop in the same order as yesterday. I unzip the interior pocket and exhale when I locate my personal cell and my handgun. I lift it out and check the chamber and the safety, out of habit. I shouldn't have let the government-issued gun out of my sight.

Chase freezes, holding two ceramic plates with our sandwiches in front of him.

"You carry a gun?"

Satisfied my gun hasn't been tampered with, I slip it into the interior pocket and zip it closed. Then, since he's still frozen in place, I take the plates from him and set them on the round table.

"Not always. I debated carrying a gun last night. It's not like it did me any good once I left my briefcase in Sam's car."

"Were you off duty last night?" The questioning angle of his head and his deep squint warns me this isn't the first time he's thought about this.

"That point is probably debatable. Technically, yesterday was the last day I was supposed to go into BB&E's office as an

278

undercover agent. Today, the plan had been for me to resume my spot on my team within FBI offices."

Chase pulls the chair out and sits down in front of one of the sandwiches. He pushes the plate away from him, leaving room for his forearms to rest on the table, and leans forward.

"Is that because indictments were going out today?"

"You saw the news?" I sit in front of the remaining sandwich, watching him, unsure of what's running through his mind and uncertain how much I can say without risking harm to our operation. I won't be a witness, so since I won't be put on the stand, the risk level from sharing information seems low. But Chase could potentially be an important witness.

"Yes. No one's been indicted from BB&E. At least, not that's made the news." His intonation rises as he finishes his sentence, leaving it open for me to add more.

I could tell him we can't find Garrick Carlson, or that additional indictments still need to be delivered to others within BB&E, but I won't. That's crossing a line. I take a bite of my sandwich.

"This morning, I spent about thirty minutes on the line with BB&E's chairman of the board."

"Really?" I ask through a mouth full of Reuben.

"Apparently, Evan Mitchell called him and told him he's expecting he and Tom Bennett will be receiving an indictment either today in Chicago or tomorrow when they return to New York. He believes Eileen Becker has shared some information that implicates BB&E. He notified Jonathan to give him a heads up."

"Jonathan is the chairman of the board?" I've seen all the names of BB&E's board but hadn't paid a great amount of attention to them as we didn't suspect any of the board members.

"Yeah. I've never spoken to the guy before. But he said they had an emergency board meeting this morning. Evan and Tom will be stepping away from the company to protect BB&E's interest, and to allow them time to devote to building their defense."

Interesting. The real question is who gave Mitchell the heads up. Did Eileen call them after her meeting with the FBI, or did Evan's childhood friend within the FBI give him a heads up?

"He wants me to step in as interim CEO."

"What?" I blurt. Chase flinches. "I mean, that's a big promotion, right?" Organizationally, that change would put Chase jumping past a whole row of SVP division heads.

"Thanks for the vote of confidence, Syd." He grimaces. "I mean, Sadie." He exhales. "But I agree with you. It doesn't make sense to me either. He said Evan Mitchell recommended it on the basis that I am the best they have at relationships, and in order to keep clients calm and with the firm through this, they're going to need someone who can lead employees and keep morale positive while also hand-holding clients."

I take another bite of my room temperature sandwich and think it through. "I can see that. I've only met three of the four division heads, and they aren't personable. I doubt communications is a core strength for any of them. But...I don't like that it's Evan Mitchell who recommended it."

"Why?"

"I don't trust him, Chase."

He nods slowly and drinks some of his water. He sets the glass back down on the table with a thud.

"I don't trust him either, but I don't have all the information you do." The statement is pointed and full of expectation.

"I can't share specifics of the case. But the team will want to get you back in to talk further about your testimony. If you ask, they may be able to share more information with you."

He rests his elbow on the table and his chin on his fist. If only his elbow was on his knee, he'd look like the infamous Thinker sculpture.

"FBI first? Job first always?"

Thoughts of my parents growing up, the coldness in our home, and frequent relocations trail through my mind. Dad's prolonged absences, the months not knowing where he was. Knowing no news meant he was alive. Mom acting as if we were like every other family, to the extent I still suspect she's an agent, and I'm not even sure for what side. There's no point in asking.

"Right now? Yes. The work we are doing is important, and I'm not going to jeopardize our case. But there comes a point when some agents do decide, or can decide, family comes first." It's a tough line to straddle. Any job that demands you be available at any time, twenty-four-seven, by definition, demands that at times the balance won't fall on the side of the family or personal life. But plenty of agents make it through for decades in the bureau, with marriages intact and healthy, well-adjusted children. "I moved around a lot growing up. My father works for the CIA based in Moscow. My mother is a professor in Great Britain. My sister is in university. I'm close to my sister."

"Are your parents divorced?"

"I don't believe so."

"What do you mean?"

"I've never asked. They don't live together for most of the year. But I don't think they've ever filed for a divorce."

"Wow." He scratches his jaw. "But your dad taught you how to shoot? So, you were close to him growing up?"

"Close is a subjective word. The definition varies by person. My father is committed to his cause. Guns are a means to an end."

"I hate guns. They should be illegal." There's an edge to his tone.

"It's a multi-faceted subject. I would never want to walk into a gunfight with a knife. I also don't see a need for civilians to own machine guns. I'm well-versed in both sides of the gun rights debate. Is that what you really want to talk about?"

He shakes his head then lifts his gaze to mine. "You said last night that we're real."

"We are." I reach for his hand and hold on to it. "I wasn't with you for this case. What happened between us in Cedar Falls, that was all me. I wanted to be with you. Once I knew you were innocent, it wasn't about the case anymore."

"Wait. I was a suspect?"

I nod. Our primary suspect to start, but there's no need to tell him that.

"So, my legal team knew what they were doing when they paraded me into the FBI with my statement and whistle-blowing piece."

"They gave you sound advice." I straighten my spine and place my palms flat on my thighs.

"But you didn't give me that advice. You were just watching what I was doing? Why?"

"I don't call the shots. We had a different plan. If you hadn't gone in on your own, we were going to bring you in today and ask for your testimony."

"You mean demand it?"

"We would have asked nicely." He squints at me. I have no recourse. I can't change the way the system works.

He pushes the plate farther away from him. He's barely touched his sandwich. He stands and picks the plate up, dumps the remains into the trash, and deposits the plate in the dishwasher. I twist in the chair and watch him warily, the way one watches a campfire on a windy day.

When he comes back to me, he leans against the breakfast bar and crosses his arms over his torso.

"Here's the thing Syd—Sadie. We, you and I, we started this on lies. And I'll be honest because we don't stand a chance if I'm not. I don't know where to go from here. Half the time I'm calling you by the wrong name in my head. I like you, I really like you. I know this for a fact because I know how fucking terrified I was last night when you were facing gunfire. But I don't know what of you is real. I don't know if the person I'm falling for even exists. And I don't know how to deal with that. And then, there's this other part of me that thinks, you know, the short guy never gets the Bond girl.

Ever." A sad, subdued smile plays across his lips. True to his personality, he's making light of something he doesn't find funny. He runs a hand through his hair and exhales. "So, why should I try?"

I place one foot in front of the other, in slow, measured steps, until I reach him and cross my palms over his heart.

"How about we start with you getting to know me, the real me? I think you got to know the real me, but you've got to decide that for yourself."

I rise onto my tiptoes, pressing my lower body against his, and brush my lips across his. At first, he doesn't open. I stand close enough that I can examine the variations of brown and gold in his irises. He wraps his arms around me, and I lift mine around his neck. He tilts his head and gives me a slow, cautious kiss.

The sound of a phone vibrating breaks us apart. I run my fingers across the scruff along his jaw, and he leans into my touch.

"Why don't you come back with me to my real apartment?" Of course, the reality is, all my business clothes are in the FBI apartment. I had planned to move them out this weekend, but other than clothes and bare necessities, all my personal life is sitting in my downtown apartment, yet to be unpacked.

"The place I've been in, that was an FBI cover?"

I nod. "Yes. FBI owns it. They use it from time to time."

"Explains the absence of personality."

"Well, don't expect more from my real place. I've only spent a handful of nights there."

"So, you really did just move to New York?"

284

I nod and back up a step, holding his hand. "Come on, let me show you."

Chase insists on getting a cab. It's not a far ride, but it'd be a long walk. I direct the cab to let us off at the corner of Reade and Church.

Chase peers around. "I'm not sure I like your hood."

I shrug. "Didn't pick it for the hood."

Church street is all business. It's a fairly major thoroughfare. He follows me as I dart along Reade Street. Reade Street is a narrow side street with limited parking. Stores line the lower level with apartments above. All the apartments feature a red brick facade and standard rectangular windows. One whole side of the building across from mine is covered in metal scaffolding. Horns beep, and sirens can be heard in the distance.

When we reach my apartment, I open my briefcase and dig deep down into the interior pocket for my key ring. I unlock the door, and he follows me inside and up two flights of stairs.

"It's not much, but it's home," I say as I push my apartment door open. There's a stale stench in the air, and I search for the thermostat to check what setting I left it on.

Unopened boxes are stacked in my den. My kitchen, if one can call it that, lines a part of the wall on one side. A narrow hall leads to the back where there is a sleeping area and a bathroom. It's technically a studio apartment, but I selected it because it has the feel of a one-bedroom.

"This place is claustrophobic." Chase says, unimpressed.

"I tend to agree with you. Would you believe I'm paying

almost three thousand a month in rent for this place?" It's truly insane how expensive things are here.

"Why did you pick this place?" He's full of derision.

"I did what anyone does when moving to a new city. I looked for apartments close to work. I can walk to work from here. It's clean. I mean, when it comes to studios, they're all equally box-like with little to offer."

"This is a studio?" He asks as he bysteps a tall stack of boxes to venture to the end of my apartment.

A mattress rests on the floor of the sleeping area. I had to sell my old bedroom set, as it wouldn't fit here.

"How old are you?"

"Twenty-nine."

"It's not bad for someone in their late twenties, but I'd encourage you to hunt for something better when your lease is up."

"Hey, we can't all live in palatial apartments like you."

"You're FBI cover pad was way nicer than this."

"Yeah, I'm aware. Thanks."

He smirks then collapses onto one side of my sofa.

"So, we're here so I can get to know the real you. You gonna open up some boxes and show me something? Because looking around this crap hole, what I see is someone who is so absorbed by work she hasn't unpacked the first box, hasn't even hung a shower curtain in the bathroom, has a pair of plain sheets thrown on a mattress, and doesn't have a single personal photograph or anything at all out to make this feel like a home. Is that who you are?"

"Your place isn't that much better. I don't think you spend much time on that firm, uncomfortable sofa. And you have to hunt for personal effects in your place."

He smirks. "Yeah, Carla took over designing my place. I let her go with it. I'll grant you I've been jonesing to make it a bit more liveable, more me."

"Who is Carla? An ex?" I sit on the sofa near him.

"Not an ex." I get the uncomfortable sense he's reflecting on Carla as he answers, "We did get to know each other while she was working on my project. I'd say it was more of a fling."

"Hmmm. So, how much is the rent on a place like yours?"

"I own. But it could rent for around ten K a month. Renting's just throwing away your money." He sounds judgmental.

"That's right. You own properties and rent them out. How'd you decide which one you wanted to live in?"

"I liked the area. But this isn't getting to know Chase time. This is getting to know Sadie time. Whatcha got?"

I'm not sure what to show him. Sometimes I'm not even sure I know myself. I make my way through the boxes until I locate the one box marked "personal." I open it and lug it over to the floor space in front of the sofa. I show him photos of my sister, my mom and dad.

"Your sister looks like you."

I agree with his assessment. "She always worries about me. I don't do a good enough job keeping in touch with her."

"Time difference. It must be tough."

I nod. "She knows about you. I did tell her."

He flips through photos. Most of my photos are landscape shots or shots of historically relevant locations that are popular with tourists. The ones in the box are photos I liked enough to print. He tosses them in the box.

"Give me your phone."

"What?"

"Clearly, you only printed photos you deemed worthy. Your phone will have the photos I want to see."

I hand him my personal cell. My photos in my Google photos file go all the way back to university. He points at a few people, asking me who they are. "After getting my MBA, I was accepted into the FBI. There aren't many photos at all from that point forward."

"Any boyfriend?" he asks as he swipes, probably recognizing he's no longer coming across human beings.

"There was one. He was FBI, too."

"Let me guess. All work, just like you."

"Yes. But, if I'm honest—"

"And we're being honest here."

"Yes, if I'm honest, I haven't been happy for a while. It can get lonely. I didn't plan on going into UC, but in some ways, I've enjoyed this time being more of a regular person. I moved here for a change, and that's what I got. A different life."

"You enjoyed life as an accountant?" He seems amused.

"I enjoyed giving myself a life outside of work. Going to the gym, hanging out with you, that kind of stuff."

"You can't tell me you didn't go to the gym in DC." He pointedly checks me out.

"Of course I did. But it was the FBI gym, and it was get in, get it done, get out. Your gym is like a spa. I can see why you spend hours there hanging out and talking. It's a social place for you."

"I'm a social guy." He reaches out for my hand and tugs me closer. His fingers toy with my hair, then he slides it behind my ear. "The picture I'm getting of Sadie is of a lonely workaholic."

"But I want to change that." And I do. I like being with Chase. I kick my shoes off and slide onto Chase's lap, straddling him.

"Sadie, I'm in for helping you." He opens my shirt, button by button. I lift the hem of his t-shirt over his head. His heart pounds beneath my fingers. My pulse throbs against his skin.

Ever so slowly, we undress each other. He takes his time, caressing my body, adoring me, and I take my turn on him. When he enters me, he is tender. Our lovemaking is slow and sensual and earth-shattering.

Earth-shattering, not because of the physical, but because as he pulses inside me, and I hold him tight, it hits me with the force of a .475 A&M Magnum that I care more about this man than I do my career. And I don't have any idea how he's going to feel about me over time, as he gets to know the real me.

TWENTY-NINE

CHASE

The sheets bear a distinct coolness. Without opening my eyes, I stretch and confirm. She's not in the bed. That's just my luck to fall for an early riser.

I rub my hands vigorously over my face, then squint into the bright morning light piercing my bedroom windows. *How late did I sleep?*

After spending the afternoon in Sadie's real apartment, I convinced her to pack a bag with some of her casual clothes to bring back here. She might end up using that place if she's working some projects with late hours, but if I have any say, we'll be spending our couple time here. Her apartment is a hole. I sometimes forget how compact New York City apartments can be.

There are no sounds of another human being moving around, but the distinct smell of coffee permeates the bedroom. After slipping on some boxers and brushing my teeth, I wander into the den. Sadie's lacing up her running shoes by the door.

"For the record, this is not the way I like to be woken up."

"I didn't mean to wake you." She stands, and I take her in. She's wearing black leggings and a tight, long sleeve running shirt. Her hair is pulled back to create the tiny bud of a pony-tail, and she's got white ear pods poking out of her ears. She looks delicious, and while I'd like to pull her back into the bedroom to show her exactly how I like to wake up, energy pulses around her. It's abundantly clear she's ready to get the day started.

"You off for a run?"

"Yeah, I figured I'd go for a run, then stop by my apartment to change for work."

"Which apartment?"

"FBI. All my business clothes are still there, remember?"

"Yeah." I take two steps and pull her against me, aware she's chomping to go, but needing to get my hands on her. "This weekend, I'll help you clear that place out. Maybe you can keep your work clothes here?"

Her eyebrows go sky high. Too much.

"Or at least some of them."

She smiles then lifts on her toes and kisses me. I'm instantly aroused, and she notices. She pushes back on me with her pretty smile in full force.

"I'll see you after work, mister."

"Looking forward to it, Ms. Frost." I cringe. "Wait, I can't call you Ms. Frost anymore. I love that name."

"Yeah, Keating doesn't have the same ring, does it?"

"Nah. I'm still using Frost. It'll be our code name. An inside joke. What do you know? I'm actually dating an FBI agent. Code names for real. I'll get you watching the superheroes, and we can brainstorm superpowers."

"I've seen superhero movies." She bites her lip and grins, all coy and sexy. "I tend to prefer movies like *James Bond* and *Mission Impossible*."

"Yeah? I dig those too. So, that's your jam, huh?"

"Well, to some degree. Now I sit there and think that is such bullshit."

That cracks me up. "If that's your take, then maybe the super-heroes aren't for you."

She grows serious. "Hey, be careful today. Alert. I believe you're safe, but—"

"Going to the office today. No reason to worry, dear." Maybe it should bother me that my woman is all protective, and can probably kick my ass, but it really doesn't.

She places those soft, tempting lips on mine once more, then she's out the door, and I watch her like a lovesick puppy until the stairwell door closes behind her. Because, of course, she'd rather take the stairs.

I lock the deadbolt then jump in the shower. I might've played a better game at luring Sadie back into bed this morn-ing, but the fact is, I've got a shit show waiting for me at the office today. I'm already behind schedule.

By seven a.m., I'm flipping light switches on in reception and along the hall to my office. No one's in yet. A slow trickle of arrivals will commence around 7:30-ish, then gradually transition to a steady flow between eight to nine.

My message light's flashing. I play the messages on the speaker as my computer powers up. I caught up on email last night. Sadie and I both worked on my sofa. It felt good. Going to bed with her last night definitely felt good. Something I have every intention of making our norm. Anna's going to be blown away when I tell her I've got a girlfriend. *Girlfriend. Damn.*

I have nineteen voice messages that entail "call me" and some version of "are you okay?" Why don't people just text? Why do I even have voice mail? In all fairness, these messages are from BB&E colleagues who have my office extension, not my cell. Still annoying to comb through.

Rhonda taps on my doorframe, announcing her arrival.

"You're in early, boss." She places a steaming cup of coffee on my desk.

"Yeah, it's gonna be an interesting day. Hey, could you start listening to my voicemail? Would you mind?"

"I already do that."

"I had nineteen messages this morning."

"Wow. That's a lot. Normally it's like one or two. But I normally get in here earlier than you. You know those slips of paper where I list who you need to call?"

"Yeah. I thought those were calls you took. Huh. Great." I slurp back my morning joe, and the warmth coats my throat.

"Everyone's grateful you're okay. I'm grateful. I don't know what I would have done." Her eyes glisten. Fuck...she's gonna cry.

"Rhonda. I'm okay. Unscathed."

"Yeah. You know, I keep thinking, if I had taken you up on those tickets, it could have been me. Or my husband."

"Hey, but you didn't go. You're safe."

She nods and sniffles. "You sure you're all right? I'm surprised you're back. That's got to be so much to go through."

"Yeah. It's a bit surreal. Like it didn't really happen." She nods, understanding. I'm still numb. And I don't want to talk about it. "What am I gonna do? Sit in my apartment all day? Besides, we've got a lot to deal with in the office. Someone from the executive floor is going to call today about setting up a meeting for me with the board. Make me available for whatever time they need, okay?"

"You mean the board of directors? For BB&E?"

"Yeah. And can you bring me last year's original documents from Biohazard Waste, Medical Supply, and McLoughlin Charity?"

"You got it, boss." She taps the doorframe again as she leaves, then bends backward with a parting message. "I really am glad you're okay."

Within minutes, Rhonda stands in my doorway. "Did you move the files?"

"Yes, Rhonda, I decided to dust them off."

"No, I'm serious. All of the files are gone."

"What?" I spin in my chair to the file cabinets that line my back office wall. I grab the key from my desk drawer and open each one. They're all empty. Even the drawer I use for my personal crap.

"Can you ask other people if they had their files removed?"

She nods. Her skin's gone pale, and something tells me my face might match hers. I pick up my cell and call Sadie's office line. I get voice mail. I call her personal cell and again get voice mail. I text her. *My work files have been stolen.*

In under sixty seconds, she calls me back.

"What do you mean? Was there a robbery?"

"Nothing's damaged. All the file cabinets are emptied out. They took everything."

I cross the hall to double-check all the cabinets that line the wall behind Rhonda's cubicle. Just like she said, they're all empty. Rhonda returns, hands on her hips, her head shaking in disbelief.

"All the files from your team have been removed. Gone. Vanished. No one knows what happened."

Sadie hears her through the phone.

"That's so stupid for them to do that," she tells me, annoyance pouring through. "There are so many charges we can throw at them for impeding an investigation and tampering with evidence."

"If you can prove who did it."

"Well, who else would it be? They would've been smarter to burn the building down. That's a ton of paperwork to remove. Is there a security camera on the hall outside your office?"

I scan the ceiling for a camera or a telltale black glass dome.

"Don't see anything. There's security footage of the elevator and lobby, probably reception on each floor. Building security has footage of all communal areas. Parking garages too."

"Okay. I'm gonna go talk to our surveillance team. For all I know, they're already tapped in, but if they're not, we can obtain the footage. I'll tell the team what we need them to look for. Someone had to have been moving boxes of files out. It shouldn't take too much work to identify who."

"You need me to do anything?"

"No. Let me go update my supervisor. We'll probably send someone over to fingerprint the cabinets. I doubt there'll be fingerprints, but you never know."

When I hang up, Rhonda peers up at me. She's curious, but she doesn't know how far she can push it with her questions. I know her looks.

"Was that Sydney?"

I swallow. Sadie and I already discussed this. Her cover's blown, so there's no reason to lie about who she is now. "Her name's Sadie."

"So, it's true? She's FBI? She was working here undercover?"

"Yeah. Rumors are flying, huh?"

She nods, eyes forced wide for effect. "Rampant. Kowabunga style. Was that really her on the YouTube video?"

"You don't watch much news, do you?"

"Not broadcast, no. But Jared shared the YouTube link to everyone in our office distribution."

"Come with me." I close the office door and sit down at my desk with a pen and my notepad.

"Give me a rundown of all the rumors. The plan is to hold a company address later this afternoon. I might as well know what's out there so I know what to cover."

My office line rings. It's an internal extension and name I don't recognize.

Rhonda pops out to her desk to answer it. I follow her, and after speaking briefly, she covers the mouthpiece. "Ms. Bellusca wants you to come up to a PR meeting on the fifteenth floor."

"Sounds good. Remember, if anyone from the board calls, that's priority. Call me. I have my cell."

The meeting with the PR team turns out to be more of a debriefing. They've been working all night on press releases and speaking instructions for client managers. They want me to review everything they've done, so I spend as much time listening to them as reading their work. Ms. Bellusca leads the team, and she's cordial, but her body language tells me she's unsure who I am and why she's been instructed to involve me. Given I'm hardly the best choice for Interim CEO, I can't say I blame her. I doubt the idea that she's been instructed to involve me because of that soon-to-be-announced appointment has even crossed her mind. But we work together well.

We're going with the key message that BB&E remains a trustworthy company and will work with authorities to ensure any illegal activities are brought to light. The suspected fraudulent activities are limited to a small number of related accounts, and all involved are no longer employed by BB&E.

Rhonda calls my cell. I wave goodbye to the PR team and head to the elevator bank, gesturing to the group gathered around the conference table that I need to take this important call. I've spent hours with them. They've got it under control. They don't need me.

"You're on a call with the board at twelve thirty."

"It's a call, not in person?"

"Yes, not everyone is in town. It may only be the chairman of the board and you. I'm not sure."

I check the time. I'm starving. I need fresh air.

"I'm gonna run out and get a falafel. You want anything?"

"I can get you lunch."

"Thanks, but I need the air."

"If you're sure. I'm jonesing for a grilled cheese, so I'm gonna head down to the cafeteria."

"One day your arteries are going to repay you."

"Maybe. But if they're gonna clog, I'd rather it be because of melted cheese than fried chickpea."

"Ha ha." I hang up and scroll through text messages.

As I wait for the elevators, the silent television in the corner of the reception area catches my attention. The weatherman is on, but the white scroll on the bottom of the screen reads *Evan Mitchell, CFO, and Tom Bennett, CEO of BB&E served indictments.*

Grand. Cat's out of the bag and all hell's gonna break loose. My phone lights up and vibrates as if it's internally combusting.

Once outside, I search the perimeter for the falafel guy then head his way, lost in the barrage, scanning for client messages, as those rank of the highest importance. Damnit. I had hoped we'd have more time before the media got hold of it.

Frank, SVP of Operations, and I are scheduled to meet at two to go through the list of clients to determine which ones need to be contacted before the end of day. Most clients will get a call from their client services manager with our prepared message. The most important clients will get a call from Frank, who technically oversees all client relationships, or from me, Interim CEO. The title makes my head spin. Frank might be pushing eighty and speaks with the speed of a tortoise, so unless he has a relationship, I'll be making all the calls. Fuck, it's gonna be an insane afternoon. I should've met with Frank earlier, but I needed the announcement about my interim post to be made.

When it's my turn in line, I step up to order my normal. I don't even get a chance to open my mouth.

"Chase, my man. I heard you were at the shooting."

"Yeah."

"So crazy. Tragic. Awful. I heard there were, like, five shooters. You must've been freaking out."

"There was one shooter. I'm pretty certain they've confirmed it was one shooter."

"No, man. I saw it on my wife's Facebook. Crazy. You lucky you made it out alive."

"Yes. I am."

He hands over my falafel, just like I like it, with extra sauce. "You need water?"

"No. I'll get it inside."

I pull out my wallet, and he waves it away. "Nah. This one's on me. Glad you're alive, man."

"Thanks, Manny. You da best," I say as we fist bump. *And that, my friends, is why it pays to be a repeat customer.*

As I step away from Manny's stand, my cell vibrates with yet another text. A large man crowds me from behind, and I step out of his way, closer to the curb. The fucker's about to make me drop my falafel.

There's a text from Sadie. *Headed over to fingerprint. See you soon.*

Something hard jabs against my side, and I spin, ready to push back. New Yorkers who push and shove are one of my biggest pet peeves. I take two steps out of the guy's way, off the sidewalk and into the street between two parked cars. *What the fuck is his problem?*

The fucker grabs onto my bicep and pushes me hard. My falafel goes flying out of my hand.

"What the fuck, man!" I belt out as another guy comes out of nowhere and grabs my other side. *This is fucking nuts.*

The guy shoves his chest out, and his buddy comes out of nowhere. Like we're about to brawl on the street. *Assholes.*

I move to get away from these whack jobs. There's nothing to gain from a fight. A van is double-parked on the street, and I go to get between it and the street parked car.

"Move it or I shoot," the giant to my side growls.

My heart stops. Like, no blood pumping anywhere when I register the glint of stainless steel jabbing into my side.

The side door of the van slides open. The guy behind me edges me forward, then at the last minute, shoves me with a hard thrust that smacks my shin against the van. *Fuck*. Pain ricochets through my leg. I go to rub the source, but the asswipe snatches both my wrists, and I hear the sound of handcuffs clicking.

The guy in the driver's seat stares straight ahead, and his right hand grips the wheel. A black cloth bag falls over my head. *Ho-ly shit. I'm being kidnapped.*

"You guys know you won't get away with this, right?"

"Shut up," a deep voice snarls beside me.

"Who hired you guys?"

"Shut up," the same voice repeats.

"This isn't gonna end well," I warn. My hands are locked behind my back, but I shift, attempting to locate the phone that should be in my pants pocket. It won't take Sadie long to track it. She'll find me. The only thing is, as I shift around, I don't feel my phone.

"I can't believe we fucking did this in broad daylight." It's a different monotone voice.

"Didn't have a choice. The feds've been staking out his apartment."

"Not smart." The guy sounds pissed.

"What do you care? You're unrecognizable. Drive."

"You guys can change your mind. Just let me out. No harm, no foul," I offer.

"You speak again, and I knock you out. Got it?"

I nod, compliant. In safety courses, they tell you getting out of the car when kidnapped is imperative. Only, I've got two muscled giants on each side of me, a black bag over my head, and I'm fucking handcuffed.

"I've already provided testimony to the FBI. Kidnapping me doesn't help your bosses."

A crushing, painful, blunt object slams into the side of my head, and I smash against the hard body sitting to my left. Pain radiates through my head and the base of my neck.

THIRTY

SADIE

The moment we enter BB&E's offices, I sense a tenseness in the air. Employees cluster in small groups throughout the lobby, heads down, and the hum of conversations fills the vast marble interior. When the elevators open onto my old floor, the silent television monitor behind reception streams news. Both receptionists are turned, reading the news alerts, although at the moment the scroll announces earnings for Apple.

Neither of the receptionists gives either Agent Connor or me a second glance as they converse in hushed tones. As I roam the hall, the first thing I notice is that no one is sitting in the cubicles. Clusters of employees gather in groups. I bypass my dark, empty office, and when I reach Chase's, his door is closed, and it's clear from the interior window his office lights are off. I knock anyway and twist the knob. The door is unlocked.

Rhonda comes around the corner with a cell phone to her ear. She sees me and presses the cell to her chest.

"Sydney…he's not here."

"I brought Agent Connor. We're going to fingerprint the file cabinets. Where is he?"

"He stepped outside for lunch…but that was a while ago." She checks her wristwatch. "He had an important meeting at twelve thirty. That's where he must be."

Her desk phone rings, and I point inside Chase's office. "Do you mind if we go in?"

"Not at all. Go ahead."

I push the door to Chase's office open, turn on the lights, and Agent Connor opens his bag and withdraws the items he'll need to fingerprint. It's unlikely we'll find anything, but it's worth the time it'll take to dust the cabinets. Surveillance has obtained video footage from the building. We weren't monitoring the building security cameras for this case, but we should be able to figure out who took the files from the footage, at least, if the files are no longer in the building. Even if they carried them down the stairs instead of using the elevator, which is unlikely given the number of boxes the files likely required, we'll see them in the parking garage footage.

"Syd…Agent?" Rhonda stands in the doorway, gripping her cell phone, her gaze flitting between me and my colleague.

"You can call me Sadie," I offer.

"Chase didn't join the 12:30. I assumed he must have gone up to sit with one of the executives for the call, but he never called in. Everyone's executive assistant has been calling me to locate him. I can't—he's not answering his cell." Her flushed skin color and fidgety stance says she's nervous and worried.

"When did you say you last saw him?"

"He called me. He was with the PR team all morning. He called to ask if I wanted a falafel. He knew he had the twelve thirty. It was with the board. He wouldn't miss that meeting." My heartrate speeds along to the staccato rhythm of her words.

"Agent Connor, I'm going to look for Chase. Are you good doing this?" He was going to be doing it on his own, anyway, as he's part of the forensics team. He nods, barely pausing preparing his brush for the task ahead.

I push Rhonda out the door. "Let's start downstairs at the falafel place. We'll make sure he made it there."

Rhonda holds her cell phone out, hitting Chase's name, hanging up when his voice mail answers, then dialing again. The repeated, frantic activity obliterates my focus. I want to tell her to cut it out. I refrain. If he's somewhere out there on a con call, and he sees her repeatedly calling, he'll at the very least take a moment to respond, even if via text.

We rush through the glass lobby doors. There's a wider concrete pavilion in front of the office building, and street vendors line the edge along the street. There's a coffee cart, a hot dog vendor, and then, to the far side, I spy the falafel guy. I take off to the shiny food cart then slow when I hear Journey playing *Any Way You Want It.*

The song stops, and I spin, searching the perimeter. The song plays again, only this time Rhonda hears it, and she holds her phone out like a beacon. The song ends once again.

"Call him again. Let it ring."

She does so as pedestrians zip around us, oblivious. I close my eyes to focus all my sensory power on the ring tone, lifting one foot after another in the direction of the song that no doubt will be playing in my head for the rest of the day. Leave it to Chase to choose a ringtone that imprints.

The ringtone stops, and I spin to Rhonda. "Again."

That's when I see it. On the street, against the curb, partially hidden by the front wheel of a parked car. A few feet away is a mangled silver wrapper. Murky orange sauce splatters the sidewalk. Unsuspecting pedestrians must have stepped in it.

"Rhonda." I point at the mess as I bend and pick up the phone. It rings, and I see Rhonda's name flash on the screen. Rhonda's mouth opens, and she covers it with her fingers. Her eyes water, and all her visible reactions are what's playing out in my insides. *Focus. Hold it together.*

I dial Agent Hopkins. I'm not undercover, and he's not my handler anymore. But of everyone on Operation Quagmire, I know him best.

He answers on the second ring. "Agent Keating."

"Chase Maitlin is missing. He had a board meeting at 12:30 he wouldn't miss. I found his phone and his falafel outside by the street."

"Why would they do that? We have his test—"

"I found his phone. On the curb. It's the only explanation."

"Shit. They knew we had agents outside his place at night, so they waited until he was at work. Where are you?"

"At BB&E's office. I'm with Rhonda, his assistant."

"Did anyone see anything?"

"I found his phone and called you."

"Okay. Let me go update the team. Ask around. See if anyone saw something."

I hang up and survey the area. The falafel cart is obviously first. But who to ask next? The coffee cart directly across the pavilion. But if they saw someone getting kidnapped, wouldn't they call the police? Then I remind myself someone could have called it in. Even if someone did, it wouldn't reach the FBI, not yet.

Rhonda stands still, an expression of shock plastered on her open-mouthed face. I redirect my attention away from her. My chest pounds. Adrenaline courses through me. I breathe deeply. Focus. I recognize the dark haired, middle aged man Chase and I have bought lunch from more than once over the last few weeks. The cart is essentially a pull-behind kitchen, and the side of the cart is maybe five to six feet wide. If he was inside, he wouldn't have had a line of sight to the location on the curb where I found his phone.

He's wiping down the narrow stainless-steel counter when I approach. A smile spreads when he looks up and sees me.

"Sydney!" He beams. I've bought from him maybe twice. He must be a savant with names. And I do not have a matching skill set.

"Hi. Was Chase Maitlin here earlier?" Yes, I would've used his name to address him if I remembered it. Yes, I should say more, but my gut tells me I don't need to warm him up.

"Yes. I gave him a free falafel. You want one? I give you one, too. After all, you are a hero. You shot the bastards." He's already whipped out the bread, placed it on a wrapper, and holds it out, expecting me to tell him if I want a spread.

"No, thank you. Maybe another time."

He loses his smile as he sets the wrapper down.

"I'm looking for Chase. I'm trying to retrace his steps. Do you remember what time he came here?"

He shakes his head and pauses, squeezing his lower lip between his thumb and index finger, before answering. "Nah. Sorry. I don't pay attention to time."

"Was he alone or with someone?"

"He was by himself. Had his phone with him. Always busy on his phone, that guy." He smiles, then frowns. "Did something happen?"

"That's what I'm trying to figure out. I found his phone over there, and a smashed falafel isn't too far away."

He leans his body out the cart's window, stretching to see where I'm pointing. As I thought, there's no way he would've seen anything. He disappears in the back of his trailer. A moment later, the side door on the cart opens, and he steps out, walking over to the area I pointed. I follow him, and we both stare down at the smashed falafel.

"This is the falafel I gave him. Extra sauce. He likes it spicy." He stares down at the falafel, then bends down to scrape it up, using the corners of the opened silver wrapper.

"Wait." I bark.

He freezes.

"Let me take photos before you pick it up." He nods and backs away.

I'm fucking this up. I should've taken photos immediately. It's not exactly evidence, but it could be useful for showing the team what I found and where. I return Chase's phone to the spot between the tire and curb where I located it and take photos with my phone, then send them off to Hopkins.

After I give the go-ahead, falafel guy bends and picks up his creation from the sidewalk. "Litter," he mumbles. "We must take care of our city."

He tosses it in a nearby trash can, somber. "You find him, okay? You find him, I give you both free falafels. I like that guy."

I smile. "Me too. Thank you. Here's my card. I know you couldn't have seen anything, but if you think of anything at all that could be useful, call me."

He runs his thumb back and forth over the card thoughtfully, nods, and returns to his cart.

I'm in route to the coffee and hot dog carts when Hopkins calls.

"Sadie, you're not gonna like this, but we found the guy who stole the files. He told the agents who interviewed him that he was hired by Chase Maitlin to remove those files and dispose of them."

"He's lying."

"I tend to agree with you. But right now we have two running theories. One, Chase Maitlin is being set up as the fall guy for this, and they plan to make him disappear so he can't defend himself, or two, Chase Maitlin is guilty, and he's done a great job of playing us."

"He's not guilty." Hopkins is aware I have a personal relationship with Chase. I sound like a girlfriend, not an agent right now. But none of that matters. I'm right.

"Chase's attorneys have been contacted. If he's playing us, he's playing them too. They don't believe for a minute Chase stole those files, but they also shared he has copies of everything electronically, and he gave copies of those files to them. So, right now, as long as his attorneys follow through with willingness to share the files, it definitely seems the first case scenario is most likely. Why don't you come back here to the office? You're too close to this to be in the field. Come back here. We'll find him."

"What's the team doing? To find him?"

"We've sent agents out to Mitchell's and Bennett's homes to ask questions."

I exhale my frustration. "That's fine, but it's not like either of them would have personally taken him. This isn't a case where he willingly got in someone's car. His phone and falafel were on the ground. If either of those guys is involved in this, they didn't do it personally. They hired someone."

"We know. But this is a logical next step. We might gain some valuable information." His tone is calm. It's a signature agent tactic to calm down someone who is frazzled. The buildings blur.

I re-focus. Scan the street for any cameras. "Do you have anyone checking street cams? He was taken on 38th near 6th. About thirty yards from the intersection."

Taking in the distance, my emotions tank, as I realize the chance that any intersection cam probably wouldn't pick up what happened here. The BB&E cameras by the front entrance are angled to view those coming in and exiting the building. It's doubtful the view would extend to the street.

I glance across the street at the buildings but know any cameras would be designed for security for the building, and the cameras would be focused on the storefront, not across the street.

"Come on back to the office."

"I haven't yet asked the other vendors if they saw anything. Let me finish surveying the area." I don't tell him I'll come back to the office. After all, I don't plan to.

The team will take this seriously, as Chase Maitlin is a key witness. The team will want to recover him, for many reasons. It doesn't look good when something happens to a witness. But I can't sit behind a desk. I need to be physically doing something to locate him. Time is ticking.

The woman inside the coffee cart seems confused by my questions. "Did I see what? When?"

"Did you see anything suspicious across the way, within the last hour or two?"

She looks in the direction I'm pointing, then back at me.

"I see nothing. We stay pretty busy. And when we're not busy, I read." She holds up an eReader and shrugs.

The hot dog guy shakes his head. I step behind his cart. It's the smallest of the three carts, and the only one the vendor stands beside, not inside. Where the man stands, he's angled with a view more to the entrance of the building, but he still could have easily seen something. The problem is during the height of lunch the now sparse concrete area is filled with human bodies, and it's likely even if he had looked at the right time, he wouldn't have had a direct view.

"I see nothing," he spits out. He sounds more annoyed than defensive.

My next call is to Hopkins.

"Can you check to see if any 911 calls were made from this area earlier today?"

"Come back to the office, Keating. You know we're on it." The call ends, and I stare at my phone. It's not like Hopkins to hang up on me. Our whole team would be swamped without this happening, given we've issued indictments and have an indictment for one individual we can't locate. Chase's disappearance has probably become priority number one, stacked onto a full list of other mission-critical priorities as we prepare for court with the rich and powerful.

He's been missing now for over an hour. They don't really have a reason to keep him alive. My eyes burn. Panic rises. My throat closes.

Rhonda touches my arm, and I jerk back, arms up in a defensive stance. When it registers she's friendly, I lower my arms.

"Any luck?"

"No. Go back up to the office. Can you let me know who comes looking for him? Create a full list of every single individual who has asked for him, including the number of times." I'm not as interested in who is asking as who isn't, but I don't tell her that. She nods but doesn't move.

"Call me if you find out anything." Her eyes are glassy. A mirror image of mine. I turn to leave.

"Where are you going?" she calls.

"I'm going to get my car and drive over to check out a hunch."

"What should I tell that man you came in with?"

I snap my fingers. "I completely forgot about Connor. I'll go up with you."

I'll return to the office, but only once I run out of things to do on the ground. The abandoned area in New Jersey lurks in the back of my mind. I don't believe they'd take Chase to the sex club. That's not the kind of place you take a kidnap victim. But those streets held many abandoned buildings. In the New York metro, there are tons of spots just like that one. But these men are familiar with that particular area. It's the only shot I have. It's a long shot. Other agents haven't been there before, and I'm not entirely sure I can talk someone else through the area. I'll visually recognize it.

I don't give Agent Connor all my rationale, but he doesn't seem to mind going for a car ride. "Sure, I'll go."

"Any prints?" I ask him as we exit the building.

"Prints are all over those cabinets. Any useful ones? Don't know yet."

Hopkins calls as I'm pulling out of my parking garage. Yes, we could use an FBI squad car, but since I don't have one assigned to me, it would be a process and take time I don't have.

"Where are you?" he asks without preamble.

"On my way to Jersey. Agent Connor and I will come back to the office after we check out some empty warehouses. It's a long shot."

"Go for it," Hopkins says, then the line goes dead.

THIRTY-ONE

Chase

Screeching tires on concrete wake me. My head throbs. A sharp pain on my wrist intensifies when I tug repeatedly, attempting to touch my head. That guy decked me. *Fuck, it hurts.*

I'm horizontal. Soft material covers my nose on the inhale. Shifts away on the exhale. Using the tips of my fingers, I feel behind me and find a hard plastic object. I can barely make out the shape of seats. I must still be in the back seat of the van.

Based on the silence, I assume I'm alone. If anyone is inside with me, he's being very quiet. A car door slams. I listen intently. Should I stay silent? Shout for help?

"You got him?" I recognize that voice.

"Yep."

"I want you to put him in this trunk, under the floorboards, and drive down 95. All the way to the Everglades. Feed the gators. Then come home. You got it?"

"I'm not driving across state lines. What if he gets away? What if we get stopped? I didn't sign up for this shit."

"Who the fuck is this?"

"It's okay, Joe. He's new." There's a beat of silence, and the same voice continues, "We'll kill him before we head down. Hide his body in the back of the van."

"He's alive?"

"Yeah, he's in the van. Knocked out."

"This the same van you grabbed him in?"

"Yeah."

"Well, you can't drive it down. Someone might've made the plates. I'll send another car over for you to use for the trip. Why the fuck's he still alive?"

"I don't have a silencer. What? I wasn't expecting this shit. This place is dead at night. Once everyone clears out, we'll off him, and no one'll hear."

"Who uses this place?"

"Small company on the top floor. There's usually about six or eight cars on top-level parking. Down here, where we are, no one ever comes."

"What the fuck are you worried about someone hearing a gunshot for, then?"

"You want this job done right? I've got no interest in going back to Rikers. What're a few hours, anyway?"

"Where is he?"

"I told ya. In the van."

The grating sound of the van door sliding open fills the vehicle. I can't see a thing, but I sense men are standing nearby. I don't recognize any of the voices except for one. The one I recognize is Joe McGurn. I'd heard rumors he had mafia connections. I thought those rumors were bullshit. Now, not so much.

"Maitlin. Fuck, man. You know, I really liked you."

"May I ask what changed your mind?"

He chuckles at my question like it's the funniest damn thing he's heard all day. Then he growls, "How much does that FBI agent know?"

"About what?"

"Don't play dumb. I know you've been banging her. What'd you give the feds?"

"The FBI has my sworn testimony. Killing me won't help anyone's case." I'm not entirely sure my meeting with the FBI constitutes sworn testimony, but he won't know that.

"You already met with the feds?"

"Yes. With my lawyers. Everything is documented. They have all the records."

"Don't matter, my man. There's this little thing called doubt. Jury gonna have to question if it's possible you're the kingpin. As we speak, a look-alike in a baseball cap is boarding a plane out of the U.S. using your passport."

Fuck. I stored my passport in a file at work. In one of the now empty file cabinets.

"And all your money is in the process of being transferred to accounts out of the country. Any jury is gonna find reasonable doubt. You know, it's really not smart to keep your passport and all your business account information in the same file folder." He chuckles again, and it's sinister. "I did like you. Fun to hang out with."

Story of my life. And now he's going to off me. I am not Houdini. There's no way I'm getting the handcuffs off. *Talk. Work some magic.*

"Why didn't you ask me if I wanted to join you guys? I would have, you know."

"Ya know, I asked the guys about bringing you in. I did. But you were always gonna be the patsy. The backup plan." His voice trails off, and desperation kicks in. I have nothing to offer. No way out. This might actually be how I die. Framed for some accounting scam.

Sadie. She won't doubt me. She'll work to prove I'm innocent. At least my parents won't have to think I'm a criminal. A disgrace. A visual of my parents graveside comes to mind. My Mom. *Okay, Chase. Get it together. Negotiate.*

"I don't like leaving him for hours in the back of the van." Joe's voice is distant. But I can hear feet on concrete close by. Someone flicks something repeatedly. Maybe the top to a pen. Or maybe it's the click of a lighter. *Click. Click. Click.*

"You know, I have all the electronic files. Don't you want those?" I'm not above begging.

"Hey, I might have a silencer." A trunk pops open somewhere nearby. Shit. This is really the end. I've been fucking around for years, acting like I have forever, and what do I have at the end of the day? A lot of meaningless shit. An apartment that photographs well. A solid list of hook-ups. An impressive net worth. Good friends. Parents. Sadie. The start of a real relationship. Not a bad list, but…a shitty obit.

"Nope. Must be back home."

"Please don't kill me. I'll do anything. I can testify for you guys. Or still be your fall guy. Just alive." Even to me, it sounds desperate. They'd be nuts to take me up on it, but no silencer means more time. *Keep the ball in play.*

"Shut the fuck up, you god damn moron. I'm going to fucking enjoy this." I'd recognize his voice anywhere. His nasty cologne fills my nostrils.

Garrick Carlson.

THIRTY-TWO

S<small>ADIE</small>

Agent Connor taps his shoe incessantly as we start and stop. Midtown tunnel traffic fires my nerves. It's all I can do to not punch the horn. A current electrifies my skin. It's an emotional response.

I breathe. The way they taught me. Deep in. Deep out. Think. When the cab let me out, what street was that?

"How well do you know Jersey?"

Now he taps the armrest. His head nods to the radio's beat. I swallow a scream.

"I live in Hoboken."

"Do you know the area when you exit the Midtown Tunnel?"

"That immediate area?"

"No. You turn left. Drive down one of the wide avenues."

"Toward Jersey City?"

"Yes."

"Get over in the left lane."

My hands grip tighter on the wheel. *Come on. Come on. Come on…*

When the phone rings, both Agent Connor and I read the name on the screen. Agent Hopkins.

I press to answer on speaker.

"Are you in Jersey?"

"Yes. Turning onto Grand Street now."

"You should've come back to the office."

I don't say anything, but simply stare at the road ahead. Agent Connor stares out the passenger window, so I can't read him. After a moment of silence, Hopkins continues.

"Maitlin's passport was used this morning at JFK. He's currently on a flight to Morocco."

"I assume by your terminology you recognize he's not the one who used his passport."

"It's a possibility. Initial airport security footage isn't clear. He's wearing a baseball cap. But, Sadie, it's also possible he is on that plane. It's possible he played us."

"What time did that flight take off?"

"1:05 p.m."

"Timing doesn't work, Hopkins. He couldn't have made it to the airport on time."

"Video shows him rushing through security."

"He was last seen by his PR team right before noon. A whole room of people. How would he make it through JFK security in time for a one o'clock flight?"

At this point, I'm weaving through a two-lane city street, headed into the bowels of Jersey City. I can't confirm the timing of Chase's PR meeting, as I haven't talked to them yet. I'm basing this on what Rhonda told me. Of course, Rhonda didn't see Chase. She spoke to him on the phone. I glance at Agent Connor. If he was listening to Rhonda, he knows that. But no. His phone, the falafel. Sure, he could have planted that, but this is Chase. I know Chase. I'm not wrong about him.

Perspiration lines my palms. My heartrate's too high, my breaths rapid and light. *Slow it down*. Focus. I inspect every person on the sidewalk. Looking for something. Anything.

"Hold on a minute, Sadie." Someone is speaking to Hopkins, and he either muted us or muffled the receiver.

Agent Connor taps my arm and points to my left, telling me to turn. Hopkins's voice returns through the speaker.

"Two 911 calls came in. Shots on Old Bergen Road. You near there?" I don't have any idea, but Connor nods.

"Yes."

"I doubt it's anything, but you might as well check it out. I'm going to head over there, anyway. I want you to show me this warehouse you mentioned."

"You know he's been kidnapped, right?"

"It's a possibility. Right now there are two running theories. But it's coincidental gunshots were fired in the area you want to check out. And you know what I say about coincidences?"

"You don't believe in them?"

"I believe they deserve investigating. Cops have been dispatched. You'll probably see at least one vehicle when you arrive in the area."

Farther up the street, a marked New Jersey police car with lights flashing, no siren, is parked beside an old warehouse building. It's not the same building that housed the sex club, but we're in the vicinity. There are a few random cars parked along the street, and the officer is talking to an elderly woman on the sidewalk. In daylight, the area shows signs of life, but the buildings need paint, and the chain-linked fence is rusted. Graffiti decorates buildings and the sidewalk.

Agent Connor and I park behind the police vehicle and approach him.

"Officer, I promise. It wasn't a vehicle backfiring. I'm old enough I know what a gunshot sounds like. You need to go in there and check it out."

She's pointing at the large brick warehouse that encompasses the block. On this side of the sidewalk, the building is entirely brick, but above, the walls are lined with windows with metal panels.

"Can I help you?" the officer asks us as we approach.

"FBI." I hold out my badge. "We're currently investigating a missing person case in this area. We heard about the 911 calls and thought we'd check it out." I scan the perimeter of the building for an entrance as Agent Connor takes a step closer to the officer.

"Calls? I wasn't the only one who called? Our neighborhood crime prevention program is working." She sounds giddy.

"Ma'am, we will investigate. Please go home now, ma'am. I want you to be safe."

I listen to the officer handling the woman as I loop back to my trunk. I pull out my Glock .22 and slip it into a waist holster. Agent Connor lifts his jacket, showing me he's already carrying. He speaks to the officer, and I stride to the corner of the building.

There's a parking garage entrance. The left paved ramp goes up to an upper level, the right ramp goes down to a lower level.

I glance back to locate the woman, wondering exactly where she was when she heard the gunshots. My bet would be she was passing this open entrance.

Agent Connor arrives at my side. "Want to circle the perimeter or head inside?"

"I can go in, you go around?"

"No. We stay together."

"Right." With one more glance down the vacant street, I step forward. "Let's circle the perimeter. Then search the stairwell."

We round the far corner, and the officer approaches from the other side. Perimeter survey complete. The stairwell door is to my right.

"Employees from the business above were the other emergency call. They were in the top level of the parking garage. They said all employees park on the upper level, and the bottom level goes unused. The caller believed shots came from the bottom level of the parking garage."

"Did you call in backup?" I ask. We could walk down the way a car would, or drive down, but it's open, exposed.

"An additional officer is on the way. Shots were reported almost fifteen minutes ago. It's been silent since I got here. There's been no activity." He's talking to us with the laidback demeanor of an extremely bored traffic cop.

"Can you stand near the garage exit? We're going down the stairwell."

He nods and turns to take his post.

Connor pulls the heavy metal door. It opens, revealing a poorly lit stairwell. Cinder block walls. Worn concrete steps.

Fifteen minutes. My insides quake. Nausea rises.

I grip the cool metal of the Glock. *Breathe in control. The shots may be nothing. Do not go to what if. Focus.*

Agent Connor lifts his gun, ready, and I do the same as we descend. A metal door with a square window marks the stairwell exit at the bottom.

I ease against the wall, descending to the door. I peer through the side of the glass. A maroon van is parked in one space. A black sedan is parked behind it, blocking it in. Men stand around the vehicle.

"Three men, minimum, two vehicles," I report back to Connor. The men are talking. From my vantage point, I can't see details, but based on proximity to car doors, it looks like the men either recently arrived or were about to leave.

I place my gun back in the holster and adjust my suit jacket to effectively hide it, or at least remove it from immediate observation. Agent Connor mimics me, and I open the door.

The door creaks. The men go quiet. One steps back from the van.

"Hello. A neighbor called in a concern of shots fired in the area. We're checking out the disturbance. Have you heard anything?" I ask as I approach. Connor trails at my side.

One of the men grimaces and balls his hand into a fist. Two men keep their heads bowed. Another turns his back to me.

We've walked in on something. I wiggle my fingers, ready. One wrong move, and it's me and my Glock.

One of the guys looks familiar. He's wearing a black crew-neck sweater beneath a sports jacket, and black suit pants. Three of the men are tattooed and could be mistaken for gang members, but this guy is a clean-cut businessman. The man who turned his back to us steps away, farther down the side of the van. Out of sight.

The familiar guy smiles the smile of a smooth politician. One I'd never support. As he does so, I remember. He was at the sex club. It's hard to be certain because the room was so dark, but I'm almost positive. All my investigative instincts flare. We're in the right place. *Where is Chase?*

"If it isn't Sydney. It's Sydney, right?"

"Yes. You've got the advantage. I'm not sure I know your name?"

The smile doesn't slip from his face, but there's a sinister gleam to his overall expression. I rest my hand on my hip, ready, and purposefully make it clear I have a gun.

"Guys, this lovely young lady frequents Casablanca." His comment has all three men looking me up and down like he just told them I'm a prostitute available at a discount price.

Connor leaves my side, walking around the van with a bored expression, scuffing his shoes along the pavement with disinterest.

"Well, we haven't been here long, but we haven't heard anything. Right, fellas?"

The men all nod. I count four guns.

"What are you guys up to down here?"

"Shooting the shit. That's not illegal, is it?" He rests his hand on the butt of the gun in his holster. "Agent?"

My fingers curve around my own gun. I scan the perimeter for Connor. I hear footsteps shuffle.

The familiar man smirks.

Agent Connor steps around the van, hands held high.

I whip out my gun and aim it at Mr. Familiar. "We're FBI. Do you have any idea what you are doing?"

The barrel of a gun appears next to Connor's head, aimed directly into his ear.

"Here's how this is going to play out. The two of you are going to climb in this van, and we're all going to drive out of here. Together. Like one big, happy family. Got it?"

Agent Connor's facial muscles are frozen; only the movement of his pupils reveal his heightened awareness. If we weren't outnumbered, he would have already fought the guy behind him.

With my gun still high, finger on the trigger, I take one step to the side, my gaze locked on Mr. Familiar. He's the leader here.

Garrick Carlson stands behind Connor. His head reaches the base of Connor's neck.

"Be a good girl. Drop the gun so I don't have to blow out your partners brains and ruin a perfectly good sports coat."

Mr. Familiar raises his gun. From this angle, I can take out Carlson. But Mr. Familiar would shoot before I have time to take him out.

A siren breaks the silence.

Mr. Familiar glances back.

"Cops," one of the men grunts.

"Get in the car. Let's go."

Mr. Familiar steps backward, his gun trained on me as he backs up to the driver side of the sedan.

I keep my gaze and gun trained on his chest. Three men pile into the back seat. One taps the front. "Let's go."

Connor flies face forward onto the pavement.

Garrick's barrel points directly to me.

I keep my gun on the driver.

He ducks into his car and cranks it, and only then do I aim at Garrick.

Cold, sinister eyes glare back at me.

"Get the fuck in," one of his buddies growls.

Garrick leers as he slides into the passenger seat.

The car squeals forward before the passenger door has closed.

I drop to one knee and fire.

The car squeals forward.

Sparks fly.

I pull the trigger. The back windshield shatters.

Pull. Pull.

The car angles up the ramp.

I sprint forward, aiming at the tires.

One hubcap clangs on the concrete.

Additional shots ring out as Connor shoots, too.

The sedan disappears.

"Did you get plates?"

Connor nods. "There's blood on the concrete."

My vision clouds. In slow motion, I step to the far side of the van.

A siren blares through the garage. Flashing lights dance on cinder blocks.

Agent Connor stands to the side of the van door.

I raise my gun.

The van door slides open.

Chase. Eyes shut. One chest wound.

I place my gun in the holster.

Agent Connor shouts, "Call an ambulance!"

He takes off.

Shaking, I crawl into the van.

My finger vibrates as I press it to Chase's neck.

Sirens flood the garage.

I press. And press. Into his cool skin. A faint, too faint, pulse.

I push back his blazer. Searching. One more bullet. In the shoulder. Of all days, he's wearing a white button down. Bright red seeps through the cloth, spreading.

I wrap my arms around him. On the garage floor. I can do CPR.

A pressure on my shoulder pulls me back.

"We've got him. Back up."

The paramedic lifts him out and onto a gurney.

One of the paramedics holds two fingers against Chase's throat. Everything fades out as I focus on the paramedic's reaction. *Is there a pulse?*

The men rush to the back of the ambulance and hoist the bed. I follow.

One paramedic works on Chase. The other jumps out the back.

"You can't ride."

I flash my badge. "FBI."

He squints, hesitating for half a second, then closes both doors and jumps into the driver's seat.

The paramedic's focus is one hundred percent on Chase. He's hooking him up to machines, getting his IV ready, removing his shirt. Preparing him for surgery. Should they get him to the hospital in time.

He must have been shot close range. There's a chance the bullets went straight through. Blood drenches the white cot. So. Much. Blood.

Come on, Chase. Stay with me.

THIRTY-THREE

"Okay. So. Motivational quotes. I'm going to read some to you. My dad, he liked motivational quotes. Fun fact. So does the FBI. Military, too. Stay Strong. Never Give Up."

I drift. Sydney's voice. Talking.

"The last guy I dated never asked to see a photo of my family. We dated for years."

My eyelids are heavy.

"If I were to score myself, I'd get top marks on every aspect of my life except the personal quadrant."

Sydney's voice is low. Her warmth surrounds my fingers. Mechanical beeps echo, louder than Sydney. I mean...Sadie. It's Sadie. My eyelids are weighted.

"I suck at relationships. They aren't easy for me. With you, it's different. You make me laugh and not take things so seriously. All those years of being so competitive, of

332

focusing on only the goal, I forgot... You know, I never wanted to be like my parents. Dedicating their whole lives to their country, at any cost. I always said I didn't want that, that I wouldn't be that, and then what did I do? I fought hard to join the FBI. Because I believed the FBI is better than the CIA. But if you give them your whole life, it doesn't really matter who you're giving it to. And at the end of the day, that choice is on you. Did I ever tell you that I don't even know for sure who my mom works for? It's true. I don't believe for a minute that she's only a professor."

Her warmth surrounds my hand and travels along my wrist.

"I hated my life growing up. It felt so lonely. We moved a lot. I worked so hard for good grades, to learn new languages, to improve my aim. Anything to win approval from one of them. All that hard work, all my training in Quantico. And I still missed it. I didn't fully understand how much danger you were in. I didn't have all the pieces, all of the connections. I should've pushed for WITSEC. I should've pushed for safety. To keep you safe. And because I screwed up... I'll probably never have the courage to say this to you when you're awake, but I've fallen hard for you. I think I love you. You have to be okay. You have to pull through this. You don't have to be with me, but you have to be okay. I can't be the reason you die."

I curl my fingers, attempting to squeeze her hand. I strain to lift my eyelids.

"Chase. Did you move your fingers? Are you?" There's a movement beside me and warmth on my forehead.

"Nurse...nurse."

My eyelids finally function, and I blink, taking in my surroundings. A thin blue blanket covers me. An IV is taped to the back of my hand. A plastic tube and wires. I yank.

"Chase? You're in the hospital."

A man in navy scrubs hovers over me. He removes my fingers from the wires. I assume he's the nurse. Fitting. Just my luck. A male nurse. He shines a bright white light into each of my pupils and checks stats on some of the machines near my bed.

"How are you feeling? Are you in any pain?"

My mouth feels like someone stuffed it with cotton balls, and my throat burns. I point at the source of discomfort, and in a weak voice I don't recognize, manage to respond, "Water."

Sadie pours water from a nearby pitcher into a clear plastic cup and silently asks his permission to give it to me.

"He can have some. A little to start. I'll bring in ice chips. You are a very lucky man, Mr. Maitlin."

Sadie holds the cup to my mouth, and her soulful mahogany irises glisten. Somehow, for some reason, she loves me.

"Your shoulder is probably going to be quite sore. We had to operate to remove the bullet. The bullet that went through your chest narrowly missed your heart. It did travel through the top portion of your kidney, but fortunately, the kidney is an organ that will repair itself. The surgeon will be by to visit you in the morning and can answer any questions you may have."

"Time?"

"It's a little after six a.m.," he tells me as he writes on a clip-board then updates a whiteboard on the wall.

"Your parents were here. Your dad made your mom go home to rest. But she wouldn't leave until the doctor assured her you'd be okay."

"You...stayed?"

"Yes." A tear escapes, and she wipes it with her fingers. The whites of her eyes are tinged pink.

"Hey," I wheeze to her.

"I'll be back with that ice. If you need anything, we're right outside. If you start to feel pain, let us know. It's important we stay ahead of your pain, so don't wait until it's so intense you can't stand it. Okay? You know what, I'm going to go ahead and give you some more pain meds through the IV now. But if you need more, let us know."

I don't look away from Sadie, but I nod to let the man know I heard him.

Sadie lifts my hand from the bed and wraps both of her hands around it.

The nurse steps out of the room, leaving the door ajar.

"Your parents will be back this morning. Oh, I should text them to tell them you're awake. You weren't in a coma or anything, but they'll be relieved to know you're awake. Oh, my god, Chase, when you were in surgery, I was so scared. There was so much blood." Her voice waffles as she chokes on tears.

"Hey." I aim for soothing but sound more like an injured toad. My eyelids are heavy, and sleep beckons. The world is drowsy and hazy. "I love you, too."

"You heard me?"

"You're amazing," I slur. Not at all sure what she sees in me, but… "I'll try."

My throat burns, and she holds the cups to my parched lips and lets me drink more.

"What are you going to try?" she asks after she places the cup of water down and clasps my hand again, warming it. I shiver. It's freezing.

"Gonna try for you."

"Did you hear everything I said?"

I blink.

"All of it?" she asks, her voice low and timid.

"Say it…again. Need to hear it. Over and over."

"I can do that."

"Sade?"

"Yeah?"

"None of this…your fault."

The room goes black as I drift.

I open my eyes, and daylight shines brightly in the room. My parents sit in two chairs against the wall, and Sadie's head rests on the end of the bed near my feet, her arm looped over the bottom of my legs.

My mom rises, a finger over her lips. "She was asleep when we got here. We decided to leave her. Are your legs okay? Do we need to move her?"

I shake my head and mouth, "Water."

A nurse comes in as my mom lifts a tiny blue plastic cup to my lips. Another male nurse in scrubs. What hospital did I end up in?

Sadie stretches and lifts her head. I can tell from her grimace her neck muscles hurt.

"Oh, honey, you're awake. Do you have a crick in your neck? I imagine you do. Why don't you go on home and get a shower? You'll feel so much better."

Jesus, Mom. "Mom. This is Sadie. My girlfriend." My throat crackles.

My dad gets out of his seat and drapes his arm around my mom's shoulder. "Abby, your boy is telling you to back off."

"I'm not doing anything. What do you mean? You back off. This is my son."

"Abs." It's Dad's name for Mom when he's aiming for tender and non-confrontational.

"It's okay," Sadie interrupts. "She's right. I probably should get a shower."

"Why don't you stay while we get coffee, then you can leave? He just woke up. When we get back here, then you can take a break. We can cover in shifts. How's that sound?" My dad looks to me, and I nod, grateful.

The male nurse seems oblivious to the discussion as he fiddles with gadgets and updates the clipboard.

"How're you feeling?" he asks the moment there's a break in conversation.

I take stock. I feel like hell. "Been better," I offer.

He grins. My mom hovers nearby. Sadie weaves her fingers between mine.

"Your doctor will be in shortly. When he clears you, I'll bring in lunch."

"We'll be back in a few," my dad says, guiding my mom to the door.

"We won't be long," Mom calls.

The doctor comes by and checks all the things the nurse did. "How's the pain level?" he asks.

"High?" I offer.

"I've always heard it hurts like hell to get shot," Sadie says as she gently squeezes my hand.

"Well, you know, not that bad," I say, full of bravado, 'cause, you know, she's my girl and all.

Thank God the doctor ignores me.

"I'm going to give you more pain meds through the IV. Then, later in the day, we'll start lowering the amount. Stop giving you pain meds through the IV. Switch you to pills."

After giving me a doctor once-over, he leaves the room and pulls the door closed.

Sadie perches on the edge of my bed. She lifts my hand to her mouth and kisses it. Some of what she said before comes back to me.

"Hey, Sadie?"

"Yeah?"

"You couldn't have possibly known. You're not responsible for what happened. You get that, right?"

She lifts her shoulders and kisses my knuckles one by one. "I like your parents."

"Yeah, they're something else, huh?"

"They are. You're lucky to have them."

"I am."

"Your mom invited me over for brunch. And to go shopping too."

"Good. Brunch is good. I recommend you skip the shop." She laughs, but she's never been shopping with my mother. Some women might be all in, but Sadie can fit all her shoes in one box. She has no idea what a shopping expedition is.

"Garrick's dead." Her lips are downturned, as is her gaze.

"How?"

"Bullet wound. Found his body near the garage. Where we found you."

"And the others?"

She shrugs. "We'll find them." She rubs her thumb across my knuckles. In a brighter tone, she changes the subject. "I'm looking forward to getting to know your parents."

I squeeze her hand until she raises her gaze from our joined hands and looks at me. "What you said about your parents? Not being like them? That's what I can give to you."

"You remember?"

"Keep you balanced. I'll do that." At least, I think I say that. My eyelids are so heavy. Once again. But I know she's still there. At my bedside. Holding my hand.

Who says the short guy doesn't get the Bond girl?

"What did you say?" I hear her ask.

"The short guy. Got the Bond girl."

Her lips press to mine, and the warmth of her breath flutters along my ear as she teases, "Not a Bond girl. But when you're up for it, if you ever want to role play, you just let me know."

And with that, I drift into the absolute best dreamland.

THIRTY-FOUR

Sydney

Three months later

Jury selection has begun for McLoughlin's court case in Chicago. He's all over the news. The current issue of *Vogue* magazine features his wife with the headline, "Standing by Her Man." In the article, she waxes poetic about what an amazing man he is and about the dangers of witch hunters hounding those who choose a career in politics. Thin, sparkly, gold bracelets from her new jewelry line debuting this fall decorate her wrists and, of course, somehow, the interview veered to talking about her new business endeavors. I read it on the subway this morning then dumped it in the nearest recycling can.

Here in New York, jury selection starts next week for Tom Bennett and Evan Mitchell's trials. BB&E isn't one of the top accounting firms, and no one really cares what happens to a few guys who falsely inflated revenues, hid losses, or laundered money. People do tend to care about men who scam a cancer research charity. A *Wall Street Journal* reporter coined the term "The Stanford Six" in his article describing how six friends from Stanford University benefited from charity funds over the prior fifteen years. It wasn't long before the term dominated headlines. Senator McLoughlin is included in the alumni list, but awareness of this fact seems to be low. We are hopeful the media coverage won't make jury selection too challenging.

Turns out the whole scam started years ago as basic crony-ism, awarding advantages to friends. McLoughlin would help his buddies get a contract through his government connec-tions. They, in turn, would contribute significantly to his charity. It seems the first time the charity bought a property at an inflated value from the Chicago Real Estate Group, the firm was in danger of going under. Then they must have real-ized how much money they could make.

Within a year, McLoughlin's charity began funding research projects from South Fork Research. Around that time, Elijah "EJ" Mason founded Medical Supply Co., and South Fork Research and McLoughlin's charity became their biggest clients. It's not clear from the paper trail how many of these deals were merely overpriced transactions and how many were real, because somewhere along the line, the friends had begun laundering money for the mafia via Joe McGurn.

Joe McGurn identified additional business opportunities. Within a month of creating Biohazard Waste Disposal, the firm won contracts with not only South Fork Research but also Tovan Hospital Group, the biggest hospital group in the midwest. Some of the work was fully legitimate, but prices were always high, and the CEOs involved were always taking an undisclosed cut. McLoughlin's charity, back in the day, did donate to cancer research, but almost twelve years ago, the company began redirecting funds to McLoughlin's election campaigns and to supporting McLoughlin's closest friends. They probably could have continued without garnering attention, except they got greedy. The real estate deals in areas where nothing would sell started to generate attention. When a company expressed interest in acquiring South Fork Research, the group decided to inflate revenue to drive the acquisition price up.

Greed and a naïve belief they'd never get caught created the notorious Stanford Six, comprised of Cooper Grayson, CEO of Chicago Real Estate Group, John Fischer and Eileen Becker from South Fork Research, Tom Bennett and Evan Michell from BB&E, and Senator McLoughlin. We believe the senator developed relationships with the mafia during his wheelings and dealings in Chicago. And it all went downhill for the group of friends from there.

Our team, and select key witnesses, will testify in Senator McLoughlin's case, but even then, the accounting piece will be the explanatory 'how they did it' element everyone won't fully understand and therefore won't care much about. As the prosecution so often has to do, our criminal case will center on all of the non-sexy ways they broke the law. These men might all be murderers, but they'll go down for boring crimes like wire fraud, tax evasion, and accounting scams.

We did catch the men who kidnapped Chase. They hailed an Uber on their personal credit card four blocks from the warehouse, around the corner from the dumpster where they left Garrick Carlson. Bullet analysis proved Garrick Carlson shot Chase. And the bullet that killed Garrick came from my gun. At the time, I didn't know I made a hit. I have no regrets.

All the captured men agreed to talk. Joseph McGurn is now off the grid, a member of the WITSEC program. The organized crime team is all over their new prized source and believe he'll be instrumental in upcoming court cases.

We never made a connection between the Stanford Six and the club shooting. On some days, I'm absolutely certain of one. On others, I doubt myself and wonder if maybe, possibly, it was all a coincidence. We happened to be in the wrong place at the wrong time. I might drive myself mad about this particular aspect of the case, except that justice has been served. The shooter himself is dead. And if the Stanford Six orchestrated it, I fully expect they will be in prison for at least the next twenty-five years on the evidence we do possess.

Media attention over the nightclub mass shooting has waned. Those first couple of weeks, every now and then someone would do a double-take when they saw me on the street. But those first few weeks I spent primarily either in the FBI office or at Chase's apartment, so I wasn't out much. Ongoing debates over stricter gun control laws linger, but I don't hold out hope anything will change. When the next mass shooting occurs, politicians will grandstand, the media will obsess, and then appetite for change will wane once more. It's the worst kind of cycle, and one I don't have an answer for.

Too many businesses make money off guns for real change to occur, and those businesses back the writers of the legislation. The flip side is there are too many guns currently in circulation for legislation to make a dent on the availability of guns to criminals. Ending payments from corporations and private interests to politicians might be one way to head down the road toward change. But then I think about the untracked payments to Senator McLoughlin through a charity aimed at raising money to fight cancer. If a cancer research charity guided funds into a corrupt politician's pockets, I lose hope that even with a sea change in public policy, we'll find an end to this vicious cycle. Especially when a crook like McLoughlin still has hordes of supporters backing his re-election campaign.

They offered Chase WITSEC. He turned it down. Said he wasn't going to walk away from his family, or me. If he hadn't thrown his family in there, I might have fought him.

Not only did he turn protection down, but he stepped into the role of Interim CEO. The day he returned, he held an employee-wide meeting in the atrium, the community area outside the cafeteria. Chase spoke of business ethics, and the importance of maintaining integrity in their work and in their lives. He reminded employees of BB&E's mission and assured them the firm remained strong and that, as a team, they would right the ship. I stood to the side, surveying the crowd, alert for any guns, admittedly possibly paranoid. Chase received a well-deserved standing ovation.

"Keating, banker hours?" Hopkins peers over his laptop, questioning me as I pass his desk, heading out for the day.

"Meeting with Chase's physical therapist. There are some specific stretches he wants me to see so I can help him with them at home." Chase is doing well, partially because he was in great shape before, and partially due to his dedication to his physical therapy. There's a good chance his shoulder will always give him some issues, but he's determined to do everything he can to reach a full recovery. We've both been seeing a therapist to work through the emotional trauma.

"You make a decision about what you want to do after the trial?"

"I'm leaning toward staying in white-collar." One of the good things about working for an organization like the FBI is that if I did decide to change to a different group in the future, it's always possible to do so. "How's Marcy doing?"

Hopkins and his wife are expecting their first child. Marcy works in surveillance.

"Nausea's gotten better since she discovered these bands to wear around her wrist. Tell Maitlin I said hello. Go easy on my man, okay?" Hopkins stopped by the hospital to check on Chase, and the two bonded. Chase sold Hopkins on the Chelsea Piers gym, so now they see each other regularly.

Chase and I have basically been living together since his kidnapping. At first, the arrangement allowed me to be there if he needed anything when he first came home from the hospital. Recovering from bullet wounds can be a slow and painful process.

During those first few weeks, Chase had me heavily involved in the redesign of his apartment. Gone are the modern, gorgeous, low-backed, curvy sofas, and in their place are comfortable, livable pieces of furniture. Last weekend we painted the white living area walls a color named Winter Calm. The color has a masculine lavender hue, and it gives the space warmth while maximizing openness. And better yet, we picked it out together.

I push the door to the apartment open, my hands full of mail. Chase sits on the sofa with a laptop on the coffee table.

"There she is," he says when I enter.

"How was work?"

"Good." I kick off my shoes by the door and join him.

"Did you call your sister back?"

"I did. Talked to her on the way home. She's good. Planning

to come visit us on her next break." I didn't think to call my sister after the nightclub shooting. She happened to see a video of me on a mutual friend's feed. That led to a long discussion and a promise to do a better job of communicating.

"Look at this." Chase angles the laptop in my direction.

"An apartment?"

"Here. Click through the photos. It's a building. An investment property I'm considering."

"Oh?"

"Look." He clicks on the arrow. "It's a full townhome currently split into four units. The bottom unit has a basement and also goes out into a small back yard. It's a two-level four-bedroom. I'm thinking we could live there and rent out the apartments above. If we needed more space one day, we could expand the living quarters and reduce the number of renters. What do you think?"

"Chase...we're not officially living together."

"That's only because you insist on holding on to that apartment downtown. You're throwing almost three thousand a month away on the place. One day you'll feel comfortable enough to let the apartment go, or at least sublet it. But this place, this is long term planning. This is for when we have kids. And the rentals make it a great investment property."

"Kids?"

"Yes, kids. You want kids, right? Remember? We talked about this."

"We talked about kids as it relates to guns. Not kids as it relates to us." Chase doesn't believe guns should be in a home with children. It's a sensitive topic, and one I haven't argued with him over because there hasn't been any reason.

"Hey, you know you're going to be an amazing mom… right?" His fingers comb through my hair, then he places the strands behind one ear and cups my jaw. He sees me, through me. Sometimes it's unnerving how well he knows me.

"I don't even have a plant." I get what he's saying, and I know others in the FBI have families, but it's hard to envision.

"Hopkins is about to have a kid."

"I know." I do know it. I'm a kid of the CIA, I know it *can* be done.

"And besides, we're a great match. I've got the flexible job, so I can be home when needed, you know, if you're caught up in a tough case." His fingers intertwine with mine, assuring me.

"You're a CEO. Flexible job, my ass." I poke him in his stomach, grinning.

"Not for long."

I raise my eyebrows, questioning.

"The board found a replacement. Great guy. So much more experience. He'll be good for BB&E. The announcement will be sometime next week."

"And what will you do?"

"Our head of client services is retiring. He was Evan Mitchell's father-in-law, so…I'll step in for a while. Be there to support the transition. But you know me. I've always got options." He grins and pulls me across him so I straddle his lap.

"Always a plan." My fingers find his shoulders, and I squeeze hard then release, maneuvering my fingers into the tight muscles, alleviating the tension. He closes his eyes and leans his head back. My hands still. "Are you saying you want kids now?" My gaze flicks back to his laptop. The screensaver now covers his long-term plan.

He grins. It's a confident grin covering a hint of uncertainty. "Not now, Frost. One day."

"With me? You want kids with me?"

"I do." His gaze sears me. "One day."

"Life with an agent isn't going to be easy, you know?" My fingers trail over his chest, exploring the hard lines I love.

"Baby, I never thought I'd say this, but I'm all about supporting you. You're my Bond girl. The way I see it, taking care of you is doing my part to improve national security. Somebody's gotta do it, and it better damn well be me." He sounds like he's posturing, but there's an underlying warmth and sincerity. It's the Chase contrast.

The door buzzes. I pop a quick kiss on his lips and hop off the sofa.

"Hello?" The intercom now functions. I insisted the building manager fix it before Chase returned home from the hospital.

"It's Laronzo. The physical therapist."

I buzz him up.

"You standing guard?" Chase asks. It's a fair question. My back is to the wall, and my hand is on the doorknob. I have the door cracked so I can see who gets off the elevator. It's not so much nerves as habit. "You look like you're about to flee."

"Flee?" I laugh. "And what would you do if I did?" He's grinning, but there's a seriousness to his expression. The way he looks at me, it warms me from the inside out.

"I'd chase you."

EPILOGUE

C HASE

One year later

"What've you got there?" Sadie's biting the tip of her tongue as she twists a pink ribbon around a bouquet of flowers.

"I thought we'd take flowers over to congratulate Anna on the engagement."

"You know he's had that ring for ages, right?"

"So you've said, but that doesn't mean it's any less of a reason to celebrate," she reprimands.

"Hey, I know. I'm happy Jackson finally made it happen. I bought champagne." I open the refrigerator to grab the bottle of bubbly, then snag Sadie from behind and kiss the curve of her neck.

One day, I'm going to follow in Jackson's footsteps and make this one mine. Officially. We've been living together for a year. She finally found someone to take over the lease on her tiny studio. All my friends are living with their significant others, and most everyone's engaged.

"Did Maggie and Jason end up coming into town?" Our friends from Chicago were hoping to make it in, but word on the street is Maggie's expecting. She miscarried a few months ago. Sam told me if Jason has anything to do with it, Maggie will be locked in a padded zero infection chamber until the baby is born.

"No, and remember, we're not supposed to know yet that she's expecting."

"Yeah, we're not supposed to know, and yet she told Anna. Anna who gabs to everyone. How's that work again?"

Sadie smiles as she continues finessing the ribbons.

"Well, I suppose Delilah and Mason are next?" *Unless you want us to be.* I watch her facial expressions closely, looking for any hint she's wistful. My old girlfriend dropped hints daily about getting engaged, but Sadie hasn't said anything. We'll talk about the kids we want to have—two—and how we'll care for them—I'll take the lead, given I'll have the most job flexibility—but she's never once held her left hand out and mentioned it needs decorating. Jackson says Anna was the same way. Olivia didn't drop any hints to Sam either. I never thought I'd say it, but I wouldn't mind a little pressure. Then at least I'd know she's ready.

Maybe I'll pull Mason aside this evening and get some advice from him. He's proposed twice, to two different women, and each woman declined. He can at least tell me what not to do.

"Do you think this is enough?" she asks, disregarding my question about who is next.

I glance down at our kitchen counter. We're just going to Sam and Olivia's for a group dinner. Yes, theoretically, it's to celebrate Jackson and Anna's engagement, but we all get together for dinner regularly.

"Flowers and bubbly? Works for me. Remember, you'll have plenty of opportunities to shower Anna with gifts. Bridal shower, engagement party."

"This is the engagement party."

"Tonight? No. It's *an* engagement party. It's not *the* engagement party. You wait. There'll be more. I wouldn't be surprised if we have to haul it to Virginia too. There's no way Jackson's parents aren't going to want to throw a party."

"Would your parents throw a party?"

"Abso-fucking-lutely." I slide my fingers through her hair and pause until her gaze meets mine. "When we get engaged, they will most definitely throw us a party."

Again, I watch her closely. She registers no surprise.

"Would your parents want us to come out?" I ask.

"To Russia?" *Now* she registers surprise.

"I speak Russian." My reminder has her rolling her eyes.

"I haven't spoken to Dad in months. Are you sure you want to marry into a family of spies? There will be no engagement parties. My parents might not even show for the wedding."

"Sadie, I don't need the fluff. All I need is you. For all I care, we could make it legal at the courthouse."

"I thought you didn't want a ball and chain?"

"That was the old me. Before you."

"Ah. And the new you?"

"I love it when you tie me down. I especially love tying you down." My fingers graze her breasts on their journey to caress her neck. I rub my thumb over her plump bottom lip, and she bites.

"Hey." I pull my hand back, shaking it, completely turned on.

"Tell me more," she teases with a sexy come-hither smile. "I rather like the handcuffs you used last weekend." God, I love this woman. I'd do anything for her.

Her fingers explore my chest, something she loves to do. Then she plucks at my t-shirt. I picked it out especially for tonight's event. *Same Penis Forever.* I wouldn't wear it if there were going to be parentals there, but it's just friends tonight. Anna will laugh.

"I'm not so sure about this." She scrunches her nose. I exhale. I can't say I'm entirely surprised. I love this woman, but her humor doesn't always align with mine.

"What about the 'To the Disco' one?" I ask.

"With the unicorn on it?"

"Yeah." My girl knows my t-shirt collection. I kiss the tip of her delectable nose.

"That's a better choice." She nods her approval. "With the black sports coat?"

"Yes." I twist her hair around my finger then slide it behind her ear. "You know, if you'd prefer, I could wear a black crewneck. I don't have to wear a funny shirt."

"I don't want to change you. I simply think tonight's saying should focus on the positive, not on the negative."

"Wait a minute, now." I spin her around, tickling her. "What's that supposed to mean? There may not be a ring on your finger, but the shirt applies to you too, Ms. Frost."

I continue accosting her with my fingers, tickling until she's crouched down, laughing hard, begging for me to stop.

"Stop, stop. You have me. You're right. It's positive. Not negative." She gasps for air, and I drop my arms, giving her a reprieve. She straightens and wipes the corners of her eyes. She grows serious and places her palms flat on my chest. "Keep the shirt on. It's definitely a positive."

And just like that, all doubts are gone. It's time to go ring shopping.

ACKNOWLEDGMENTS

Chasing Frost wraps up the West Side Series. It's with mixed emotions that I write this. This series is an exploration of romance tropes and I've had a blast writing it. Of all the books, Chasing Frost was probably the most fun to write. I know that Chase can come across as a bit of an ass, but I love him. I also thoroughly enjoyed researching the FBI.

I read Jerri William's *Armchair Detective,* then had the great experience of talking to her on the phone and listening to her podcasts. If you're a podcast person and you like hearing about FBI true stories, I strongly recommend her FBI Retired Case Files. She's also a writer and you can find her books at http://www.jerriwilliams.com

AmyClaire Majer, as development editor, helped tremendously with Chasing Frost. My beta readers had great insights and helped point out when I needed to pull Chase back a bit and also when I needed to soften Sadie. Evan Dave proved helpful with all things guns. Evan and I met in a class years ago, and I'm grateful we've kept in touch. He's a Sci-Fi writer with a side thing for romance. Jennifer Pezzano, Kia,

Allison Miller, and Keri D. James, my critique match partners and beta readers extraordinaire, thank you. And a special thank you goes out to Lori Whitwam from Furwood Forrest for editing this entire series. When I write, I can now hear her comments in my mind. And I'd like to thank Heather Whitehead from Capstone for line editing and for eliminating any and all errors.

Sara Hansen from Okay Creations designed not only the Chasing Frost cover but several of the covers in this series. Most notably, she stepped in and saved me at the eleventh hour on the Lost on the Way cover when AMS ads determined the original cover was too provocative (my newsletter subscribers know it SO was not at all) but I digress. The point is one book later and I'm still feeling grateful to Sara.

Chasing Frost is also the first book of mine my husband read. And he actually liked it. I think he might have been more surprised than me. His exact comment was something along the lines of, "Wow. This is like legit." Not a stunning endorsement, but I'll take it. I'm sort of jesting. If it wasn't for my husband, I would have never even attempted this venture or rolled the dice to see what happens. They say that your partner in life should be someone who helps you to be the person you want to be, and he does that for me in immeasurable ways. I haven't dedicated any of these books to anyone (it didn't even register until mid-way through the series that sometimes authors do that). The fact is, I should dedicate this entire series to him in gratitude for his support and love. In so many ways, he melts my frost.

ABOUT THE AUTHOR

Isabel Jolie, aka Izzy, lives on a lake, loves dogs of all stripes, and if she's not working, she can be found reading, often with a glass of wine in hand. In prior lives, Izzie worked in marketing and advertising, in a variety of industries, such as financial services, entertainment, and technology. In this life, she loves daydreaming and writing contemporary romances with strong heroines.

Sign-up for Izzy's newsletter at https://isabeljoliebooks.com/#newsletter to keep up-to-date on new releases, promotions and giveaways.

 facebook.com/isabeljoliebooks

twitter.com/isabeljoliebook

 instagram.com/isabeljoliebooks

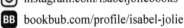 bookbub.com/profile/isabel-jolie

ALSO BY ISABEL JOLIE

When the Stars Align (Jackson and Anna)

Trust Me (Sam and Olivia)

Walk the Dog (Mason and Delilah)

Lost on the Way (Jason and Maggie)